the sex education of m.e.

L.B. DUNBAR

www.lbdunbar.com

Sex happens.
LB Dunbar

L.B. Dunbar

ROMANCE. FOR SEXY SILVER FOX LOVERS.

The Sex Education of M.E.
Copyright © 2016 Laura Dunbar
L.B. Dunbar Writes, Ltd.
www.lbdunbar.com

All rights reserved. No part of this book may be reproduced or transmitted in any form or by any means, electronic or mechanical, including photocopying, recording, or by any information storage and retrieval system, without permission in writing.

This is a work of fiction. Names, characters, places, and incidents are the product of the author's imagination or are used fictitiously, and any resemblance to any actual persons, living or dead, events, or locales is entirely coincidental.

The author acknowledges the trademarked status and trademark owners of various products referenced in this work of fiction, which have been used without permission. The publication/use of these trademarks is not authorized, associated with, or sponsored by the trademark owner.

2022 Cover Design – Shannon Passmore/Shanoff Formats

Original Edits – Kiezha Ferrell/Librum Artis Editorial Services

Proofread – Karen Fischer

Other Books by L.B. Dunbar

Lakeside Cottage
Living at 40
Loving at 40
Learning at 40
Letting Go at 40

The Silver Foxes of Blue Ridge
Silver Brewer
Silver Player
Silver Mayor
Silver Biker

Silver Fox Former Rock Stars
After Care
Midlife Crisis
Restored Dreams
Second Chance
Wine&Dine

Collision novellas
Collide
Caught

Smartypants Romance (an imprint of Penny Reid)
Love in Due Time
Love in Deed
Love in a Pickle

The World of True North (an imprint of Sarina Bowen)
Cowboy
Studfinder

Rom-com for the over 40
The Sex Education of M.E.

The Heart Collection
Speak from the Heart
Read with your Heart
Look with your Heart

L.B. Dunbar

Fight from the Heart
View with your Heart

A Heart Collection Spin-off
The Heart Remembers

THE EARLY YEARS
The Legendary Rock Star Series
The Legend of Arturo King
The Story of Lansing Lotte
The Quest of Perkins Vale
The Truth of Tristan Lyons
The Trials of Guinevere DeGrance

Paradise Stories
Abel
Cain

The Island Duet
Redemption Island
Return to the Island

Modern Descendants – writing as elda lore
Hades
Solis
Heph

Dedication

For my readers, especially those in Loving L.B. Thank you.

And for women over forty everywhere: you still got it, girl.

L.B. Dunbar

Chapter 1
Match Me

[M.E. = Mary Elizabeth = Emme]

A mother and a widow. These things defined me. Forty-something, I stopped counting once the second digit rolled past another zero. It's funny...as a child, I couldn't wait to get to double digits. Ten seemed so important. Thirteen entered another realm. Eighteen, twenty, twenty-one. The counting slowed down when I got closer to thirty, but the years sped up. I wanted time to stand still at forty.

Whoever said forty was the new twenty clearly didn't live in my body. It was curvy, but not in that seductive, luscious, twenty-something way. There were no toned abs and sculpted thighs on my body. These were the lumps and bumps of a woman who'd bore children, nursed them until her breasts sagged, and carried them until her back spread. Each child added pounds, and each decade refused to remove them.

It has been one year since my husband's death. This isn't a story about the dead, however. It's about re-birth. After my husband died, I had two choices: I could continue to sleep away each day and feel sorry for myself, or I could get my ass out of bed and take charge of my life. The life that remained after my husband's ended. A difficult year followed after the loss of a man I'd been married to for nineteen years, but I had two children, and they needed me. The past year was a blur of firsts I didn't wish to recall.

What I wanted to recall was sex. More than recall it - reinstate the practice of it. To be perfectly honest, I hadn't had sex in the last year either. The desire just hadn't existed. I remembered it, but guilt kept me from doing anything about it. I didn't want to dishonor the memory of a man I'd been with for twenty years. One man. It was no small feat. People wanted to glorify him after death. Nate Peters was a good man, but he wasn't an angel. At times, I was angered by people's praise of him; at other times, I wallowed in self-pity that I had lost a respectable man. Then one day, I snapped out of it. I still had a life to live.

So here I sat at a Fourth of July block party, a few streets over from my home. My best friend, Gia Carlutti, asked me to attend. The theme was screaming children and drunken fathers letting off fireworks, but what the hell, I had nothing better to do. Besides, Gia had been a huge source of support during the last year. Divorced long ago, she'd been gently encouraging me to date—something I'd refused to do.

"It will be good for you," she said. "Meet some people. Go to a club. Be wild again." She swung her large hips back and forth, fluffing out her hair like a teenager. She acted like one, and I loved her for it. I'd lost track of all the men she was dating at once. She lived the life, according to her, and I needed to live mine, too. I wasn't convinced yet that living life meant sleeping with seven different men, one for each night of the week, but what did I know? The last time I'd dated, I had gone out each night of the week. With one man, who became my husband.

Sitting on her front steps, we sipped Moscato while her two young children rode up and down the block on their bikes, dodging laughing groups of adults and narrowly missing toddlers on tricycles. Admittedly, Sam and Sara were out of control, but Gia didn't pay them much mind. A single mother of a six- and eight-year-old, she did the best she could. According to her, their father was the one who made them unruly. He'd disappeared after only a few years of marriage. Parenting tips were not shared between us—what Gia offered was man advice.

"Here," she said, reaching out for my phone that lay on the stoop next to me. I don't know why I carried it with me. I was only a few blocks from home, but it became more and more of a security measure for monitoring my teenage daughters. They were both out on this crazy night. Mitzi went to the northern suburbs with a group of friends to watch the fireworks. Bree wandered the neighborhood with other teenagers not yet old enough to drive. The phone was mischief control.

Before I knew it, Gia had my phone in her hand, downloading an app. Another thing I hardly understood in the modern mode of communication. Other than maps and messaging, and of course, calling someone, I didn't see the use of a variety of apps my children and Gia told me I needed. In seconds, she had something loaded and then began a litany of questions. Muttering to herself, she stated my name, birthdate, eye color, and hair color.

"Weight?" Side-glancing at me and pouting her lower lip while rocking back and forth, she answered her own question. "Ahh…let's say one-fifteen."

I snorted into my plastic cup of wine.

"One-fifteen? Unless you are discussing the time for a meeting, that is clearly not my weight."

"You can't be much more than that," she mumbled, continuing to type.

"I can. And I am. What are you doing anyway?" I reached over her arm, attempting to retrieve my phone. She held it just out of my reach, but faced my direction, and I was able to make out the logo, if I squinted. That was the other thing about age. Slowly, my eyesight was failing. I refused to give into the need for an optometrist visit and be diagnosed with reading glasses. This over-forty-thing was the pits.

Narrowing my eyes, I read the blue swirl: *MatchMe*.

"Oh no." Leaning into her, I reached for the phone again. "No, Gia, absolutely not. I'm not that desperate." As soon as the words escaped me, I was apologetic. MatchMe was the dating site where Gia got all her men.

"I didn't mean…"

"It's fine." She cut me off with the wave of a hand, manicured with red nails for the holiday. "I am desperate, and actually, so are you." Her eyebrow rose at me. Gia knew some of my deepest secrets, one of which was I hadn't had sex since my husband's death, and I was getting…horny. As a college professor, the profession did not provide much mingling with other adults my own age very often. Other than the fellow faculty members, most of whom were either married, too old, too young, or gay, I didn't meet many potential candidates for my pent up frustration. In a drunken stupor one night, when I learned I couldn't drink like a college student any longer, I confessed to Gia I wanted someone to sleep with. Just that. No dating. Just sex.

"Friends with benefits," I suggested.

"Fuck buddy," Gia said.

"I don't even know what that is."

"It's someone you call, and if he's available, you get together for sex. Not friends. No dates. Just sex," she explained. I laughed, but Gia

was serious. Her dark eyes danced with pleasure at teaching me my first lesson in modern sex.

"Yes," I said. "Then I need one of those." Saying "fuck" seemed a little extreme. "Why couldn't he be a 'sex friend'?" I asked, to which she replied: "You could call him a boy toy." That just sounded all kinds of wrong. I didn't want a boy. I wanted a man.

She'd set me up with an account on her favorite dating site in hopes of finding me someone. Here's the thing: I was scared out of my mind. I didn't want some sex addict. I didn't want an ax murderer. I didn't want someone sleeping with fourteen other women ages twenty to twenty-one. A dating site wasn't going to factor all those characters out. Every person there was like me - desperate to find someone for sex. I hung my head in shame at the thought. I was running out of choices unless I simply propositioned someone.

"Honey, it's perfect. Most of these men are no strings attached. It's just what you need."

The fireworks were about to begin, and we entered the street like the rest of the neighbors. At the opposite end, in the cross streets, stood the first of many large displays the resident on the corner would release to celebrate the birth of our nation. Gathering in close with other adults, while children settled closer to the activity, I noticed Gia's neighbor and a few of his male friends near us. Todd Swanker was just that – a wanker. He was crude and abrasive in his language, with no filter for all things inappropriate. Every neighborhood has one of those neighbors; the harmless, married one who flirts with every female above sixteen. Our neighborhood was not unique. Todd was our guy.

"Ladies," he said, stepping up to wrap an arm around each of us, letting his fall from Gia almost instantaneously but lingering on my waist. A gentle tug toward him compelled me to pull back out of his grasp as he began the first of his unfiltered comments.

"Another year of fireworks, but of course I see them nightly," he boasted, pausing to let the images of him and his wife sink in.

"Bet it's your wife who sees colors each night. The inside of her eyelids as she holds them shut tight," Gia muttered causing me to giggle at the thought of Todd's sexual prowess.

"Of course, if Emme needed help in this area, I'm sure I could work something out." He twitched his eyebrows and rubbed his hands together, as if it wouldn't be a problem for him to provide his services to me. My name rolled over his tongue made me shiver.

With a brief, "No thanks," I looked around the gathered crowd.

Nearby, but not too close, was a man I hadn't seen before. He dragged his beer bottle up to his mouth and took a long pull before releasing the lip of the bottle. His throat rolled slowly as he swallowed, and for some reason, I was mesmerized by this motion. The slight glow of a streetlight illuminated our small patch of street and offered a backdrop that highlighted his features from the side: large arms with a hint of tattoo, flat stomach under a tight t-shirt, low-hanging shorts. I continued to stare, transfixed by the movement of his throat under a layer of scruff. Removing the bottle from his mouth, he turned in our direction, and I quickly looked away. My face heated, and I thanked the heavy black of night. I stared forward just in time to see another wave of fire light the sky ahead.

"That's Chief," Todd offered in my ear, startling me like the buzz of a mosquito. I turned to him, and followed his gaze to the man he referenced, the same man I'd been ogling seconds ago.

"Hey, Merek!" He motioned for the man to come closer. "Come meet Emme!" The tall man turned in our direction, and his dark eyes narrowed in on me. His hair looked thick, with a hint of salt at his temples. His face displayed a few days' growth. His skin was tight, but the crinkles by his eyes gave away his age.

My face flushed again, and I wanted to melt into the sidewalk, disappearing under the weight of his returned stare. Dark eyes twinkled with specks of gold met mine and playfully sparked the reflection of another round of fireworks. He held my eyes for a moment, and I noted the glassy gleam that winked at me before he took a step: an uneven, swaying step. The man was drunk. A slow curve crept up one side of his perfectly puffed mouth and tugged the other side to join, revealing a dimple I wanted to trace. My panties smoldered. The next spark of fireworks in the sky matched the instant pulse between my thighs, igniting my sensible cotton underwear. I squeezed my thighs together, imagining this stranger's mouth on the most intimate parts of me. My sex clenched, and I looked away. Oh God, I *was* desperate, if I was imagining a stranger doing such things to me.

"Merek Elliott, meet Emme," Todd offered. "Emme, Merek."

"Yummy," he muttered with a chuckle. Instantly, I was enveloped in a sloppy hug. A dribble of beer from his bottle poured down my back as his mammoth arms engulfed me. He inhaled deeply next to my head, before he pulled back. With a slur, he said: "You're lovely." A hint of Irish brogue twisted into his drunken compliment, and cursing myself, I blushed again.

"It's Emme," I emphasized when he released me. "It's short for Mary Elizabeth. M. E." Using my finger, I traced the letter M and E in the air as I enunciated my nickname since childhood.

"That's what I said, Yum. Me."

"Okay, Chief. Don't be hitting on my ladies." Todd reached out a hand to steady the man beside us. Drawing back, Merek held my gaze before his eyes slowly drooped downward to close, and then snapped open again. He swayed back on his feet, one kicking out to catch himself.

"I'm not hitting on her," Merek said. "No hitting," he said, raising his beer bottle and taking a final long pull. I turned to Gia, who shrugged her shoulders, before glancing ahead again at the crowd near the end of the block. She returned her attention to my phone.

"MatchMe?" Todd asked, squinting at what held Gia's interest. "Don't you already have like twelve of those accounts?" he teased.

"Thirteen," she said without batting an eye, "and it's not for me. It's for Emme."

"Gia," I squawked, raising a hand to cover one side of my face, as if it would shield my embarrassment, while she shared this information with our most notorious neighbor and a sexy stranger. Why didn't she just mark me with a giant D, like the scarlet letter? D is for desperate.

"MatchMe?" Merek questioned with a slur. "The dating site?"

I couldn't respond. Reaching for my phone again, Gia relinquished it to me, and I stared down at a picture of myself. I hated having my picture taken, and this one didn't flatter me anymore than any other might. I instantly found a hundred things to criticize. My chin sagged. The skin under my eyes had darkened with age, suggesting I didn't sleep. My eyes didn't sparkle cobalt blue like they once had. My nose was too pointed. My hair was almost white-blonde, and I had an age spot on my cheek.

"How do I delete this?" I scowled at Gia and anyone else standing too close.

"You don't," she offered. "You use it. Just see what happens. Who responds."

"I bet you'll get plenty of offers," Todd commented. "But mine still stands, of course."

I glared at him, and I sensed the weight of Merek's eyes on Todd, too.

"I'll make you an offer," Merek suggested. All three of our heads turned in his direction.

"Oh yeah," Gia teased. "What offer you going to make her?"

"What do you need?" He tilted his head ever so slightly to one side.

"Nothing," I blurted at the same time Gia said, "Sex."

An audible groan escaped Todd, and a shaky hand wiped down his face then slid over his large belly and lower, adjusting himself at the mere mention of sex. I looked away, willing the ground to open up and swallow me. I wanted to kill Gia at the moment, just strangle her right in the street. I could read the headline now: *Friend Murders Friend for Soliciting Sex with a Stranger on Her Behalf.* I covered my own face in horror.

"I'm leaving now," I said, spinning away from Gia.

"Wait," Merek's voice froze me in a half-spin. "I'll give you a ride." He swayed back on his feet again. He righted himself this time with a firm stomp with his left. Legs straddled, he put in the effort to hold himself still. Something softened in those dark eyes, but I assumed it was nothing more than the sleepiness that takes over a drunken man at the end of his limit.

"You're too drunk to drive. Besides, I walked," I said, swiping the hand that held my phone before me. I didn't live far, and the two-block walk was what I needed to burn off the shame and fury.

"Here," he suggested, holding out a hand for my phone. "I can delete your MatchMe account. I used to have one."

Reluctantly, I held my phone out for Merek. He pressed several buttons and pushed down the home key. The phone went to the main screen. Returning the phone to me, I pushed the home key, and the first window to open was my contacts.

"What's this?" I scoffed, holding out the phone for him to read.

"My number. Think of me like Uber. You need a ride, I'm your man." He winked. Gia snatched my phone from my hands and laughed as she glanced at the screen.

"Oh, my God." Forgetting all about my phone, I turned and stalked toward my home on the other side of the park.

Chapter 2
The Arrangement

[M.E.]

Sitting at the bar, I stared at my phone. I didn't know what else to do with myself. It had been years since I'd gone to a bar alone, and I felt like everyone was looking at me. Of course, they weren't. Who would notice a forty-something woman with blonde-gray hair at a bar? Only men over sixty, which, no offense to that age category, but it didn't describe me. Yet.

I couldn't believe Gia had talked me into this. After returning my phone the day after the party, she explained I already had a "connection" on MatchMe. It wasn't even a date. It was simply a meeting of sorts. She showed me a few of the hits I had, which were unacceptable.

You like me long time.

Nope to the person who can't speak English.

U look hot 4 an older woman. MILF all the way. I'm in.

Nope to the younger person who couldn't seem to spell.

I like piña coladas and getting caught in the rain.

Nope to the guy who smoked a big one before sending out the message.

She assured me the request for tonight was a good offer. This matchmaking thing seemed hopeless, and besides, I didn't want to date. The idea of starting over, getting to know someone, trust them, and spend time coordinating my life with theirs just didn't appeal to me. I recalled the awkward moments when I first dated Nate. We didn't click immediately. It wasn't love at first sight, but more like a slow progression of connection. He was smooth and patient. He wined and dined me, like I'd never experienced before. Intrigued by his interest in me, the quiet one of our bunch in college, I hesitated to form a relationship. In hindsight, it seemed like circumstance kept us together, moving us forward, until marriage was the natural next step at twenty-two years old.

I was comfortable with myself. Not in my skin, but by myself, I was good. I didn't mind going to a movie alone, just not on a Friday night. I had no problem eating alone at a corner deli with a good book as my date. At times, I wished for a companion, but I was so busy with work and the girls, I was okay alone. I was. Sitting at the bar was another story.

I was self-conscious of my pencil skirt that might or might not be cutting off my circulation, and my heels that kept slipping into the rung of the stool. With the air conditioning on high, my skin chilled in the lightweight, flouncy, sheer blouse Gia encouraged me to wear.

"Just wear your black bra," she argued.

"No. No way am I only wearing my bra and nothing else under this see-through material," I countered. Besides, if my breasts were on full display, so was my stomach. A strappy tank camouflaged some of the lumps across my lower abdomen. Conscious of it rolling up a little, I tried to sit straighter on the stool.

Everything was Gia's fault. She'd accepted an invitation through MatchMe to meet someone. Assuring me she hadn't picked someone too young or too old, too cheesy or too suave, I currently sat at the bar waiting for my "arrangement." It wasn't a date. It was a meeting. Fifteen minutes. If either of us decided we wanted more, we could go from there, but the initial in-person conversation arranged for only a drink.

"You're going to be fine," Gia soothed as she smoothed back my hair like I was a child. *"You can even time it if you wish."*

Did people really do that? I wondered. I worked well with schedules, a trait I'd picked up from Nate over the years.

"I'll can even call you and fake an emergency, if you wish."

O'Malley's was a nod to the Irish nature of our neighborhood. Old-world-pub-themed with dark wood, dim lighting, and banners of Irish bands decorated the small space. I'd been here a multitude of times with my late husband, with ladies from the area, and with my daughters. It was strange to sit here alone, and I worried that someone I knew would walk in and see me. On the other hand, Gia thought this was the best place to meet as I was close to home. This environment felt comfortable, and I had the protection of possibly seeing someone if I needed another excuse to end the meeting.

Still fiddling with my phone, aimlessly clearing out my emails, I hardly noticed the person who took the seat next to me. The stool pulled back, so I looked up in curiosity. A man, I noted, and then returned to my phone. Quickly, I did a second take.

"Merek," the bartender said, addressing him. "Long time, no see, you old bugger."

I blinked. It was more than a man that sat next to me. It was that guy from the block party. My eyes roamed downward, assessing him: dress shirt rolled to the elbows, nice pants, and flip-flops. Dressy, but understated by the casual footwear, he certainly looked more pulled together than the cargo shorts and tight t-shirt from the street party. He turned to face me, and my breath hitched as his dark eyes captured my stare. I blushed, while he extended a hand to me.

"Merek Elliott," he offered.

Wide-eyed, I took too long to respond, and he lowered his hand. He shifted toward the bartender, who took his order, and I spun away from him, returning my attention to my phone, frantically scrolling through emails though not reading a thing. My breathing was shallow and goose bumps rose on my skin. The damn air conditioning. *Was there a chill in here?*

"You don't remember me?" he asked, and my attention twisted back to him.

"I…well, how could I forget?" I scoffed. "You made a memorable impression."

His eyebrows pinched but his face was full of mirth.

"Oh yeah? What did I say?" The crinkles by his eyes teased me. That sassy dimple peeked out.

The heat in my face racketed upward. "Something about Uber," I muttered.

"Well, that certainly explains it." He slipped his phone out of his pocket and shook it in my direction before setting it on the dark wooden bar.

"Explains what?" My eyebrows pinched as I glanced in the direction of the screen.

"You asked for a ride." The curve of his lips while he smirked lit up his eyes. The call of that lickable dimple magnified under the end-of-the-day scruff, and his eyes sparked with specks of gold and green mixed among the dark streaks. There wasn't enough air in the bar. I reached for the edge of my blouse and fanned it outward to cool myself. *Was it hot in here?*

"I did no such thing." My tone sounded like a child denying he stole a cookie before dinner. Sitting up straighter, I reached for his phone which he tapped. A text message conversation lit up the screen.

Would love to take you up on that offer of a ride?

The speech bubble was green.

Pardon me?

The response was gray.

At the block party, you offered me a lift. (winky emoticon)

The reply was green, followed by a second green invitation.

Say 7 pm at O'Malley's.

Blinking rapidly, my heart raced. My throat dried and my stomach fluttered. It couldn't be. I mean, I'd have to have his *num*— the thought faded away and a horrifying truth surfaced. I did have his number, but I hadn't contacted him.

Gia, my brain growled. Letting her touch my phone had obviously been dangerous. I felt foolish and more than embarrassed, like get-the-mop-ready-to-wipe-me-up-because-I-wanted-to-melt-on-the-spot, mortified.

"I'm so sorry," I offered, "there's been a terrible misunderstanding."

"So you didn't want to ride me?" The dimple toyed with me. His lips rolled to suppress his laughter.

"I...oh my God, you didn't just say that to me," I chuckled. He smiled, a genuine, full-on smile, and another part of me needed a mopping. I crossed my legs. His eyes wandered to the motion, lingering as one knee climbed over the other. My skirt rode up, exposing more than my kneecaps. I tugged at material that wouldn't go back down.

"I think there's been a mistake," I began again.

"You didn't send this text?" He waved the phone at me. Well, it was my number, but it wasn't me. How could I explain that this was a sick joke from my ex-best friend? I planned to disown her as soon as I escaped from this awkward situation.

"Actually, I didn't," I responded, but he cut me off.

"Yet, you're here," he said, raising an eyebrow over those teasing eyes. The dimple flashed again, blinding me with thoughts of tracing it with my tongue. *How would those lips taste?* I wondered. Blinking hard and turning away from him, I took a hearty gulp of my wine.

"I have a date." I choked on the words. Merek gazed exaggeratedly over his shoulder, and then turned back to me.

"Well, don't let me interrupt." His lips puckered in distaste.

"Well, I mean, he's coming."

Those damn eyebrows rose again. The slight wrinkles by his eyes danced in delight.

"I mean…"

"I got it," he smirked.

A thought suddenly occurred to me. "Why are you here?"

"Having a beer." He jiggled the draft in his hand before taking a long swallow. I stared as his Adam's apple rolled along his throat, and my mouth watered, my mind drifting to thoughts of kissing along that path. A shaky hand came to my forehead. I was a mess. I needed to get laid. No, correction, I just needed to get my mind out of the gutter.

"So, you didn't come to meet me?" My eyes lowered, troubled by the thought.

"Guess not." He shook his head. "So where's your date?"

Could Gia have done this? My brain was slow to compute that there was no date. There was no arrangement. Instead of setting me up with someone random from MatchMe, Gia had lied and set me up with someone more realistic. A friend of a friend in the neighborhood. This was suddenly worse. I didn't need the neighbors knowing my business.

"I think there's been a mistake." Reaching for my clutch purse on the bar, I fumbled for some bills to cover my wine.

"How much?" I asked, but it came out like a holler at the young man serving me.

"That's $7.50."

I nearly choked. I wasn't a recluse, but I didn't go out much on my own to drinking establishments. For seven dollars and fifty cents I could have purchased a whole bottle of wine, stayed at home with a good book, and spared myself all this humiliation.

"Let me get it," Merek offered, reaching for his back pocket.

"No," I snapped. "I mean, no. Thank you."

His eyes softened a little, the lines around them becoming more prominent. I was making a fool of myself, and I wanted nothing more than to walk away, while I still had a shred of pride left.

"I've made a terrible mistake," I stated again. "He isn't going to show, and I think I'm just going to go home." I brushed off the idea that I might have purposely been set up with Merek. Standing from the stool, forced me into Merek's space. My heel caught on the rung, and as I stumbled forward, Merek's hand shot out to steady me at my waist. While the thought of his hands on me ignited wayward images through my brain, the idea that he just squeezed the flabby part of my waistline made me flinch. I was out of my mind thinking someone like him would touch me in pleasure, and I was out of control with the whole need-for-sex thing. Excusing myself, I walked toward the front door of O'Malley's.

Chapter 3
The Date

[M.E. 2 = Merek Elliott]

I watched her sweet ass walk away from me. Shaking my head, I turned toward Thomas O'Malley, the young son of the proprietor of this joint, and winked. I finished the rest of my beer and twisted toward the front door to see Emme trapped by four men. They obviously knew her, and she smiled politely in return to something one of them said. She nodded, laughed, and squeezed between them, continuing her exit of the bar. Each man took his turn to admire her backside as she passed by them, taking a moment too long, in my opinion, to follow the sashay of her black skirt exiting.

For some reason, this pissed me off. She had a nice shape, but there wasn't anything else that stood out to me. She wasn't my typical type. I'd gone after younger women. At first, the youthful twenty somethings were a decent age to conquer; full of spunk and discovery, but in recent years, the age group hit a little too close to home. I'd moved up to late twenties or early thirties. I found flirty-thirties were too needy, though. In the childbearing age, wanting a little more than I was willing to offer, these women were confident and willful in experimentation. At forty-two, I was growing too old for their shenanigans for emotional entrapment. I refused to date for this very reason. I didn't want to get too close to one woman again.

Strutting to the booth behind me, the men sat, and I lingered when I heard one of them say, "I'd tap that." The others laughed heartily, and I returned my focus to Thomas across the bar. He watched the men over my shoulder. Preppy types, in basketball shorts and athletic shirts, the rowdy bunch showed their age. Paunch stomachs, bald heads, and reading glasses filled out their images. Their type was one I recognized all too well. Their wives were probably home alone reading about sex instead of having it because their husbands were assholes who went out with "the boys". I shook my head and stood from the stool.

"Good to see ya, old man." Thomas laughed as he took my ten. I waved before leaving the small local pub. I liked O'Malley's, but I didn't hang out there often. It was too close to home – literally. I knew Thomas' dad from the old neighborhood by my parents' house.

While I walked past the parking lot on the side of the building, I noticed Emme talking to another man: Mike Murphy. He was a city police officer, and I'd had some run-ins with him on occasion. He was an odd guy, and for some unknown reason, I never trusted him. Just had that gnawing suspicion about him. I don't know what made me do it, but I stopped. Emme looked uncomfortable, despite the smile pressed across those pink lips. I'd been trying not to get caught staring at those lips while she spoke to me. They looked ripe for kissing. In fact, I think they needed a swift kiss. A breathtaking, heart-stopping, dick-straining kind of kiss. And I wanted to give her one while she stared at me all wide-eyed and horrified at the bar.

Her eyes flipped up and met mine across the lot. Her forced smile turned back to Mike, and she stepped back. He followed. She was almost pressed up against her car.

Sauntering into the lot, I came close enough to hear Mike asking her if she'd like to go inside for a drink.

"I was just leaving," she stated. "But thank you."

He started talking again, but I cut him off.

"Emme, everything okay?"

Mike turned toward me, his mousy face pinching as his narrow eyes skimmed my face.

"Emme and I are just having a chat. We haven't seen each other in a while."

I stepped closer to the two of them. Emme's eyes weren't leaving my face, but I couldn't read her expression. She shook her head infinitesimally and I took another step. Mike had this nervous quality about him, almost jittery, and his hand shook as he addressed Emme again. "Well, if you ever want to have a burger, they have the best ones. Monday night, it's the special."

Something told me Emme did not want to be alone with Mike, and I refused to move. I easily stood six inches taller and at least fifty pounds heavier than the scrawny man before me. Mike's eyes shifted sideways to me before he mumbled, "Nice to see you again, Emme." He stepped away from her. Waiting until Mike was around the corner of the building, I turned on Emme.

"Mike Murphy? Really?"

"I…he…" Her voice fumbled before she stood up straighter. "Truthfully, he creeps me out. He used to see me at the gym and follow me around the track, as if we were old friends. I'd like to thank you for interrupting him. I think you scared him."

"Me?" I laughed.

She smiled slowly and my breath hitched. Those lips again begged mine for connection. Her eyes were bright blue, and her hair practically glowed under the streetlamp. She definitely wasn't in her twenties, but there was something about the way she looked at me that made me feel like a young man again. I took another step closer to her.

"I didn't mean to run you off from your date." My voice lowered with the apology.

She waved a hand dismissing me. "It wasn't a date. It was just an arrangement." Her pretty eyes shifted away from me, and she twirled the flat purse in her hands.

"An arrangement? Like a MatchMe thing?" I growled.

"Well, I thought so, but I don't know." Her eyes refused to meet mine.

"You thought so?"

"I mean, that's what Gia told me. She set this all up for me, I guess." Her shoulders drooped.

"Why MatchMe?"

Shaking her head, she refused to answer. My fingers tipped up her chin. Her skin was soft, slightly tan from the summer sun. When she smiled, her teeth gleamed pure white. She wasn't smiling at the question I'd asked.

"Tell me." I softened my tone but refused to let go of her. My skin prickled where it touched her. I didn't want the sensation to end.

"I just…I don't need commitment," she whispered. My eyes widened.

"What do you need?" My voice graveled, raspy and rough. I swallowed and my pants tightened at the nearness of her.

"I just…" She closed her eyes and shook her head despite my hold.

I waited her out. She'd tell me. I filled the gap between us and her lush breasts brushed against me. The tender ripple of that flimsy shirt against my crisp oxford made me hyperaware of her. She was shorter than me, my chin coming to her forehead. If I dipped lower, her lips were all I'd need. Cursing myself for such thoughts, I held my breath while I cupped her chin. Her ragged breathing forced her breasts to lightly skim up and down my chest, the sensation a teasing tickle of what lay beneath that sheer blouse. Her breasts were large, nipples peaked. I had a sudden suspicion about her needs.

"Were you looking for a one-night stand?"

Her face jerked back from my grip, and she fumbled. My hand instinctively reached for her waist and manicured nails scratched at my chest to steady herself. The effect rippled through me. She hadn't answered me.

"Too bad for your date," I muttered, my lips twisted in frustration.

"It wasn't a date." Her voice was barely a whisper. Her eyes focused on my mouth. Her teeth sneaked a tender bite of her lower lip and the desire to capture that lip with mine flamed uncontrollably.

"About that date, by the way…" My nose skimmed along her jaw to below her ear. Her breath hitched and I pulled back. "He showed."

Chapter 4
Said Too Much

[M.E.]

After giving Gia a huge what-the-hell lecture, I stopped speaking with her. The humiliation was debilitating, and I returned home crying over my pathetic needs. Why couldn't I be like normal people? Why didn't I have toys to take care of this or just handle it all myself? Those weren't legitimate questions, though. I wanted sex—the physical connection with another human being. Note, I wasn't saying emotional connection. I wasn't a love-sick teenager in need of assurance that a man felt the same about me. On the other hand, whoever I finally slept with couldn't belittle me. I needed someone sensitive enough to accept my body, even if they didn't care about me. I was pathetic.

A week passed after my embarrassing encounter at O'Malley's. I'd given up hope of solving my problem, and I refused to check my MatchMe account. It just wasn't going to be the way I met someone. I fumbled with groceries while my phone went off in my purse. Scrambling over receipts, loose change, and something unidentifiable, my fingers blindly searched for the phone. I didn't find it quick enough, and the call passed. Finally, setting down the groceries, I checked my phone for messages from Mitzi and Bree.

As teenagers, they were hardly home. My beautiful brunette, Mitzi, was involved in swimming and coached younger girls for a local swim team. Blonde-haired, blue-eyed Bree starred in most of the school's plays. Summer freedom left them with less time at home. Other than occasional food refueling and nightly rest stops, the girls worked at a summer day camp. Six weeks of preschool-aged mishaps, middle-grade frustrations, and young teenage antics highlighted stories told on rare nights they were home to have dinner. Summer was always a conflict for me, as I worked the summer session at North East University. I hated leaving the girls alone while I had to work. Mitzi was going to be a senior, while Bree was a sophomore, and having summer jobs made this summer easier.

My messages showed Mitzi had a date with her boyfriend. Bree planned to meet a group of kids at the movie theatre for a summer blockbuster. The night would be mine. Again. Then I noticed one more text message.

Need a lift tonight?

I stared at the gray conversation bubble.

Merek Elliott. I smiled in spite of myself. Looking around my empty kitchen, I realized I didn't have any other plans. Maybe I should just be honest with him. Tell him what I wanted. Gia told me that's how modern women did it. They were open about their bedroom desires. I didn't think I could ever be open like that. What I had with Nate had been good. We were compatible in the sex department. I'd dare to label it an area we clicked, but there were moments I thought it could have been better. We were pretty missionary. The occasional times we mixed it up seemed fleeting and reckless. Afraid Nate would question my sanity, my morals, or my desires, I never mentioned things I'd like to try. Cursing the memory of Nate finding other means for his sexual adventures, I responded to Merek.

Sure.

Well don't overwhelm me with words, he responded, and I laughed out loud.

O'Malley's? I offered, dreading the suggestion.

I was thinking of something more out of the hood.

Hood? Was he twenty? I lived in a respectable neighborhood of Chicago that was more suburban than some suburbs. A park where all the kids played. A local eatery where the owners knew your name. My hand paused in mid-air, the phone weighing heavily in my hand.

He suggested a place named NorthSiders, located in Bucktown.

After responding with the lame, single word: **Okay**, I called Gia.

"Am I setting myself up to be ax murdered?" I breathed into the phone. She laughed immediately and I continued on, while sweat trickled under my arms, and my skin chilled despite the evening heat.

"Or tied up and tortured?" Stress apparent in my tone.

"Have you been reading again?" she admonished with a tease. "Seriously, why would you ask?"

"I think I'm getting laid tonight and I need some advice," I blurted.

"Well, honey, the long thing sticking out of his body is a penis and it gets inserted into your…"

"Not that," I laughed, as she used her nurse tone with me. As if Director of Nursing for Swedish Covenant Hospital wasn't enough for her, she also taught a basic health course at North East. That's where we'd met three years ago.

"I don't even know where to start," I breathed heavily.

"Shower. Shave. Everywhere," she emphasized.

"Everywhere?" I choked. She couldn't be serious. Armpits, check. Legs, check. Landing strip, check.

"Every. Where," she stated confidently. "Guys like that," Her voice teased with schoolgirl excitement.

"Like shave *it*?" I choked for clarification.

"It's okay. You can say the word *va*—"

"I got it," I interrupted her. "Won't I cut myself? Something vital? It's all folded and lumpy down there." I laughed nervously.

"Just take your time. Be careful. You'll be great. He'll love it," she assured me. "Bare is the new there," she added confidently.

What?

I wasn't convinced and risking a *Fried Green Tomatoes* moment of self-discovery with a mirror between my legs, I decided against it. I didn't want to assume we'd make it that far on the first night. What would it say about me if we did? Then again, this wasn't a date. Plus, this wasn't about his thoughts of me. This was about getting laid with no strings attached. Wasn't that how the modern dating world worked? Sex friends, or whatever it's called?

I readied myself and pulled up near NorthSiders. Parking was difficult on a summer's evening, and I had to turn down a side street, and then look for places that weren't marked with "permit necessary". Although I arrived early, the circus of parking made me a few minutes late. My hands shook, and my underarms were moist. The night was warm but not so warm we couldn't sit out on the patio of the bar.

Merek sat comfortably, leaning back in a chair, a beer dangling from his hand. I spotted him before he saw me. Thankful in some ways he actually showed, I was well aware this was a pity date when I saw the brilliant smile he flashed the young waitress. She might have been too young for him in my opinion, but she wasn't too young to notice a good-looking man. He was the epitome of casual, in his flip-flops and khaki shorts. He noticed me saunter through the tables, but the waitress remained until I approached.

"Nice to see you again, Lettie," he said, reaching out a hand to grip hers lightly. She blushed and walked away from the table. He stood as soon as I was close enough and reached for my chair, but I already had a hand on the back of it. I wasn't used to a gentleman, honestly. My late husband hadn't always been one. It was one of the things that bothered me as time went on. Nate never opened a door without entering it himself first. He might have waited until I sat, but he didn't hold out my chair, and he never opened the car door for me. It was an annoying fact that he would actually get in the car first, then press the unlock button after I stood in the rain or cold for a minute, while he fumbled to clear the passenger seat. Reminding myself it was disrespectful to curse the dead, I sat across from Merek, who raised his hand to grab the attention of another young thing who was a waitress.

"Find the place alright?" he asked casually, before sipping from his beer.

Explaining my parking woes and struggles with parallel parking, I realized I talked too much, mainly afraid if I stopped, I'd shatter. I shook with chill despite the heat, and for some reason, the presence of Merek this night seemed different. Maybe it was because he sat across from me and had a better chance to observe me versus when we sat side by side at O'Malley's. Maybe it was because the question of sex gnawed at me. He was attentive while I rambled. Then he cut me off.

"Still registered with MatchMe?" He sat back again, crossing an ankle over his knee. His hair wasn't long, but it ruffled in the breeze. Flecks of gray never looked so good on a man. Those playful eyes gleamed under the lowering sunlight, and that dimple, my heart raced in a place that needed attention.

"It's Gia's fault. I'm confused when I'm on there," I explained. "I mean how hard can it be to find a man? No whips, no chains. No spanking, no plugging. No gray ties. No restraints. No flogging necessary. I just want a man to have sex with me." My hand swiped through my hair. My voice rose then faded as I realized I'd definitely said too much. Swallowing hard, I sat up straighter and reached for my glass of wine.

"How hard indeed," he mumbled, before taking another sip of his beer. He raised his hand again, signaling for our waitress, and I was glad he looked away for her attention because unbearable shame washed over me. I lowered my head and rubbed my forehead. I hardly knew this man and I'd just spewed a laundry list of conditions that had no meaning to him.

"Sorry," I muttered. "That was definitely too much information."

"So tell me more about yourself." He blatantly ignored my apology. I sighed, knowing this was the part I feared. How do you tell someone about the past twenty years of your life? Do you start with college? Do you jump forward to your career and then speak in a reverse timeline about yourself? I wasn't good at small talk, but I began the boring litany of how I was a college professor of English at NEU. How long I'd worked there, what I liked about the university, and what I'd really wanted to be instead of what I was. Again, it was all too much information.

"Children?" he asked. That's where I drew a line. I didn't want to be defined by my two amazing daughters. This night was not about them, and the moment I spoke about their accomplishments, I'd be a mother, instead of a woman having a drink with a man.

"What about you?" I interjected, hoping to divert our conversation to him.

"Not much to tell you, my dear," he smirked, hinting at secrets. He reached for his beer and took another deep sip. His eyes didn't leave mine.

"Don't call me that," I sputtered, uncertain where the tone came from, but knowing why I didn't want him to say that endearment.

"Why not?" He rested an arm along the side of his chair.

"My husband called me that."

"And he's…"

"Dead." The word was definitive, and the cocky smile on Merek's face fell flat. Nate was gone, and tonight was not about raising his memory, either.

"I'm sorry," he said, sitting forward. His hands rubbed together while his elbows rested on his knees. He looked downward for a moment, thoughtful for a second, before sitting upright so quickly it startled me.

"What would you like to be called instead?" His mouth tweaked slowly.

"Emme." I drew out the sound of my name. Mary Elizabeth O'Grady Peters was a mouthful. When I was a child, I wanted something more glamorous, and I took the nickname Emme for the M and E of my formal name. A second passed before I realized he was flirting with me.

"I meant as an endearment," He further twisted the side of his mouth. His tone teased.

"I always thought baby was sweet, darling, maybe, or love would be nice. You know when men say it in those English accents, it's just so…" I shivered excitedly then realized I was speaking too much again, and what I said was just garbage spewing from my mouth.

"Uhm…I don't actually know what you mean," he teased.

"You had an Irish accent the other night."

"When I drink too much it slips out, or so I'm told. If I'm that drunk, I don't know what I'm saying." He laughed as he finished his beer.

"So, you don't remember asking to be my Uber?" My eyebrow rose in question. He smiled slowly, like a mischievous child. Then his expression shifted.

"Husband didn't say, 'Sweetheart, I'm home' each time he entered the house?" His lips smirked.

Actually, he didn't do that. In fact, most nights he'd walk in the door and go directly to our room to change out of his suit. He'd come down for dinner and mention his day. He didn't ask about mine and when I wanted to speak, he was too distracted to listen. Calling me *dear* had been Nate's patronizing way of dismissing me. Other tender terms were out of the question. The memory hit me hard, and the guilt at the negativity made me feel like a bad person. The memory caught up to me and my eyes filled with liquid.

"Don't mind me." I waved a hand dismissively. Crying *before* sex would certainly make an impression, but I already convinced myself I'd dug enough of a hole that I'd never see Merek naked or again.

"I'm just a silly, frustrated woman." Blinking rapidly, I took another sip of my second wine. The taste was suddenly bitter, and I understood why MatchMe had timed arrangements. I was so awkward, even I wanted to get away from me in fifteen minutes or less.

Merek sat forward again, his hands clasped as his elbows braced on his knees.

"Want to finish that?" he offered, nodding in the direction of my wine. The dismissal evident. Merek really was finished with me.

"I'm good," I said, and his head shot up to stare at me for a long moment. Dark eyes danced while the slight lines of skin around them crinkled. My stomach fluttered. His good looks left me breathless. For the millionth time, I wondered if his lips would be tender or rough.

He stood abruptly, dropped two twenties on the table, and I followed him. As we sauntered through the tables, making our way through the main restaurant area to the front door, an older gentleman smiled at me. Noticeably older with full onset white hair and over-tanned skin, he muttered "Lucky man" as we passed him and Merek's hand made contact with my lower back. I always thought this touch was a tender show of possessiveness. If only that were true with Merek. I smiled kindly in response to the elder man's comment. It was sweet but deflating. He was exactly the type of man I attracted. Older.

Suddenly feeling ancient, I prepared to part ways with Merek.

"Where's your car?" he asked, and I pointed in the general direction of the side street.

"I'll walk you," he offered. Raising a hand, I decided to end the misery of my evening.

"I've got it. Thanks for the drink." Awkward once again, I didn't know whether to stick out a hand to shake his or to reach in for an air hug. Instead, I did neither. I just pointed over my shoulder, motioning the direction of my car. I turned and took a step when his hand hit my back again.

"I said, I'll walk with you. I'm going that way, anyway."

Chapter 5
The Proposal

[M.E. 2]

I was convinced, she didn't see what I saw. While she wasn't young like my typical partners, she was something. Drawn to her, I wasn't ready to let her go. In fact, my curiosity was piqued. She rattled off her list of hard limits, and I nearly lost it in my shorts as the list continued. I wouldn't admit whether I'd practiced most of what she listed, but the mere idea that someone sweet looking in a yellow sundress knew what most of those things were, was shocking.

To say she seemed innocent was an overstatement. If I had to guess, nerves made her ramble. I'd learned from Todd that her husband had been dead for a year, but I'd forgotten in the playfulness of calling her "my dear." The expression of confusion at the term twisted to a hint of hurt and I cursed myself for asking about him. I didn't want her to think of someone else when she sat across from me, especially someone who evidently caused her pain. It was one of the reasons I preferred the younger, unattached girls. No ex-husband or deceased one to contend with from the past. Occasionally, an old lover, maybe an ex-boyfriend, but that's where I came into play. I relieved the memory. Young, free, and emotionally unavailable – that's how I liked them.

Emme was definitely emotional. It didn't escape me that her eyes filled with tears and her sad expression chipped at my heart. Her openness was refreshing, but inside her was a closed-up woman. Frustrated, that had been her word. A plan slowly formed in my mind, but I couldn't get a read on how receptive she'd be to it. This wasn't some MatchMe arrangement I planned to present to her. This was more.

We walked in silence down the side street. The irony of the location wasn't lost on me. She had parked in front of the apartment. I had two choices here: a road well-traveled would mean saying goodnight and never thinking of her again, but the uncharted path intrigued me. When she stopped on the sidewalk, midway between the apartment entrance and a parked car, she spun toward me. Her mouth opened, but before she could speak, I cut her off.

"I'd like to make a proposal." Her blue eyes twinkled. The bright reflection of the setting sun softened the blue.

"I wonder, if you'd come inside?" My hand directed her attention to the building on my right. Her eyes narrowed for a moment before opening wide.

"You're not an ax-murderer, are you?" she blurted. Her face turned a sweet shade of pink, highlighting her subtle tan.

"Last time I checked, no," I smirked. "I also don't do whips, chains, spanking, or plugging. I don't own any gray ties. No restraints. No flogger either. Did I miss anything?"

Her eyes opened wider, if that were possible, and then she laughed. My heart melted.

"Oh, my gosh. How did you…I mean…you memorized…you actually listened to me?" The surprise in her tone emphasized the shock on her face. My first thought was: *why wouldn't I listen*? My second recognized she hadn't been heard very often. It was a shame. One skill I prided myself on was listening and observing the reaction of women.

Emme intrigued me, but I prepared for her to turn away. Older women weren't interested in playing games and the second I had her in the door, she might regret the decision. She'd be talking futures and children and coordinating schedules. I didn't want any of that. I just wanted one night with her.

Continuing to stare at me, her eyes dewed over for a moment and then she blinked. The mask returned, and she looked away instantly.

"So, would you like to come?" I nodded in the direction of the apartment. The innuendo was intentional

"I'm sorry." Blue eyes hammered me to the sidewalk.

"Inside. Will you come inside with me?" While she hesitated for a moment, she stepped toward me, and I had my answer. She was intrigued, as well.

Chapter 6
A Proposal of Sorts

[M.E.]

The inside of his second-floor apartment was very masculine. The living room had a black leather couch with a glass coffee table. A flat screen television hung on the wall with a series of cables and wires running under it to a gaming system. For a moment, I wondered if I'd entered the home of a grown man-child. Boys and their toys, but there was something else that caught my attention. A shelf on the wall had an array of photos. I attempted to step toward it when Merek cut me off.

"Here's my proposition," he started. "Let's not make things complicated. I think we both know where we want this to end, but let's just take our time to clarify things," he said.

A sigh of relief seeped out of me as I wasn't certain what I was doing or how to do what I wanted. My body was wound tight but another part of me literally dripped with desire. There was no doubt what I wanted: him. His body exuded sex. The way he quirked his lip. The sparkle in his mossy brown eyes. The hint of mischief in his expressions. The scruff on his jaw. It all begged for my attention, and he had it. My body hummed with need that was almost audible. My problem: I didn't know how to seduce him.

Being here was the craziest thing I'd ever done.

While I'd met my husband at a college party, and left with him that first night, we didn't have sex until many nights later. We went on a real date first. But this night felt different, wild and reckless, yet not dangerous. I was not frightened of Merek per se. I was terrified I'd make a fool of myself. Before I knew it, my body pressed against the wall with Merek's body holding me in place. His hands were above my head on both sides. My breath came heavy, forcing my breasts to brush ever so lightly against Merek's dress shirt. The sound was a tender rustling, but all I heard was my erect nipples against my satiny bra, crying out to press against him, naked.

"I thought you said, take our time?" The words tumbled out of my mouth on a whisper. My eyes were trained on his lips. He twisted them and it snapped my attention to his full face.

"I have my own hard limit, and it's important." His voice took on a smoky harshness that teased but warned me. "No kissing on the mouth."

This startled me enough that my lingering eyes on his jaw shot up to his eyes. The sparkle had flicked out. Those eyes told me he was earnest. I felt like I might be in a scene from *Pretty Woman*, only the roles reversed. A kiss was too intimate, or something like that, I remembered Julia Roberts saying. Merek set the same standard. Kissing would be intimate. This night would not involve emotion. It was like he read my mind, or at least I hoped he could because I wanted him. This could work. Kissing would be too personal. *Keep kissing out*, my mind whispered. I could do that. If there was an emotional burn, I'd have to deal with the fire afterward. Right now, I wanted to play with the flame.

"All right," I swallowed as a thick hand came to my cheek and caressed the skin so tenderly goose bumps rose across my skin. It had been a long time since I'd been touched in this manner. In a way that hints of things desired. He slipped his fingers down to my neck, his thumb cascaded over my throat before his index finger dipped along the top of my dress, over the curve of my breast. My hands had been at my side, but inched behind me, forcing my breasts forward for his attention. His mouth slowly curved upward. He read my body language.

Surprising me further, his mouth crashed to my neck and sucked delicately down the angle of my throat to the juncture of my shoulder.

"I thought you said no kissing," I whimpered when he suddenly nipped my neck hard enough that my knees buckled, and my sex pulsed.

"No kissing on the lips. Everywhere else is fair game," he groaned into my skin, sensitive and alive with the contact of his mouth. Prickling sparks covered me and I vibrated with the need to touch him in response. My hands followed their own will and rubbed up his thick arms to his broad shoulders. While one of his hands remained braced above me, he lowered the other to wrap around my back and tugged me against him. The moment our bodies collided, I ignited.

"Oh God," I moaned at the very nearness of him. I hadn't touched another man, aside from Nate, in twenty years. The feel of this one was so different. Refreshing and exciting in a way I shouldn't have compared in my head. In fact, I didn't want Nate anywhere near what I was doing. My mind needed to remain clear in order for my body to stay in this game. Merek's responding hum returned me to the present.

"Your proposition?" I questioned as his mouth worked its way to removing the material over my shoulder. His teeth covered the strap of my dress and tugged it down my chilled arm.

"I propose we only think of each other and tonight," he muttered as his lips continued the sparking attack along my collarbone. "Tell me what you want. For tonight."

Remaining silent, I reveled in the tenderness of his kisses over the surface of my skin. The tiny suction and moist lips, washing my skin, like a baptism.

"I'd like to offer you a deal," he muttered into the crease of my shoulder. "Sex. No strings attached."

Hyperaware of his presence and making assumptions about his body, my concentration faltered.

"Emme?" he questioned, snapping me out of images of his bare chest and firm length.

"Yes," I exhaled, wantonly, until both his hands lowered to my hips. Suddenly, I stiffened. He couldn't touch the soft rolls and ridges formed by the boy shorts Gia talked me into wearing. Made to give a smooth look under my dress, the waist was cut higher to hold my tummy flat. It wasn't sexy under there, but utilitarian for appearance's sake. I was suddenly self-conscious of what I wore that shouldn't be seen.

My dress rose, slowly dragging up my thighs as delicious distraction and dangerous diversion. My hands instantly came to his wrists and froze the motion.

"I…"

He pulled back from the make-out session with my neck and stared at me. His dark eyes were almost black with desire; his lips were slick and puffy from his attention to my skin.

"You want me to stop?" He wasn't angry. He was curious.

"I just…I might not be like what you're used to." My eyes lowered, avoiding his penetrating gaze and feeling the potential prickle of tears. Tears would be a deal breaker and I couldn't afford this deal to not go down. But I had to warn him. I wasn't a slim twenty-year-old with flat abs and a tight ass. I was a woman who'd birthed children which widened my hips, massacred my stomach and sagged my behind. Not to mention, the weight of my breasts made them more *National Geographic* than national treasure when un-holstered from a bra.

"Emme," he smiled slowly, "if I heard you correctly, you said you wanted sex."

"Well, yes…but…" I stammered.

"And you asked how hard could it be?" His tone teased.

"Yes, but…"

He tugged my hand forward to cover the bulge at his zipper.

"Is that hard enough for you, darlin'?"

The only motion I could make was a nod. He held my hand over him, and I risked a squeeze. His reassuring moan encouraged me to explore the shaft straining against his shorts. The thickness of his extensive length sent my body into overdrive with desire. My dress continued upward until a smooth hand caressed the outside of my thigh, up to my hip. I tried to suck my stomach in, but my concentration faltered.

"Just breathe," he whispered into my neck, as he inhaled against me. "Mmmm…you smell like sunshine."

I exhaled and his fingers skittered over the damp cotton between my legs. I moaned. No, groaned. I might have even grunted. Whatever the sound was, it was hard to imagine it came from inside me, but other things were happening inside me that outweighed any noise. The flutter was indescribable; a million tiny leaves rustling in a breeze. My toes curled. My core pulsed. My lower abdomen flittered. Then he touched me full on, fingers brushing over me, and my knees crippled. Without the wall for support, I was going down.

Thick fingers pushed aside my underwear and curled through wet folds. Since embarrassment was my theme, it was almost shameful how damp I was. His sounds of approval and the resounding moan against my neck increased the building pleasure.

The sensation of his groans tingled over my skin, and a choked giggle stalled any thought. The idea of sex on the first night seemed a little overboard. As much as I wanted this, I wasn't convinced I could follow through with it. His nose tickled me.

"What's so funny?" His mouth curled into a smile while he trailed over my collarbone. Before I could answer, I was sweetly impaled with a finger and my hands wrapped around his biceps.

"Is my proposal funny?" he teased. The breathy *no* I released encouraged a second finger to enter me, and I was lost. Working in and out of me, his thumb joined the party and circled that sensitive nub, triggering the fluttering flits to full flight. My knees locked, and my hips bucked forward. In my head, I made promises to God and any other deity that wanted to listen, to give me the release I craved. My body teetered precariously on edge, tensing, bucking, clenching, responding. Finally, the flutters detonated, and a sound I didn't recognize escaped me as I slid down the wall. Merek caught me, still cupping my core, forcing me to remain upright as his fingers continued their attention until I felt myself drifting down from a high taller than the Willis Tower itself.

"Oh, my God," I muttered, my eyes closing, as my head fell back against the wall. Merek's mouth paid a final kiss to my neck before his fingers released me. My dress slipped down to my knees and my eyes slowly opened to see his mouth twitch upward. Breathing heavily, I stared at him. His expression was hard to read. While I felt satiated and replete, his face looked…confused.

"I think this just sealed our contract," he said as he stepped back. "Just give me a minute."

Chapter 7
Taking Time

[M.E. 2]

Here's the thing—she was unlike any other woman. How did I know that in less than an hour? Because I'd been with many. Enough women to drown out the past and escape the present. Young, supple, experienced, innocent, all shapes, sizes, color. Women were my addiction, in some ways. More like a drug to numb the pain of things I didn't want to admit to myself.

When Emme went for the pictures on the shelf, I didn't want her to focus on people that didn't matter. Well, they mattered, but not in the moment. I didn't want her to think about anyone but us. Not that we were an *us*, but I wanted her to be in the here-and-now, which her body proved, she certainly was. Wet didn't describe her. She was drenched, and it was heavenly. Her reaction to me was distinct. She wasn't exaggerating the experience. She wasn't overacting. She was savoring it, memorizing it. She was lost in my touch.

From her innocent comments, which rather forcefully fell from her mouth, she admitted she hadn't been with someone in a long time. Maybe too long, if the tears in her eyes, while we sat on the patio at the bar, were a testament. She wanted sex, but she wasn't willing to throw herself at me. In fact, she seemed a little awkward about the whole seduction thing. She wanted it, but she didn't know how to ask for it. And honestly, I found it refreshing. Some women were so demanding; others I had to command. Emme let me take control, but she was all in.

My dick was so hard, I felt a loss of circulation, and I just needed a second to calm down before I went in for round two. I didn't want to lose it too early. It sucked getting older. I couldn't recover as fast as I used to, and Emme was someone I wanted to repeat.

Her body was shapely but that didn't matter to me. I actually liked it that she wasn't stick thin or so athletic I feared she could kick my ass. She'd ignored my comment about children. Her omission was admission that she had them. Her eyes were expressive. They widened when she got excited, as she had with her list of hard limits. They narrowed when she was annoyed, as she had when I called her *dear*. But I couldn't read her thoughts. While some women told a story through their eyes, Emme didn't. She was a cluster of mixed signals. Most importantly, though, those eyes grew lusty and heavy with the excitement of being touched. Realizing again that it had been a while since a man's hands caressed her, my dick pulsed back to life.

Down, boy, or we aren't going to make it.

Bracing my hands on the edge of the counter, I leaned over the sink and exhaled deeply. It thrilled me a little that I had been her first. Closing my eyes, I heard the soft click of a door. Damn this apartment. The walls were thin here. The slightest noise could be exaggerated. With that thought, my lip curled. The noises coming from Emme had been unrestrained. As much as she seemed a little uptight, pressing the right button would make her come undone. The pun was not lost to me. I wanted to press her again, and sincerely hoped she'd take me up on my offer. Commitment was the last thing I wanted, but an arrangement of types would solidify that I would see her again. Allowing myself one more deep breath, I pushed off the sink and headed to the living room to find it empty.

I searched the bedroom next, thinking she might have been more a temptress than I gave her credit, but the bed was vacant as well. Returning to the living room, my hands came to my hips in frustration. I couldn't believe it. She'd walked out.

Chapter 8
Fresh Fruit

[M.E.]

I'd thought a lot about Merek and his proposal. Too much, actually. To the point, I was wet and ready for him at the most inappropriate times. Not one to "take care of myself," I suffered through the agony of desire, after I chickened out and bailed from his apartment. The sensory overload swept through my body and a strong case of he's-out-of-my-league moved in. Self-doubt took over when he said he needed a minute, and other than the split-second I thought he was headed for the ax to murder me, I couldn't get my head back into the moment. I panicked.

Days later, I cursed myself. I had a problem; it needed rectifying. Gia didn't know I hadn't followed through on sleeping with Merek, so she encouraged me to date, since I'd broken the proverbial ice, which was the cold lower region of my body. My frustration scolded me. Maybe it was time.

My evening graduate class finished late, and I wandered into the grocery store after ten o'clock. The place was actually peaceful at this time, in an odd sort of way. Not many customers, yet there was a camaraderie. We were all here this late for a reason. Each person had a story, and some nights I'd make one up as I stood next to the display of apples, but I was too tired for imagination. My nighttime interaction from a few nights prior still haunted my thoughts to the point I was exhausted. Overthinking, that's what I did. *How hard was I making it?* Of course, the word *hard* set off a whole string of images in my head like a pubescent teenager. Internally scolding myself, I moved onto the banana bins. That's when I saw him.

Quickly glancing up and across the open cases to the salad section, I noticed Merek, his defined muscles hidden under a dark gray suit jacket. The back pulled tight against the firm strength of him. The color did nothing but enhance his sexy, silver features and he caught me staring when he swung to face my direction, holding a cucumber in his hand. *Forget it, I am an adolescent.* My eyes shifted downward, and my hands shook as I examined the bunches of yellow fruit before me for far too long. My feet weighed heavy, and circulation flowed directly to another part of my body, which seemed rather inappropriate for standing in the fresh fruit aisle.

Suddenly, a body bumped into mine from behind. As I made to turn, ready to rip into the rude intruder of my personal daydream, I was pressed forward enough that my hands fell among the bananas.

"Not going to talk to me?" The sound of his soft groan near my ear was a live wire to sensitive parts of me. Leaning against my backside, he bent us forward and reached around me to grab a clump of bananas. He didn't move, and we remained frozen in this compromising position for a moment too long.

"I didn't think that was allowed," I whispered, turning my head to the left, wondering if people noticed us. There didn't appear to be another soul in the produce section. For a second, it seemed like there wasn't another human in the whole store.

"You could at least say, hi." His warm brush of air on my neck convulsed my body, and unknowingly, I pressed into him. His erection was pressed firmly against me. His arm still braced around my waist, and I noticed his fingers stroking the fruit.

"What do you think of these…bananas?" he questioned, brushing the length of himself tenderly from side to side against my behind.

"Hhm…I like mine a little firmer," I responded, swallowing hard at the implication.

"A little…or a lot?" I heard the smile in his voice as his other hand slipped to my hip, drawing me back and forcing me upright.

"A lot," I whispered, despite the emptiness of the space. My voice could not have projected louder if I tried. All my concentration centered on one part of my body, and it sang a song I hardly recognized.

"That's what I remember," he said, letting his hand skim down my hip to rest on the outside of my thigh. Still dressed in my skirt and heels from class, my legs separated slightly to balance my weight and force my trembling knees to lock. Melting on the floor or falling over onto the display were my only two options. I reached for a bunch of lightly green fruit.

"Those look a little green," he said, and my eyes shifted to the ones not quite ready.

"They'll ripen over time," I purred, and his hand slid back up my hip bone. When he reached my side, the edge that pinched and rolled a little over my waistband, I flinched away. His large hand tightened his grip on the area once labelled love handles, and now considered lusty lumps.

"Yes, all the best fruits do." His sultry voice made me shiver. "Over time."

I swear, I wet myself. A trickle escaped and if his hand delved under my skirt like I wanted, no, needed, he'd find an area over-ripe with desire and ready for ingestion. I squirmed at the thought. My nipples peaked under my bra and the firmness of my shirt exposed my excitement.

"Looks like another delicacy might be ripe." His voice rolled seductively slow across my breasts, the brush of that sound a tender, teasing tickle. My nipples stood further at attention as his head gazed over my shoulder.

"God, I wish I could read your mind," he said, a smile in his tone. He squeezed at the hunk of tough flesh on my side, and then stepped back from me. I spun and searched into those dark eyes that mesmerized me. Despite the youthful face at his age, the crinkles near his eyes spoke of wisdom. And something more: pain. The gleam in his eyes hid a secret. He actually looked tired.

"Mary Elizabeth?" someone questioned, and I turned to face a man I didn't recognize. My mind was too clouded by the nearness of Merek. When Merek took another step to the side and returned to his inspection of the bananas, I got a better glimpse of the man who called out my name.

"I'm sor…" Then it hit me. His rounded, clean-shaven face was more weathered than I remembered. Vaguely familiar, detailed wrinkles marked his murky green eyes which sparkled in recognition of me.

"Rod?" I questioned. "Rod Stanton?" I stepped away from Merek, still conscious of his presence, but uncertain how to proceed. *Did I introduce him? Did I acknowledge him?* He answered my unspoken questions for me.

"Thanks for the tip with the bananas, ma'am," he spoke, his eyes narrowing. His calling me ma'am, implicating my age, made me wince.

It seemed cruel, and he didn't need to be. He set the rules, not me. It was just sex, nothing more. I watched Merek retreat. His taut back in the dark suit spoke volumes. I was dismissed.

Spinning away from Merek, I stared at eyes that haunted my memories. Rod Stanton. He certainly didn't look like I remembered from high school. A little slimmer back then, the shy boy smile that greeted me was the trigger of reminiscence.

"It's been a long time," he said, running a hand through his sandy blond hair. I was a bit jealous he still had his original hair color. It wasn't exactly fair. *Why did men age well?*

Entering the parking lot, I paused next to my van. The lot was dark, and I lowered my forehead to the driver window.

Rod Stanton just asked me out.

Could I do this? Could I flirt? Could I date?

"Just pick someone. One date. Test the waters again," Gia had said. *"Who knows? The temperate lake might heat to hot tub levels!"*

Rod was sweet, but I just didn't know if I could go back in time. I rolled my head side to side slowly against the glass, and then stood up straight.

"If you need anything…"

"Jesus!" I yelled, spinning to face Merek. His eyes searched my face, fierce looking for a moment, and then softening.

"You scared the bloody hell out of me!" My heart raced under my hand, letting one set of grocery bags dangle from my wrist before my body as a shield.

"If you ever need anything, have an itch to scratch, remember to call me," he said, lowering his head and leveling his eyes with mine. "I'll scratch it for you." His mouth twerked up and my heart nearly exploded at the onslaught, startling me. Then he further surprised me by leaning forward and brushing his lips along my cheek. I held my breath as he pulled back, the wetness of a milk jug, chilling the plastic bag against my chest. I didn't respond as he walked away, my breath coming in ragged gasps.

Shaking my head, I opened the side door of the van and set the bags inside. The ice cream shop was right around the corner and Rod waited. I don't know what I was waiting for. I did have an itch, and it needed more than a scratching.

Chapter 9
Breaking the Ice

[M.E.]

When Rod asked me if I had some time for coffee, I laughed with my rejection. I didn't drink coffee; it was that simple. His smile told me I hadn't offended him.

"I should have remembered," he grinned sheepishly, and my heart blipped at the thought.

Rod Stanton had been a summer fling before my freshman year of college. Handsome as a teenager, he was a little paunchy around the middle as an adult. However, his face and his hair looked nearly the same as his youthful self. I saw in him the boy he was, and his smile was a reminder of a time long ago.

He asked me to have ice cream instead, and the suggestion wasn't lost on me. It was how we had our first date. He had friends. They dared him. I said yes. We hit it off and I was in love: summer love, that is. He wasn't from the neighborhood but visiting his aunt. She'd introduced him to some of the neighbor boys and they were instant friends. I was a casualty of acquaintances, but it had been a long time ago.

Seeing Rod again brought on an onslaught of memories. Young, fresh, and exciting ones. I giggled awkwardly like a teenager as we sat and licked ice cream cones.

"So how have you been?" His eyes questioned me, and that's how I knew, he knew. Nate was dead. I was alone. I sighed heavily but didn't want to give in to sad memories.

"I'm good," I offered, my voice rising an octave higher than necessary. I grew so used to the lie I actually believed it over time. In fact, I *was* good. I survived that dreaded first year. Milestone complete, I was ready to move on. Slowly, but moving forward, nonetheless. Sitting here with Rod was one small sign of that happening.

"What about you?" I asked.

"I've actually moved here."

I nearly dropped my ice cream. Twisting the sugar cone, I used my tongue to reposition the scoop of ice cream and Rod's eyes focused on the motion. He swallowed hard, and averted his eyes briefly, but they returned quickly. I swallowed down the frozen lump I'd bit off in an effort to cool the slight heat I felt when he looked at me. We locked eyes as I tried to recover from what he'd said.

When Rod returned back to his home in Florida, at the end of that summer, the euphoria of our love affair came to an abrupt end. I'd really liked him, but we were young. I'd seen him on occasion when he returned to visit his aunt, but by then the feelings had passed. Still, there was always a special place in my heart for that type of summer affair: a connection of shared memories, simple pleasures, and first discoveries. Rod was it for me, and here he sat again in my life.

"Wow, what brings you here?" I asked.

"Job. I lost mine six months ago. When something opened up in Chicago, I jumped at the chance. I'd inherited my aunt's place a few years back when she passed." He gave me that awkward look again. Like mentioning the death of someone else would lead me to recall the death closest to me, which it did, but I wasn't going to start crying hysterically because people died.

"Anyway," he grinned slowly. "I've always wanted to come back here." His eyes narrowed in on me, "and now seemed like an opportune time." Something in the tone of his voice made me smile and shiver.

Chapter 10
Clean Up, Aisle 3

[M.E. 2]

I hated grocery shopping late at night. It was lonely and depressing. Lost souls were the only ones in there after dark, which explained why I was there so late. Alone seemed to be my middle name, although that wasn't really true. I was surrounded by people often, but it didn't fill the void I often felt lately. What a pleasant surprise, then, to see her. Fresh fruit — the section suited her. She was refreshing, even if she had ditched me. Initially, I intended to blow off what happened, telling myself I would never think of her again. It seemed incredible that the woman who wanted sex would disappear before it happened. What I really wanted was an answer.

Why did she walk away?

I didn't think I had done anything wrong. Actually, her response led me to believe I'd done everything right. The way she melted against my fingers. Her sighs of pleasure, genuine and intense. The way her hands clutched at me, like she couldn't hold tight enough. So, it weighed heavy on my mind that she'd left. Most women wanted to stay. They wanted to cuddle. They wanted breakfast and a sparkling ring the next day. I'd already been in that position. Once.

I hadn't intended to lean against her. It was a reaction. I was ready to ask her what happened, why she'd left, but she distracted me by the subtle reflex of rubbing against me. I lost thought, and the bananas sidetracked me. *Clean up, in aisle three*, they were going to call over the loudspeaker, if her ass swiped against me again. Ripe for release, I was rock solid.

Asking her to join me for a drink, or even worse, a romp in the car, the words were on the tip of my tongue when some wanker interrupted us. He was large, polished, and a little too pleased to recognize Mary Elizabeth. The expression on her face was priceless. She didn't know what to do, and her awkwardness showed. It shouldn't have hurt my feelings. It didn't, but the urge to be spiteful arose.

"Thanks, ma'am," I spat politely, my innuendo about banana advice clear. The sudden confusion in her eyes pinched my chest. Glancing back at the man in his open suit coat, too comfortable in his own skin and sporting perfect hair, I took the opportunity to escape before more damage was done. It was only my pride. I could walk away. I'd done it before.

After startling her in the parking lot, I realized I was bordering on stalker level, especially with my open invitation. I itched all over and I wanted those delicate fingers to scratch me. She was parked in the row opposite me, and I decided I'd wait for her to leave the parking lot. I watched for the taillights to reverse from the space. Instead, I saw her walk to the ice cream shop around the corner. I pulled my truck forward through the open spot, and that's when I noticed the polished wanker in the shop with her. She smiled up at him, and that pinch turned into a clench inside my ribs. It shouldn't have mattered. Walking away from me proved she had no interest in my proposal, but the memory of her leaning against me returned me to my question: *Why not?*

Chapter 11
Second First Dates

[M.E.]

Seeing Rod had renewed so many memories and a few old feelings. He was the one that got away, in some respects. When summer ended, so did the relationship, especially when he had to return to his home in Florida. But he lived here now and the possibility of exploring who he was presently intrigued me. Rod was safe. He wasn't a random MatchMe hook-up. He wasn't a friend of a friend that my friend tried to set me up with. I knew Rod. Or at least, in the past I had.

We chatted easily while sharing ice cream. He told me more about his aunt's death and his inheritance from her. His new job was with the firm of Becket, Bennett, and Walters as a corporate attorney. He'd been married briefly. He was easy to listen to, animated in his storytelling, drawing me into his experiences. Here's what he didn't do: He didn't ask about me, and my mind drifted at one point when I heard the burning rubber screech of a muscle-sounding truck in the parking lot outside the window.

"Damn kids," Rod scowled, shaking his head in disgust.

"So, no children for you," I teased.

"I never thought I wanted them, until it risked my marriage. Then I begged for one. It was a pity child," he said sadly. "She got pregnant to save the marriage, but when she miscarried, I took it as a sign. It was time to part ways."

My heart ached. I'd always felt fortunate to have my children: two healthy daughters. I wanted more, but Nate didn't. *There's enough estrogen in this house as it is*, he had teased. Not able to guarantee him a boy wasn't worth the risk to him. Rod watched me while these thoughts swirled in my head.

"So, tell me about you?" he finally asked, and I suddenly felt tired. How could I possibly shove twenty years into one ice cream shop? Smiling slowly, he interrupted my thoughts.

"You know what, why don't I take you to dinner and you can tell me all about you?" His green eyes twinkled and the idea of being asked out without having to proposition someone, like a certain rugged-looking man on a patio bar, was refreshing. The possibility of being wanted warmed my insides, and I agreed to dinner on Thursday.

There I stood in front of my full-length mirror, dressed in clothes I might have worn to work because I didn't know how to dress for a date. I didn't own flirty, fun clothes, as my daughters generously pointed out to me when I asked for help. I had casual work clothes, slumming at home shorts, and an informal sundress which I wore to meet Merek, who hadn't called me since our run-in at the grocery store. *Whatevs*, as my girls would say, but I didn't feel so cavalier about the situation. It was me who walked away, and yet I'd sadly hoped Merek would chase. *Stupid*, I reminded myself. He was too good looking. He probably dated young girls like that waitress at the patio bar. He was out of my league with his polished suit in the grocery store late at night. Not knowing what he did for work, I imagined he must be some high-powered businessman. It was the aura he gave off. Take charge.

As I stared at myself, one more time in the mirror, my phone rang. Fumbling to find it under a pile of rough notes on the nightstand, I missed the call. When it was finally in my hand, it binged a text.

It's ME.

I had to giggle.

Hey, ME, it's ME, too.

I laughed harder then realized what a dork I sounded like.

It's Merek Elliott, actually.

I sighed as he obviously didn't appreciate my silliness. Hovering over the keys, wondering how to respond that would rectify sounding like a child, a message came through instantly.

Want to take a ride?

Oh, my God. I laughed in spite of myself. The euphemism wasn't going to go away.

L.B. Dunbar

Got an itch to scratch?

What felt like an eternity passed, while I once again cursed myself for trying to sound witty and failing. I didn't understand text messaging. It was part of the reason I had limited social media experience. I loved human conversation. I couldn't interpret what was behind a screen.

I do, but this is a bona fide offer.

I could have gone all kinds of places with the *bone* in that phrase, but I was trumped into silence. *Was Merek asking me out?* My answer came in another text.

How about a boat ride on the lake?

My head shot up to glance out my bedroom window. The evening was glorious, blue skies, with a lazy setting summer sun. I hadn't ever been on a boat ride on Lake Michigan, as crazy as that sounded considering I lived here my whole life.

I... My finger hovered. *I'd love to*, I instantly wanted to respond, but a sinking feeling told me I couldn't respond so easily. Erasing the letter I, instead I typed: **When?**

Now?

My shoulders sagged as I assumed this would be the timing. Merek appeared to live in the moment; I was a planner. The only way to make it day-by-day and week-by-week after Nate's death had been to schedule small milestones. Grocery store on Monday. Laundry on Saturday. While I'd lived by the calendar previous to his passing, it wasn't the same after he was gone. I wanted to be spontaneous. I wanted to say yes.

I can't. I'm so sorry.

Hot date?

Envisioning the smirk of his lips, I smiled weakly. Yes, after twenty years with one man, and one year alone, two men had asked me out for the same night. What are the odds of that happening? Unfortunately, only one of them had my curiosity. I didn't know how to answer, other than honestly.

Yes, actually, I do.

The silence that followed was endless, but the message was loud and clear. When there was no further response, I finally dropped the phone on the bed. The doorbell rang, and I took one last look at my phone before powering it to silent and exiting my room for my "hot" date.

Rod took me to a local mom-and-pop Thai restaurant. He produced a bottle of red wine while I scanned the menu for something mild to eat. I didn't have the heart to tell him; I didn't like Thai food. I didn't typically try new things. I wasn't a risk-taker like that. I wanted to be, though. This whole night was a risk. If I was going to jump into dating and new experiences, trying different foods had to be on my virtual menu. Spontaneous had to be a theme. So I ordered the chicken ginger and sipped the dry red wine that Rod offered as I began a narrative of my life over the past twenty years.

Marriage. Children. Career. I had wanted so many things over the years, which included for better or worse, richer or poorer, until death did us part. The wine was making me melancholy as I listened to my life in rewind. I defined it by things I did as a stay-at-home mother before returning to work, then continued to define it by the accomplishments of my children. Listening to myself, I realized it hadn't been about me, but about them: my girls. This list should have made me proud. Raising amazing daughters was praiseworthy. Returning to work as a college professor was notable. Twenty years of marriage involved dedication, and yet it didn't seem like enough. Listening to my life pour forth like the wine, I bored myself with what I heard.

Rather, it was what I wasn't saying that surprised me. Where was the excitement? Where was the spontaneity? What happened to all the promises made for travel, companionship, and adventure? The wine soured in my throat as I had one of those moments of dismal regret for what I hadn't done compared to what I had. The conversation slowed while we ate, and I determined I'd talked Rod into boredom. We fell silent.

"Remember when we went to the condo?" he asked, interrupting the gentle scraping of forks against plates, and the quiet process of chewing spicy poultry.

The duplex had been owned by the McCarthys, a family who lived next to Rod's aunt. Reese was their son, roughly the same age as us, and his family rented the home to families visiting Chicago for a one week stay. There was a lull between the Saturday departure, and the Sunday arrivals, and it led to Reese using the place for private parties. Rod and I had gone to a summer bash celebration. People branched off into separate rooms for whatever nefarious purpose. Eventually for Rod and I, it had resulted in teenage sex. It was a strange memory to disrupt my rambles. My mind wandered at the simplicity of young decisions, drifted to the difficulty as an adult to be so carefree and careless, then skipped to Merek. Sex only. It seemed simple enough. It certainly was spontaneous. Rod's mention of the past was an attempt to reminisce about our youth, but my body knew it could only live in the present.

"We were so young," Rod stated, a bemused look on his face as he pushed his Praram Chicken from side to side on the dish. "You were so beautiful," he said quietly before his head shot up. "You still are. Beautiful, that is," he offered with a smile, and it warmed my insides to be complimented. Nate hadn't been the complimenting type.

Maybe I could do this. Sweet talk and a nice smile could lead places, right? But thoughts of fresh fruit innuendos and the moans of desire outweighed what sat before me. Rod was safe ground, if I wanted to step back into the past. Merek was an unchartered path, if I wished to hike forward.

"Thank you. I remember you being beautiful then, too," I laughed. He had been beautiful: sandy blond hair, green eyes and a tempting smile on a solid, growing body. Rod looked at me with held breath before I added, "And, of course, you're still very attractive now."

He exhaled at the comment, smiled sheepishly, and returned to his chicken. And that was the end of the flirting. It hit me like the glass of ice water before me. I didn't want to go backward. My relationship with Nate had been one of awkward flirtation in the beginning. While I couldn't recall with clarity what that was like, I knew we had to have begun somewhere. Through time our relationship grew to one of comfort. We were compatible and structured. Being with someone like Rod would be similar to Nate. A spark that fizzled instead of a flame that burned hot. Merek was a flame. More like a bonfire, and I wished to dance around the potential inferno. That was a risk I longed to take.

The Sex Education of M.E.
A sudden bout of stomach over-activity from chicken ginger was the excuse I used, and asked Rod to cut our date short. I was surprised when he did, and then asked for a second date.

Chapter 12
Unexpecting

[M.E. 2]

Dammit. My phone died. And she had a date. The wanker in a suit was probably heading for her panties after I'd opened the flood gates, and it pissed me off. Tempted to throw my phone in the lake, I accelerated back to Montrose Harbor. I hoped she'd say yes, and I'd meet her at the Sheridan Shore Yacht Club, but she had a damn date. She didn't give off the impression she wanted a date. She said she wanted sex, but then again, that's why she was in O'Malley's that first night. She thought she was meeting someone.

I didn't do dates. It was too complicated. I don't know why I went that night, but there was something about Emme that intrigued me. A boat ride was the perfect excuse to see her again. Also, it would prevent her from running, and we could finish what we had started nights ago. But she had a fucking date.

Returning to Montrose Harbor, I pulled into the boat slip, focusing on the task at hand. I tied the boat to the dock, hosed off the bow, and replaced the canvas covering. Owning this boat and securing this coveted slip had been a dream come true for my brother and me. With the death of our father, years ago, we used the money for something he always wanted: a boat on the lake and a space in Montrose Harbor. It wasn't really my thing, the prestige of being here, but my younger brother, Marshall, wanted the image. It fit his growing need to prove himself as more than a fireman's kid. He didn't want the labor involved with being a civil servant and having a side job in a trade, as many Chicago firemen did. As our father had done, being a plumber.

I swallowed my disappointment and headed for my truck. Marshall had been out of town the past week. His availability was limited. He played the bachelor more than me, and his climb to the top of the financial establishment he worked for prevented him from any formal commitment. The boat was a networking investment he argued when he convinced me to purchase it with him. The thing he was missing in his prestigious ladder-to-the-top was a better apartment, but it served its purpose for him and me. I plugged in my phone and a text flashed, as if he sensed my thoughts of him.

You available?

Heading to Bruno's, I replied.

I'll meet you there.

Bruno's was a dive bar off Wilson Avenue. It was a throwback to our firemen connections as many of the men we might find there were from the firehouse nearby, which had been our father's command post when he was alive. Old friends considered family returned often.

"What's up, man?" Marshall greeted, handing me a beer before I even sat. My younger brother was my opposite. While my hair shifted to salt and pepper, Marshall's hair remained a rusty red, from a bottle, with a touch-up every three weeks. It countered his deep blue eyes and gave him a youthful look. My brother delayed growing into a man, even more than me.

"Just returned from China. My time schedule is so off." He took a long pull from his beer. His hands looked manicured, so opposite mine which were thick and roughed from work. His lips twisted in concentration, and my eyes narrowed at him.

"What's going on?" I questioned. My brother was an open book. Marshall ran a hand through those thick reddish locks.

"Bridget wants to get married."

"Who's Bridget, again?" I teased. My brother had so many conquests it was hard to keep up. He topped me and keeping straight who was who in his list of weekly arrangements provided good fodder. Bridget McMahon was a name I recognized, however. Dark-haired, wild girl who was the daughter of one of our lifelong family friends. She was from the old neighborhood. An Irish Catholic girl who grew up down the block from our parents' home.

"She's the one I got pregnant," he stated plainly. The bottle coming to my lips froze in mid-air.

"What?"

"She's pregnant."

"Is it yours?" I blurted and instantly regretted it. Bridget had been crazy for my brother for years when we were younger. She'd been married and divorced with children, much to her parents' dismay. Recently, a relationship of sorts rekindled between Marshall and Bridge, her childhood nickname, which gave me the idea to proposition Emme. Marshall and Bridge had an arrangement where a simple phone call was all they needed. The Bat Signal, Marshall joked. It meant *I'm horny; I need assistance.* Despite the teasing of my brother, I questioned the possibility of growing emotions between Marshall and Bridge. They had history, compared to the random pick-ups in bars and hook-ups from MatchMe that I dealt with. Over time, I questioned if the arrangement meant more to him than he let on. A baby changed everything, especially at thirty-five years old. My heart dropped. The pain on my brother's face proved my words hurt.

"I'm sorry, man. Of course, it's yours."

His hand worked faster through his hair. If he kept it up, he'd have more than coloring to worry about; he'd suddenly have hair loss.

"What am I going to do?" His blue eyes questioned mine, and for a moment, he was the little pest following me around when I was a teen.

"What do you want to do?"

"I don't know."

I shuddered at the thought of a child at my age. Marshall and Bridget weren't kids. They needed to be responsible adults.

"You want the kid, right?" I stared at him, willing him to answer in affirmation. This wasn't a joke to me, this was life. He needed to respect that.

"Of course," he said. "I think… I mean, yes." He exhaled then inhaled deeply and sat up straighter.

"Then marry her," I said, as if that resolved the issue.

"I can't marry her. I'm not the marrying type. I like the freedom to roam," he quipped.

"Well, you should have thought of that before you tapped it uncovered," I snipped, raising an eyebrow at his stupidity.

"I wasn't uncovered. It ripped."

The noise of Bruno's filled the silence.

"How the fuck do we get into these messes?" He shook his head before his eyes darted up to me. "I didn't mean that," he added.

"Yes, you did." I smiled weakly. "And it happens because you can't keep your dick in your pants. And neither could I. Be thankful you aren't a kid yourself, though." I tipped my beer at him before taking a long pull to drown out memories I didn't wish to discuss. Marshall knew all my secrets, anyway.

"I don't want to grow up," he pouted, and the little boy image flashed again. I laughed.

"Too bad. At some time, you have to bite the commitment bullet."

"Oh yeah, and when will you do that?" he chuckled.

"Never gonna happen again," I smirked.

"I noticed you had someone at the apartment," he stated, eying me over the lip of his beer.

"How'd you know that?" I barked, thinking back to any evidence after Emme left me.

"The expression on your face just admitted it," he laughed.

"That...that was nothing," I lied. "Like I said, never gonna happen."

"You never bring people to the apartment." He teased. He was correct. I didn't, as a rule, bring women there. I went to them, so I could leave, or we used the convenience of wherever we were located.

"I'm not having this conversation. So, I brought someone there. Once."

"You want to bring her again, though?" he questioned, and I hardened my face, hoping to hide any expression of guilt. I did want Emme to return.

"How did this conversation turn to me?"

"We were talking commitment," he laughed. My eyes narrowed at him. There was no way he could know about Emme. Then I blinked in shock. Her name crossing my mind startled me. She had a date. She walked away. She didn't want my proposal. I didn't do commitment, regardless. That's why I propositioned her.

"Never gonna happen."

"Wanna bet? Cubs tickets say it's gonna happen."

"You're on. Cubs tickets. I want a nice sunny day game in September. I look forward to the box."

My brother's company owned a box that could be reserved for personal events. If I did lose, bleacher seats would be the place I could afford. I didn't worry about losing.

Chapter 13
The Call

[M.E.]

"You need to call him," Gia encouraged, waving my phone at me.

"He made himself perfectly clear, Gia. I had a date and that was a signal he wanted nothing more to do with me."

"That's not true," she said, reaching for her glass of wine as we sat on my back deck. The night was warm, and the girls were gone again. Gia's ex had the kids for a few hours, and she took a breather to be an adult, as she liked to call it. She was only in her early thirties, but the age difference didn't matter to either of us. At some point, being a mother halted all barriers of age discrepancy and bound women to each other.

"Explain to me how you know this about Merek. And again, how you got him to show up at O'Malley's?" My lips twisted as I shook my head. "Look, I know you're a pro at this dating thing, but I'm not so ancient I can't read a sign."

"Can you just trust me on this? You have to proposition the man, nowadays. Just text him. If he doesn't respond, I promise, I'll stop hounding and go back to MatchMe. You have like thirty requests."

"I do?" My eyes shot wide. It was obvious Rod was interested. He'd asked me out again. But I couldn't imagine who else would want to date me. Then I remembered the site was full of predators and those looking for cougars (older women who craved younger men) and those with MILF obsessions (younger men looking for mother types).

"Yes, you do. Emme, how many times do I have to tell you, you're a beautiful woman. You have a great personality. You're funny. Don't let whatever it is that keeps you down, keep you down."

Gia knew Nate wasn't always forthcoming with compliments or affection. The lack of attention over twenty years proved a subtle assault on my self-esteem. I couldn't imagine who would be interested in a forty-something with two kids and a mortgage.

"You know what?" I reached for my phone in Gia's hand. "I'll text him just to prove he isn't going to respond."

I want a ride.

"There." I showed Gia the message. "He isn't going to…" Aimed toward Gia, the phone pinged with a response. She choked on her wine. Flipping the phone to face me, I read the reply.

I'd love to drive you.

Oh, my God, I mouthed to Gia. Her eyes danced as she waved for me to respond.

"I don't even know what to say."

"You say, Now. Yes, now." Her eyes started fluttering. "Oh, yeah, now. Right there…"

"Okay, I got it." I laughed, raising my hand to stop further description. My fingers shook as I typed three simple letters. **N-O-W.**

The following text was the address of the apartment where we previously went.

To say I was nervous was an understatement. *Was I taking the risk of a lifetime?* In the grand scheme of life, no. *A risk with my body?* In many ways, yes, but I tingled all over at the thought. *A risk with my heart?* My head overruled.

"Don't overthink," Gia warned me.

"He'll only go as far as you want," she encouraged.

"This isn't love," she snorted. "This is lust."

She was correct on all accounts. Even though I hardly knew him, I trusted Merek. This was Sex Ed 101. My body was out of control, and I wanted the touch of a man. I could do this, I pep talked.

Finally stepping out of my car, Merek waited for me on the front steps outside the apartment building. In typical Chicago style, the two-flat looked like a house, raised several steps above ground level. There were two entrances as soon as you entered the front door. Merek's place was on the second floor. A city home, the surrounding houses were similar in fashion. The cookie cutter line-up was slightly different from the neighborhood I lived in.

"I was beginning to wonder if you'd changed your mind." He smiled slowly. The golden spark to his eyes made my heart race.

"If we're going to stand on the stoop, I might." Sweat trickled under my arms and my hands shook. He reached for me, and I stumbled as he tugged me forward, teasingly, to rush us inside. He slowed as we climbed the stairs to the second-floor apartment. Stopping before the door, he spun to face me.

"We'll only go as far as you want." He tucked a piece of hair behind my ear, "but I'm going to admit, I'm hoping it's far. I like long drives."

I laughed. His flirting shattered some of my nerves. Still holding my hand, we entered the apartment and he led me to the couch.

"Drink," he offered. He crossed behind the couch and returned with two glasses of wine. Mine was pink; his was red.

"White zinfandel?" I questioned. "You remembered what I ordered?" His mouth curved slowly, rolling up on one side, then the other followed, like he had a secret he wanted to tell, but the smile hid it. He didn't answer my question, just watched me over the rim of his glass.

"So how do we do this?" Nerves caught up to me again as he sat next to me on the couch. *How did one jump into sex?* It wasn't like we'd been on a date first where I was plied with wine, laughter and the occasional compliment. My date with Rod certainly didn't lead there.

"Slow down." He smirked, placing the glass on the table beside him. His hand landed on my thigh as his body twisted toward me.

"Tell me about your date." His husky voice was not the tone I'd expect for such a question. I swallowed hard.

"Why do you want to know about that?" I squeaked as his hand slid up and down my skirted thigh. The material slowly danced back and forth with each stroke.

"I'm curious about it." His tone lowered, his words directed at the attention to my thigh. He stopped abruptly and reached for my hand instead. Turning it over, he rubbed his palm over mine, caressing my wrist, and then dragging the calloused pads of his fingertips back over my sensitive palm. One digit drew along the creased lines in my skin.

"Why?" My eyes followed the motion. He spread his fingers to slide between mine briefly, then returned to stroking each one.

"Tell me." Clasping them together, he raised our hands and kissed my knuckles.

"Rod is an old friend," I began. "I knew him as a teenager."

"Rod?" he choked. "Like nimrod," he muttered. Flipping our combined palms, his lips lingered, and his mouth sucked tenderly on the flat of my hand.

"That's not nice." I stifled a laugh, distracted by his mouth.

"Sorry. So how well did you know Rod? Are you familiar with Rod's rod?" His voice was still low, but not threatening.

"I'm not sure that's any of your business."

His mouth stopped. His eyes searched mine. His chin tipped.

"Did you get reacquainted with Rod's rod?" His tone roughened. His fingers closed around mine again, and he twisted my arm to expose my wrist. His mouth met the tender skin. He sucked gently, his tongue darting forward and caressing the delicate veins. He lapped lightly, and my breath hitched.

"Nothing happened the other night," I breathed. "In fact, I went home early." His eyes shot up to mine.

"That good, huh?" He chuckled. His lips continued to serenade my arm with kisses, dotting a path to my elbow.

"It was fine." I exhaled slowly, trying to concentrate on the conversation but completely distracted by the movement of his mouth.

"That's a word I never want you to use with me." The playful edge disappeared from his tone. His tender attention stopped, and I instantly missed it. His touch soothed, distracted, and if it's possible to be turned on by fingers petting and unique kisses, I wasn't going to make it past first base with this man. Moisture pooled between my legs, and I didn't dare rub my thighs as they already touched. The slightest movement would only increase my excitement.

"Okay." My voice was so low I wasn't certain any sound escaped my mouth. His lips brushed against my shoulder. My eyes closed under the weight of his kisses.

"I'm relieved you didn't sleep with him," Merek muttered against my skin.

"Who said I didn't sleep with him?"

His lips stopped, and I laughed. My hand covered my mouth.

"I'm sorry." I laughed harder at the momentary expression on his face. Then he playfully narrowed his eyes and shifted his body to kneel before me.

"You're going to pay for that." The curve of his lips was pure seduction. Then those lips hit my knee. I jolted. His mouth opened, and he sucked the skin above my kneecap. My head fell back, and a shaky hand reached out for his hair. It was coarse, the salt mixing with the pepper of age, but slipping my fingers through it, rubbing over his scalp, made him moan. The vibration of his mouth tingled up my thigh, igniting the steady spark into a full-on inferno at the apex. With a will of their own, my legs parted, extending the invitation for him to continue higher.

"Will you take a payment plan?" I whispered toward the ceiling. His subtle laughter tickled my skin. The air sizzled and my nervous giggle turned serious. We were really doing this. He was really going there, *there*, and I wanted it like nothing I'd ever wanted before. My skirt rose and firm hands removed my underwear without missing a beat. Kisses continued uninterrupted. My knees opened farther as his broad body wedged between them. His mouth drew seductively closer to where I wanted it to go. His tongue dragged hesitantly along my inner thigh before he lapped through tender folds. I bucked, suppressing the chuckle of nerves threatening to escape. His tongue strengthened and the pressure increased to full-on devouring. I held his head between my thighs. The seduction of his tongue increased to part my lower lips and he sucked that nub of pleasure hard. I sighed as he guided one of my legs up to perch on the couch. I was completely exposed.

He tugged me closer to the edge of the cushion without missing a beat of his connection on my core. His mouth was on a mission. His fingers joined the adventure. One thick digit slipped into my wet channel, which sucked him deeper, while his tongue circled around me. My toes curled, and my legs quivered as the fluttering crawled from my ankles, rapidly curled around my calves, and burst forth at the top of my thighs. I screamed. Or I think I screamed. The strangled sound coming out of me wasn't a noise I recognized.

My body shuddered with aftershocks. My fingers tightened in his hair, and I tugged gently to let him know I'd had enough. My thighs shook, but my insides felt languid. Replete for the moment, I stared at

Merek as his head rose and he faced me with moisture enhancing his red lips. His mouth curved into that delicious smile, and I longed to kiss him, regardless of his rule. I was tempted to ask about it, but he asked me a question instead.

"Like that?" As confident as he came across, it seemed strange he would even ask such a question. Then he added: "If you say fine, I'm going to punish you again."

"Fine, fine, fine," was the mantra my mouth sang to tease him. He stood methodically, pulling me up by my hands as he went. Shaky legs quivered, and his mouth landed below my ear.

"My turn," he purred. I assumed what he meant; I just didn't know if I could do that. Oral sex wasn't my specialty. While I often felt guilty I rarely performed it on Nate, I also never felt I was any good at it. Being with Nate was also more often about getting the act done, than experiencing each other.

Merek surprised me by reaching around me and slipping his hands firmly under my behind. Lifting upward, my reaction was to wrap my legs around him. My skirt rose up, and the sensation of bare skin against the material instantly rekindled my excitement. The hard length of him on the edge of my entrance enhanced the experience and teased me with what was to come next.

"You can't carry me," I whimpered, clasping my arms around his neck as he adjusted me before turning us. "I'm too heavy," I cried. He didn't respond. If he struggled, I didn't have the slightest notion as his nose traced my neck while he blindly guided us into another room. I was dropped on a bed and bounced with the connection.

"Oh my," I laughed as I flopped against the mattress. Brushing back my hair, I looked up at Merek whose face appeared thoughtful.

"I'm sorry. I shouldn't have tossed you down like that." His expression shifted; his eyebrows pinched in question. Fear rose inside me. Did he have his own doubts about what was going to happen next? Because the next step was going to be sex — pure, unadulterated sex, unless he changed his mind. He reached for the collar of his t-shirt and slipped it over his head. Guess I had my answer.

For a man in his forties, before me stood a god who rivaled a twenty-year-old. In fact, the solidity of his chest and the thickness of his arms

The Sex Education of M.E.

proved he was a man of age, not a youth newly out of puberty. His stomach rippled, and my fingers twitched to travel the bumpy road before me. Forget it, my mouth watered to trace down the treasure trail that peeked out of his jeans. To top it off he had tattoos, and while I didn't personally have any, I was so intrigued by them on others. The color, the images, the meaning behind the art always made me curious. I didn't have long to ogle him, though, as his hands came to mine, tugging me upward so he could remove my skirt and t-shirt.

Here's where it got tricky. My body did not compare in physique to his. I wasn't solid, anywhere. A slight bulge typically peeked over my underwear and my thighs had grown together. Skin dangled under my arms and my stomach had the scars of childbirth. One arm rested around my stomach as if I could wrap myself up. My other arm instinctively crossed my chest. My breasts still stood large in a black bra, and my boy-cut shorts, which had been removed in the living room, were not chosen to flatter but rather a futile attempt to hold things together in the midsection.

"Don't do that." His eyes were trained on my chest. Mine shifted away. His fingers gently circled my wrist, forcing it down to expose my breasts. My heart raced with inadequacy. A deep breath was necessary to calm my fears. I licked my lips. The aroma of my desire perfumed the air, and I added another line to my list of insecurities before this man. He removed my other arm.

Holding my wrists at my sides, his eyes caressed over me. It was too much, and I had to look away again. I couldn't watch him inspect my body. My heart beat so wildly, I worried he'd see it through my skin. Instead, he nudged me to step back until I hit the bed. I sat on instinct, and then he asked me to scoot back. He followed me like I was his prey, but I wasn't afraid. In fact, I longed for the attack. When I hit the pillows with my back I stopped, and his mouth landed on the deep ridges of my stomach. My hand flew to cover where he had kissed. The barrier wasn't strong enough and he instantly removed my weak attempts to prevent him from looking at the scars.

"Children?" he muttered as he continued to kiss up and over deep grooves that did not match the sharp ripples of his structured abs. Instead, it looked like a semi-truck rolled over my abdomen.

"I have two," I mumbled. He continued his attention on marred skin before his hand spread over my stomach.

"It's beautiful. You're beautiful."

"Right," I snorted. Literally. His eyes shot upward.

"You created a miracle in there. Your body wears the proof of that, and it's beautiful." His tone turned rough as he spoke, as if the harshness would ingrain in me the seriousness of his words. I didn't know how to respond. I didn't need to; his hands slipped around my back and with only a minor fumble, unclasped my three-hook support bra. He dragged it forward, and then flung it behind him. I laughed only long enough for his mouth to engulf one nipple. Then the sound became a strangled moan.

His warm lips sucked hard on a nipple sharp and peaked. A tingly letdown sensation filled both breasts and it shot like an arrow straight to another part of body. My body responded to Merek by wrapping a leg around his and letting my hands trail his hair again. He dragged his tongue down the hill of one breast, crossing the thin valley between them to climb the other and pay it equal homage. The prickling sensation struck again. The throbbing between my legs needed to get closer to him. My wet center pressed against his bare chest.

Reaching for his shorts, I wedged a hand between us to unbutton them, but he sat back to continue the rest. Standing before me, his length was firm and large underneath boxer briefs. Sight unseen, he was larger than another man. Nate flashed between us, and I cursed myself for letting my mind wander. Before me stood a man, a god, of perfection. His dark treasure trail led to something golden, and I didn't wish to compare him to anyone else. Merek shook his head.

"Only you and me in here, or this won't work," he said, twisting his lips.

"It's only you and me," I whispered, ridding my mind of any other thoughts. He removed his boxers and mesmerized me with the sight of him. He climbed my body again but kept himself balanced over me. The weight of his length pressed upward against me, his solid head braced at my entrance. I needed him closer. My hips inched toward him, calling to him. His response was to drag his firm tip through sensitive folds. Nudging forward, the motion replicated what I wanted: him inside me.

His nose trailed along my collar bone as he thrust forward one more time but held back from slipping deep inside.

"Merek," I moaned.

"Mmmm...I like the sound of my name on your lips."

"I have..." I didn't think I could continue with: *condoms in my purse*. Gia had dumped a truck load in there. Not needing one for twenty years, and even before that, I wasn't certain what was in the collection she gave me.

An assortment, she teased, before explaining color, size and flavors.

"Flavors?" I questioned. Who puts those in their mouth? I actually didn't want an answer.

"I'm covered." He saved me. "I don't suppose you're on the pill," he asked, pulling back from me.

"Uhm...no," I laughed. There hadn't been a need. Nate didn't want other children after a scare, as he called it, when Bree was five. He took care of it himself to assure there wasn't any future risk.

"I can't get you pregnant," he hinted. "But I still like to have it wrapped."

Merek reached awkwardly for the top drawer of the nightstand, and my mind wandered to the number of women that had been in this room, on this bed, with this man. Being curious was dangerous as my thoughts wondered if he had an assortment in that drawer. Removing a square foil package, I panicked that he'd ask me to put it on him. Wasn't that the way romance novels wrote it? The woman covers this action, but I couldn't recall the first thing about how to apply a condom. Thankfully, Merek ripped the foil and rolled the latex over himself. Admittedly, this was freaking sexy. My wanton mind was all in suddenly, as he knelt between my legs. Naked, fully exposed to him, my heart raced, but my lower region sped into overdrive. It had been a long time.

Merek ran teasing fingers over tender folds, hypersensitive and alert. I moaned, spreading my legs, begging him to take me. With my pelvis tipped upward, the tension built again. I'd never had a second orgasm. One per customer, and the sale was finished. But this, this was the wave of a second coming. I wanted this like nothing I'd ever wanted before. My toes curled into the sheets. My hips rose for greater friction.

"Again," Merek mumbled in encouragement, and I risked a peek at where his attention was focused. Watching him stroke me was too much.

"Come on, darlin'," he said. It wasn't a command. It was wanton in its own right. He was waiting for me. My concentration was intense. I needed this release.

"I…" My breath hitched. "Oh, God." The wave took me by surprise. My legs shuddered and collapsed. My head rolled to the side. I gripped the sheets as my back arched upward. The sensation washed over me in a manner I'd never felt before. I would not stop. I would not say *enough*. I would not offer that I was done, so he could take me. I rode the unchartered waters until I was dry and exhausted.

And then I felt him.

His head poised at my entrance, and I opened for him. Romance novels talk about young girls having sex; they are always tight. This channel had been discovered long ago, and yet I felt like a virgin. It had been so long, and Merek was thick, and solid. Good God, I felt each ridge of him as he entered me, and my eyes rolled back. He took his time, slowly dragging out the anticipation, filling me completely. Then he paused.

"You okay?" His voice was rugged, strained, as if he held back. A tear escaped the corner of my eye. Overwhelmed and worshipped was a heady combination. As I looked away, I blinked rapidly.

"Eyes on me," he groaned, emphasizing the words with a gentle thrust.

"Again," I whispered, drawing my attention back to his face. *Do that again*, my head silently pleaded. All of it. Any of it. *Again, again, again.*

He dragged to the edge of me, but muscles clenched to hold him inside. My knees bent and squeezed his hips. I would not let him leave me. Not yet. Painstakingly slow, he slid forward. A hissing sound circulated in the air above us. I think the noise was me.

He withdrew a little faster this time. My legs hitched up over his hips. A hand reached under my backside, and he tilted me upward. Thrusting forward quickly, he filled me to the hilt, and I grunted.

"Okay?" he questioned.

"It's…it's…" I couldn't describe what was happening to me, or what he was doing to me. The fullness. The completion. The ecstasy. Another tear escaped, but I ignored it. I wasn't sad; no, I was far from sorrow

He repeated the motion, increasing each time until we developed a rapid rhythm, a beating pace that bordered on out of control.

"Darlin'." His voice strained, and he stilled over me. A vein ran down his neck. His eyes closed tight. The pulsing inside me was not my own. Three quick beats and he collapsed over me. I couldn't bear his weight for long, but then again, I wasn't ready for him to withdraw from me. Not yet.

Chapter 14
The Response

[M.E. 2]

My pulse beat rapidly as I took calming breaths. Her frame was crushed under me, but I didn't want to move. Her arms came around my neck, holding me in place as I covered her. She held tight, and a tear trickled along my neck. I didn't want her to cry. I didn't want her to be sad about what we'd done. I wanted to blanket her and cursed the thought. This wasn't like me. *What just happened?* My mind was a jumble of confusion while my body was replete with satisfaction I hadn't felt in a long time.

The way she purred and gasped with each thrust. The way her nails scratched tenderly up my back. Her legs wrapped around me and her body in rhythm with mine. I'd had so many women over the years. An embarrassing amount. They were a means to an end, and so was this, but somehow that was a lie. She had needs, but was not desperate, and I selfishly liked that I had been her first. After all the time she'd been with one man, I was her first. I didn't intend to replace him, though. That's not what this was about.

I was suddenly uncertain what this was about.

Emme wasn't someone I was prepared for. She was nearly the same age as me. She was short on sexual history. I shouldn't have tossed her on the bed. The young things liked that. Throwing them down. Spanking their ass. Tying them up. Not that Emme didn't want those things. Hell, I didn't know what she wanted, but tonight wasn't about the tricks. This was simple sex. Although, it was hardly simple.

She was expressive. Combined with her lack of experience, she was unique to me. Unusual, but in a good way. Those tears haunted me, though. I wanted to ask, but then again, I didn't. I didn't want to hear she felt guilty, or she thought of someone else instead of me buried inside of her. I didn't recognize the emotion that crept inside me, and I rolled off of her hastily, using the excuse of cleaning up to separate myself from her.

I slipped out of the room, taking a second to collect my thoughts. Images of Emme writhing under me, undulating with me, sparked my dick to long for her again. I wasn't ready yet. I needed another minute. Would she even let me have her a second time? What if once was all she wanted to fulfill the need, scratch the itch. I stood tall and looked at myself in the mirror. I didn't normally care what women thought of me. I wasn't young, but I didn't feel old. I took care of my body. The graying shade of stubble on my face contrasted with the dark tone of my hair. I'd been told it made me look distinguished. Why wouldn't she want me again?

On second thought, what if she wanted me to hold her. What if she wanted to talk about what we'd done? I didn't cuddle. I didn't have to. I never brought women to the apartment. Tonight, I was stuck. But, that wasn't quite the right word. I didn't feel stuck. I didn't know what I felt. I wanted her to stay, at least for round two, maybe a round three. There was more I wanted to discover about Emme. Just how far would she be adventurous.

When I heard a thump from the floor below, I panicked. Rushing into the bedroom, I found her seated and mostly dressed. She reached down for a shoe when doubt struck. *She was leaving?* She flipped her longer hair over her shoulder and that white-blonde color made her beautiful. Her blue eyes were hazy with lust and exhaustion. If she left, I was an ass. If she stayed, I was an ass.

"What are you doing?" I crossed the room and scrambled for my boxers on the floor.

"My girls will be home around midnight. I need to go. Besides you probably have to work tomorrow." She made it sound like she was leaving for my benefit. A trait of women I hated: turning a situation around so it seemed like they were doing me a favor.

"I…" *Did I want her to stay? Did I want her to go?*

She finished strapping her sandal and stood slowly. A sheepish smile brightened her face, but her eyes avoided mine. She was sweetly shy as she approached me. A shaky hand came forward and pressed hesitantly against my bare chest. I swear she could feel my heart racing.

"Thank you," she whispered, then smiled weakly. Kissing me chastely on the cheek, then she stepped around me and left. Again.

Chapter 15
Head Trumps Heart

[M.E.]

My head quickly overruled my body. While I'd love to bask in the afterglow of incredible sex, something on Merek's face was off. When he rolled away from me, the connection with him was lost. I didn't know what to do next. My desire to curl into him and sleep was completely unrealistic. I hadn't slept wrapped around a man since Nate and I first dated. After twenty years, once the act was complete, Nate and I rolled our separate ways, each to our corner of the bed. Had we ever slept wrapped around one another? I couldn't remember a time and recognized romance novels tainted what I thought should happen next. But this wasn't a book; this was life, and mine caught up to me. I noticed the time on the nightstand clock and realized I needed to get home. I had children. It's not that they expected me to be home, but the inquiry if I wasn't, was something I wasn't ready to explain to my growing girls.

I slipped out of the bed and wrapped myself back in my clothes. Straightening my skirt, Merek entered the room. Without much exchange, he watched me dress. I explained briefly why I was leaving, begging him silently to ask me to stay, but knowing I couldn't. For once in my life, I wanted to feel like someone didn't want me to go. I shook my head at the thought.

I stepped around Merek, held my head high, took a deep breath and left the apartment. I only made it to the car before tears blinded me. Blinking hastily, I pulled away from the curb. My hand trembled as my thoughts conflicted with what my body had done. The way he touched me. The way he filled me. It was so intense. But my inadequacies overwhelmed me. Worried I didn't satisfy him, I took his abrupt departure from the room as evidence he wasn't. My tears dried only enough to make it in the front door. Stunned, I found both my girls home.

"Mom?" Bree called out.

"Mom, where were you?" Mitzi expanded.

The Sex Education of M.E.

The collective questions warranted an answer, yet I didn't want to explain myself. How could I tell them where I'd been? I went to have sex with a man who wasn't their father. Doubtful that was an appropriate response. Swiping briskly at my cheeks, I took a deep breath and walked into the family room.

"Hey. You girls are home early," I said, sounding a bit too cheerful. My voice cracked.

"Allison went home early tonight," Bree offered.

"Kevin got a stomachache," Mitzi said. Her eyes pinched, giving off an appearance of scrutiny. My oldest knew me well. She would notice the swollen eyes. She would question the blotchy cheeks.

"Mom, you okay?" Mitzi asked. Bree didn't shift her attention from the television.

"Yeah." My hand wave dismissed the concern. Her wide eyes proved she didn't believe me, but my girls were used to seeing that sad expression on my face. It had been a while, but Mitzi would excuse my appearance as thoughts of her father. Shaking her head in dismay was confirmation of my prediction.

"I'm going to bed," I offered, and stepped toward the front hall. I hadn't made it to the stairs when I heard the murmurs of the girls.

"Bree, did you see Mom's face?"

Silence. Bree couldn't pull herself away from a good movie.

"Bree?" Mitzi snapped.

"What?"

"I think Mom's been crying again."

Silence. My Bree wasn't one for words.

"I thought she was done with tears. I can't watch her be sad again," Mitzi answered herself.

"She's not sad. She misses Dad," Bree replied softly. "There's a difference." My psychology-loving daughter had tried to diagnose me the past year.

"She needs to move on," Mitzi said.

"She can't," Bree replied.

"I just want her to be happy again."

"Me too," Bree answered. The room fell quiet again and I climbed the stairs. *Me, too*, I thought.

Chapter 16
Clubbing It

[M.E.]

Gia decided I needed further indoctrination into being single, so she took me to a dance club. Chicago was filled with them, in a variety of themes. That night was Ladies Night at The Square, a place on the edge of the city, near the airport. Despite the Ladies Night moniker, the place was packed with men. Old men. For older women. Anyone who had stock in thick gold chains might find one here around the neck of someone whose shirt was unbuttoned one button too many. A quick survey of the place and instantly I realized I had entered a parallel universe or something. There was too much testosterone in the air and any second someone would pee on me to stake a claim.

Gia believed I needed a place to let loose. I was still uptight over my night with Merek. He hadn't contacted me, and I didn't have the emotional strength to contact him. He'd scratched my itch, as he might have said, and I didn't want to turn into a needy rash. I held strong to the conviction that I got what I had asked for—sex and nothing more. Still, my heart ached. It hurt that he hadn't called me. My imagination ran away with grandiose ideas of Merek finding our night together life-altering, like it had been for me.

I wasn't a good dancer. I had been. At one point in my life, I loved to dance. Music was addicting, and when at home, alone, cleaning bathrooms or dusting furniture, letting loose was no problem. I'd sing in my off-key way and gyrate like a backup dancer. But in public, forget it. It was one of those weird hang-ups. Nate once told me I couldn't dance, like I didn't do it well, and so I never did again. I shouldn't have harbored the insult, but I could never let it go. I hung onto it. Feeling self-conscious of my body, added to the discomfort of public exhibition. I wasn't comfortable in my own skin and shaking for others wasn't my thing. I envied people who could do it. Work their body, and not think twice, but I was definitely thinking twice about my decision to be here.

"You can do this," Gia encouraged with a squeeze to my hand, and I took an empowering breath. "Relax. Deep breath in, deep breath out," she mocked. "That's good."

Risk-taking. That was tonight's theme. I needed to let the night lead me. I tried to rid my mind of Merek for days and the dance club was the distraction I needed. Only within minutes I wondered what it would be like to dance with Merek. My body recalled the press of him against me. The way his hips rolled. You know what they say about a man that can dance? In reverse, I knew Merek would be an amazing dancer if there was any comparison to his sexual ability. I shook my head to erase the thoughts.

We'd sauntered to the bar. The strobe lighting reflected in the place like a disco horror movie. The lights were so dim I strained to see more than ten feet away and the red flashing bulbs, laser beamed over the dance floor, enhanced the 1970s feel of the place. I waited patiently to order a drink. I wasn't good at interrupting, but it seemed like the bartender was taking an extraordinary amount of time to notice I wanted to place an order. He was more interested in helping anyone but me. Gia eventually wedged between me and a man with his back to us. Speaking to him, he raised his arm and the bartender approached. Gia yelled our drink order over the loud music. The man with his back to us twisted, and Gia was suddenly in a deep conversation with him.

I took the opportunity to scope out the place again, as best I could. I'd never seen so many black button downs in my life. A man with solid gray hair approached, and my heart sank. This had happened before. Men nearly twenty years older would flirt with me. I smiled politely and his mouth opened wider to display a row of yellowed teeth. I stood taller than him in my wedge heels, which wasn't saying much, as I wasn't a tall woman. His skin was weathered, a gold chain prominent at his throat.

"Come dance with me, baby."

It wasn't a question, so I didn't have an answer. There was no way I was dancing. Fortunately, Gia handed me my drink and I held it up as a response.

"Maybe when I finish this."

He didn't get the hint, as he remained nearby, clearly willing me to hurry up. I sipped slowly.

"So, come here often?" His white eyebrows wiggled, and I choked on the sweet wine. He couldn't be serious. *Did men really still ask that question?*

"She's a virgin," Gia yelled over the music, and it was his turn to sputter. His eyes undressed me and, for once, I didn't have the urge to cover my body in shame. I wanted to scrub it clean.

"Square Virgin," Gia clarified, and the intensity of his smile grew.

"Well, let me de-virginize you." His open mouth displayed his yellowed teeth. I laughed uneasily at his persistence.

"I think I'm all set," I retorted. "I can take care of myself."

"Oh, I'd like to see that, too," he whistled, his eyes still roaming up and down my body, and I shivered.

"Okay, killer, she'll be around later for a dance. Let's not pressure the virgin," Gia interjected, her facial expression admonishing him, and he dipped his head as an exit. Within seconds, he moved onto a group of women standing at a high table.

"This isn't real," I shouted to Gia. "I mean, men don't honestly still act this way." I laughed.

"Yeah, well, he wasn't exactly a man." Pinching her fingers an inch apart, she mocked him.

The place was hot, but I shivered with nerves. Sweat pooled under my pits and I downed the glass of wine. Gia's new friend asked her to dance, and she agreed, but not without pulling me toward the floor. I laughed again, tripping over my own feet. The tempo pulsed through me, and my one glass of wine became liquid courage, until I saw him.

I'd hardly moved two swaying hips when I noticed a familiar face with a young girl near the corner of the bar. His hand wrapped around her upper arm, but she was doing all the conversing. In fact, she looked like she was arguing with him. Her free arm flared, her hand waving in response to something he said. He wasn't letting her go, though. The dark t-shirt he wore bulged under the strain of his bicep muscles. He didn't wear the standard uniform of the place: a black button down. The tight black tee accentuating his broad chest was pure Merek.

The girl appeared roughly the same age as the waitress from the patio bar. This girl could have been one in the same person, for all I knew, with her long, straight hair and thin, youthful body. Her arm jerked, and she freed it from his grasp.

Gia bumped me with her hip, and it set me stumbling a few steps into someone. Reaching for the stranger in desperation, I prayed I wouldn't draw attention to myself by falling flat on my face. My focus so intent on Merek and the girl, I hadn't noticed who I grabbed until it was too late: cheesy old man.

"Well, well, well, ready for the virginal sacrifice?" he teased, as I looked into his older eyes. I shook my head. Glancing to the corner of the bar, I noticed Merek staring in my direction over the shoulder of his partner. His eyes narrowed, as if he couldn't quite make out if it was me. Shaking off the cold hands holding me upright, I stepped back from the older man.

"Oh look," Gia sing-songed in my ear over the thudding sound of the music. "It's Merek." Her high-pitched squeal teased, but I wasn't amused. The thought of Merek here, amongst all these men hunting for a one-night stand, made my stomach roll. The idea of Merek with a younger woman, someone slinky and sexy, forced the bile to rise.

"I need to go," I whispered, positive Gia didn't hear me. Twisting away from my pursuer, I faced Gia shaking my head. Liquid pricked my eyes. Her hand reached out for me, but I backed away, making my exit.

The contact with warm bodies, as I pushed my way over the dance floor, increased the heat radiating off of me. It was mostly nerves, but it added to the layer of hurt. While I had been hit on by an older man, Merek was at this bar with a younger girl. My imagination featured him with her, filling her the way he filled me, enjoying the lithe body of a younger woman who was slim, and trim, and experienced in ways I wasn't. Pushing through the main doors to exit the club, I gulped the refreshing summer night air and swiped a shaky hand over my damp forehead. I fumbled for my keys as I hurried across the darkening parking lot, vaguely aware of footsteps following me. My heart raced, and I braced my keys between my fingers in a form of defense.

When I rounded the corner of my car, I risked a glance in the direction of my follower.

"Emme?" Merek called out, but I ignored him. I tried to press the unlock button, but my thumb hit the lock instead and the door gave no response. Flicking to the correct button, the locks clicked upward as Merek wrapped a hand around my upper arm. My fingers clasped the door handle, but his free hand reached around me and held the door shut.

"Emme." He breathed into my hair. "Why are you always running?" His voice teased against my neck. He gently tugged me against him, and I briefly reveled in the feel of him behind me before I spun on him.

"What difference does it make?" I snapped. His dark eyes sparkled in the dim parking lot light. His grin widened and I wanted to slap him. To see with my own eyes that he was interested in someone younger, sucker-punched my gut. I didn't need a visual. My imagination was wild enough.

"I wanted to call," he offered, and I groaned. *Did men still say this excuse, too?* There could be no reason not to call in the modern age. I used that line a hundred times with my daughters. *You have a cell phone, so you can call me anytime, from anywhere.* It wasn't acceptable.

"But I had to work," he said. Exhaling hard, I read his black t-shirt: Security. My eyes flicked up to his. His lips tipped upward as the truth registered with me, and he twisted that seductive mouth to hold in a laugh.

"You work here?" I choked.

"Every Thursday night. Ladies Night," he answered.

"How convenient for you," I bit out, not appreciating his teasing tone. His face grew serious.

"Why would you say that?" His brows arched. His eyes opened wide.

"I saw you with that girl," I stated. "Very pretty. Very young."

"That girl?" His forehead wrinkled. "She's...wait a minute, I saw you with that man on the dance floor."

"You can't be serious?" I laughed without humor. "He was old."

"Oh, Henry's harmless." His twisting lips struggled against another laugh. I didn't let his familiarity with said Henry deter me.

"That doesn't answer my question." My voice lowered as did my eyes and he loosened his grasp enough I pulled my arm free.

"She's too young to be here. I was escorting her out." It seemed plausible based on the average age of the clientele. The Square was clearly for the over thirty crowd, if not even older. But someone twenty-something might find that age interesting, even financially beneficial.

"Oh my God, was she a prostitute?" Merek's fists clenched at his side in response as he hissed: "She better not be." The determination in his tone frightened me. His anger instant. His eyes flitted toward the exit door, out of sight from my car.

"I guess you should get back to work," I said, as the silence fell between us.

"Why are you leaving?"

"This isn't for me." I flipped my hand in the direction of the club. Without warning, his arms enveloped me, and I fumbled against his chest. My hands awkwardly reached for his waist as his broad biceps crushed me. His nose found my neck and he placed a tender kiss under my ear.

"Is this your car?" His voice rolled seductively across my skin. "You drive a minivan?"

I was ready to defend the minivan. The convenience of this vehicle was purposeful. I could cart carloads of kids and haul large items. I didn't have time to answer when the hand on my back opened the side door.

"Get in," he said, twisting me. He wasn't pushing, but he was definitely guiding me as I climbed into the second row. I sat with a thud as he climbed in, then slid the door hard enough it slammed.

"What are you…" I started, but he knelt before me and enfolded his arms around my back, drawing me closer to him. His lips met my neck, caressed my jaw, and my mouth watered to taste his. The kissing thing I ignored in our tussle at his home, but tonight I wanted an answer.

"Why won't you kiss me?" I questioned, but as his mouth brushed aside my shirt and he nipped my shoulder at the juncture to my neck, my resolve disappeared.

"Someone's going to see us." I worried. Merek picked his head up, taking note of the steam forming on the inside of the stifling car. His eyes drifted back to me.

"I've been thinking of you."

"You have?" My voice squeaked, and I cursed myself. My thoughts too hopeful. My response too quick. I'd been thinking of him constantly, to the point of total distraction. I was continually wet and ready, and wanting. It had been three full days.

Laughter outside the van brought out the reality of where we were. It had been a long time since I'd made out in a car, or more.

"Don't you have to work?"

"I'm on a break." He dragged me off the second seat.

"How do you feel about being on your knees?" he asked, but he wasn't waiting for an answer. I heard the zip of metal on metal as the two middle seats moved forward. He positioned me to lean over the third seat in the van, my knees rubbing on the rough car carpet. We were below window level. Thankfully, the tinted windows, furthest back, allowed some privacy. My legs wedged open as his knees fell between mine. His chest crushed my back. He twisted my hair over his fist and raised it, so his mouth could suck on the nape of my neck. His arm was wrapped around my waist, and he tugged me back to grind against the length of him pressed on my ass. The spark ignited instantaneously.

Wanton woman, hear me roar. My hips rolled. My back arched. I rubbed against him like a waking kitten. My claws dug into the seat where my elbows braced. I might have actually purred.

"Are you wet?" he growled, throaty and low, and the moisture between my thighs increased. My dress slid upward while his hand traveled around my hip to cup me. The touch forced me back. Thick fingers slipped into my underwear and impaled me sweetly. My back arched again as I sucked him into me.

"Is this what you came here for tonight, Emme?" His tone, one of condemnation. "Are you wet and willing because you wanted someone to take you tonight?" His words cut through the air

"No," I groaned as his fingers rotated inside me and I thrust backward, tugging him deeper inside me. "Oh God," I moaned, thanking every spiritual deity for the way he made me feel. He moved the collar of my dress for access to my shoulder. His warm mouth brushed over it, nipping me as he had before. If I wasn't already on my knees, I would have fallen on them.

"Were you hoping to dance with someone, then go home with him?" His voice roughened, accusatory.

"No," I hissed. The attention of his fingers rough, yet welcome. After several deep strokes, my underwear was removed.

"Are we really doing this here?" I gasped, looking up briefly at the dark windows, where condensation formed from the heat of our breaths in a warm van.

"Yes."

The sound of his buckle clicking open filled the back seat. A slight jumble of his clothes and the warm length of him dragged through cool globes. I stilled instinctively.

"Uhm...I...uhm..." My hands gripped the seat belt, if only for something to hold onto.

"You've never done it this way?" he asked sultry and deep as he continued to caress my seam with his hard length.

"I...I have in this position...just...not...*there*." I sounded like an inexperienced imbecile, but then again, I was. I read books. Too many books, and I knew this was a popular style. Men apparently did want to go in the back door. I just hadn't ever experienced that position and I wasn't certain doing it for the first time in the back of my minivan was something I could handle.

"We won't be doing that tonight," he assured me, as if he read my mind. He paused, teasing his thick tip between my ass cheeks, before sliding further down my center. "That would take preparation and time we don't have." His voice lowered as a firm finger slid seductively close to my back entrance. He paused momentarily. The sharp rip of foil behind me could only be him sheathing on a condom.

"But I am going here," he said with little warning, and slammed into me in just the right place. I cried out in awkward pleasure and a sharp dash of pain. He stilled, and I took a deep breath.

"You okay?" he asked. Firm hands slid up my still-dressed back. Then one hand wove into my hair again while the other landed on my hip, warm and steady, while he waited for my answer.

"God...yes..." I exhaled. I curled back to draw him deeper. His rhythm increased instantly as he thrust forward over and over. The hand on my hip slipped around to that nub of pleasure that wept for friction. He gently tugged my hair while he rubbed sensitive folds and continued to impale me in a steady beat. On sensory overload, I worried I wouldn't get to where I wanted to go.

"Relax, beautiful," he grunted. "Let it happen. I'll wait."

I took a deep breath, encouraging myself into taking the pleasure. My hand tightened its grip on the seat belt. I might have pulled it from the seat. I thrust backward, forcing him deeper inside me as I practically sat on him. My legs spread wide over his thighs, exposing me, and I bounced up and down on the sharp length of him. Our skin slapped. The van shook. My toes curled in my shoes as a new sensation skittered up my legs. A guttural, animalistic sound escaped me, and I rolled my hips, letting loose three days of pent-up tension. The release washed out of me, intensifying my jungle cry as I rode Merek in a way I'd never done with anyone before. And then he came apart inside me. His hands stilled my hips, and the pulse rushed deep, giving me a euphoric high. My channel clenched, holding him in, responding of its own will to Merek filling me.

"You okay?" he asked, cautiously, his head resting between my shoulder blades as we both breathed heavily.

"I'm...yeah...I'm good."

His head rose.

"Good? You can't use *good* to describe that. It's like using the word *fine*. It's not allowed." His tone teased despite the hint of seriousness.

"It was incredible," I offered, smiling to myself.

"You're incredible," he whispered to my hair, and my smile deepened.

Chapter 17
Dancing In the Dark

[M.E. 2]

Who knew a fucking minivan could be so hot? I typically didn't do the vehicle thing. While I wasn't too old for one-night stands, I was too old for fumbling in a back seat. But when I saw the horrified expression on her face as I argued with Cassie, I had to make things right. I didn't want to explain myself, or Cassie, but I also couldn't let Emme leave without giving her something. This something in her backseat wasn't exactly what I had in mind, but I would not complain.

When she left the other night, I was pissed. Even though, I'd argued with myself whether I wanted her to stay or go, I was irritated after she walked out. I understood she had kids. I'd been with women who had them before, and typically, it was a good reason *not* to spend the night. But I wanted Emme to stay. I argued that my decision was made only *because* she walked out. She'd gotten what she wanted from me, like most women. As I breathed in the summer sweet scent of her, mingled with the smell of us together, I knew it wasn't true. Emme wasn't selfishly taking from me. In fact, I wasn't sure what she was doing to me, but I couldn't let her leave the club without speaking to her.

I slid out of her, unfazed by the noise that escaped. Emme, however, was mortified.

"Oh my God. Was that me?" The car was dark, but I sensed her deep blush.

"It's nothing. Just the friction release," I clarified as I pulled off the condom, suppressing a chuckle. Some nights I was sick of these things, but it was for my own protection and that of my partner. Of course, Emme hadn't been with another man in twenty years. I would wager it was safe to say she was clean.

Her retreat happened quickly. She scrambled to face me and quickly reached for her underwear that dangled off one ankle. She fumbled, hastily tugging it up under her skirt, before straightening the material to sit prim and proper. She shifted on the back seat where she now perched.

I was still on my knees before her, and I took a moment to observe her. Her reaction to Cassie surprised me. *Was she jealous?* If only she knew the truth. I suppressed the chuckle. Emme was different. Her body was a woman's body. What we did just now might rival a twenty-year-old and Emme proved she could handle it. She was more than a bang in the back of a truck. She was beautiful. Really beautiful. Her body showed signs of life that I wouldn't find in someone younger. She had experience. She lived life; she didn't just float from one night to another. I wanted to wrap up what she offered and take it with me. Bottle it and carry it in my pocket like a new drug. One whiff would restore me.

She caught me staring, so I struggled to right my pants.

"What do you have on?" She wore those sexy boy shorts again, and tonight's pair was black. She smoothed down her already flat skirt and glanced at her knees.

"A dress."

The seriousness of what she said made my laughter release. I rose up on my knees to adjust my belt buckle. When I sat back, she was staring at me.

"I'm so glad I amuse you." Her tone sharp. I don't know what made me do it, but I lunged forward, my mouth eager to crush hers. I stopped. An inch separated us and her gasp told me I surprised her. While that was my intention, I shocked myself. Her breath mingled with mine, and I wanted a taste of her. But I wouldn't kiss her. That was my hard limit. My fine line. My breaking point. It was a weird fetish, but I had my reasons.

"Kiss me," she whispered, and I swallowed hard.

"I...I can't." My attempts at love had bitten me hard and I hadn't recovered. My eyes averted from hers, but the pressure weighed on me. She wanted an answer, and I wasn't willing to share. This was casual. We had agreed.

"Who's the girl inside?" Her voice shook.

"She's..." I couldn't find the right words. I couldn't say *no one*. This was another line, more like a deep divide, and I wasn't certain I could offer even a nugget of information.

Emme looked away from me while I knelt before her. Her sideways gaze was brief, and she returned to me with a false smile.

"I think I should go," she said softly. My lips smashed together and twisted in frustration. She was running away again. *Damn it.* I maneuvered myself out of the back seat, and Emme followed me out the side door. She stepped aside while I slid it closed.

"Wait! You aren't going back inside?" My body blocked her from reaching for the door handle. I don't know why I assumed she would return to the club, but I had hoped. I didn't want her to leave. Not like this, not again. Even though I had to work, I could still keep my eye on her. Working security was a second job. It paid well, and I had hours to fill.

"I think I'm just going to go home." Pinched lips aimed at me. Her hand smoothed down her hip. The skirt fit snug and hugged her curves. So beautiful, I thought again. Her platinum hair practically glowed under the dim parking lot lights and the just-fucked look was sexy. Her blouse was sheer, hinting at what I was well aware hid beneath it. I had to look away as I was already growing hard for round two.

"You don't want to dance?" I asked, nodding toward the club. I didn't really like the idea of her dancing with other guys, even that harmless old man, Henry. He'd be having fantasies of her for months. Hell, if he knew what her body could do, he'd die from cardiac arrest, but he'd be a happy man. The thought made me shiver.

"I don't really dance. My friend, Gia, made me come here."

"Gia, huh." Then I realized what she said. "You don't dance?"

"I…I just don't…" She was so adorable when she was flustered, and I bit back my smile.

"Tell me," I asked softly, brushing back a stray hair. My hand rested on her neck, just under her ear.

"I…" Avoiding my eyes, she spoke. "I can't dance. I mean, I can, I just don't."

"What?"

"I don't dance."

"Why not?"

"I'm not…" She wasn't looking at me, and I tugged at her neck to force her focus to me. "I'm not really comfortable dancing. Besides, Nate said I wasn't very good at it."

"He…" *Bastard.* Who tells his wife she can't dance? Her blue eyes warned me not to speak.

"Well, I can't let you leave without a dance."

"Merek, I just told you, I don't dance." Her tone grew angry, but I tugged her toward the end of the van.

"Just one dance. With me." My arms circled her, holding her close to me. For only a second, her arms dangled at her side before her hands reached for my biceps. I took one hand with mine and tucked it between us. My hips swayed. She stiffened.

"I can't do this here." She softly laughed, the sound like butterflies flapping tender wings.

"That's what you thought a few minutes ago and look what you did." She stared up at me and her blue eyes crushed me. "Think of it like what we just did. Follow me," My voice dipped. She nodded. Pulling her closer, I hummed my favorite song and her smile pressed against my shoulder. And that touch warmed me deeper than being inside of her.

Chapter 18
Round 2

[M.E.]

I didn't want to do it, but Gia said I should go out with Rod again. We decided on a movie. I hadn't seen a movie in so long I didn't even know what was playing, so I let Rod decide. The comedy was something straight out of a fraternity boys' wet dream. Tons of T and A, with lots of laughter about drugs and raunchy college kids hooking up. This wasn't my kind of movie. The predictable scenes were not hilarious to me, while Rod couldn't control his laughter. When the third sex scene started, he reached for my hand, and that became my focus instead of the film.

Rod's hands were large and meaty. There wasn't another way to describe them. I honestly couldn't remember the touch of his hands from our teenage years, but it wasn't like this: clammy, moist, and heavy. There was just something not right about his touch. It wasn't Merek's. I'd been trying not to think of Merek since he hadn't called me again. Thinking of him was like my own sordid fraternity wet dream. Thoughts of the young girl he left behind in the bar continued to haunt me. He probably preferred someone like her. Young and lithe, she was most likely more experienced than I, sadly. Which made me think of my youth and wonder what happened to that girl.

That girl I had been...the one who had dreams and goals. The one who felt sexy in her twenties and used it. The one who wanted a soulmate experience, who was supposed to be my husband, but had sadly turned out not to be. I'd disappeared along the way. I'd lost myself. It took years to find her again, but I didn't feel complete. Merek popped into my meandering mind.

Gia wondered where I disappeared to the other night. While she didn't pry, she noted Merek followed after me. She hadn't noticed if, or when, he returned, so she could offer no report if he had a repeat performance with another woman. Or that girl. My stomach lurched at the thought of him sleeping with others. We didn't have commitment or stipulations in his proposition. Only, I struggled with the terms of agreement. This was what I wanted, and yet, it wasn't. Add in the whole lack of kissing thing, and I started to think he had some strange Vivian thing going on. Only I was the client, when I wanted to be considered the pretty woman. I sighed while Rod laughed again and then squeezed my hand.

"This really puts me in the mood." A harsh whisper hit my ear. Then he growled. Literally. He sounded like a sick tiger, and it was the first thing I found funny all night. It occurred to me that while Merek might be sleeping around, I couldn't.

Thankfully, the movie ended.

"My place or yours?" he teased. The flirtation unsettled me, but I offered my home. I found it odd that Rod didn't ask for an after-movie drink or an ice cream dessert. He claimed he had to work early the next morning, but he wanted to go to his house or mine. It puzzled me at first, but the excuse was reminiscent of poor ones from the past. Nate had them all the time. He couldn't do this or that because he had to work late. He had to wake early. I understood the code. Nate wasn't interested in spending time with me. He only wanted occasional sex. Merek used the excuse as well. He hadn't called because he had to work.

Rod kissed me.

It was a surprise attack that threw me so off guard it took me a moment to catch up to what happened. He pulled back with lazy, hooded lids before opening them and addressing me. We hadn't moved from the car parked in my driveway.

"You taste exactly the same," he said. "Just how I remember."

"Is that good or bad?" I asked, realizing I'd had popcorn during the movie, and probably had salty-butter-kernel breath.

"It's good." The words struck me. I didn't want to be good, like Merek teased. Taking up the challenge, I leaned toward Rod and kissed him back. I tried to throw into his lips what I would do to Merek's. How I wanted to tease the bow and lick the curl. How I wanted to suck his tongue. How I wanted to nip those lips in hopes he'd beg me for more kisses. Only this wasn't Merek, and Merek didn't kiss me.

When Rod pulled back for a breather, his heavy lids plus another growl sealed the deal. I couldn't do this with him. Rod and I had our shot twenty-five years ago, and it wasn't going to happen twenty-five years later.

"Want me to come in?" The implication of what Rod wanted was clear and I had my own excuse. I had children.

Chapter 19
Headaches Are a Poor Excuse, or Are They?

[M.E. 2]

I need a ride, I texted to her.

Isn't that my line? she responded.

I'd like it to be your line.

There was a long pause while the three dots rolled and bounced signaling her response.

I can't.

This better not be another fucking date, I thought. While I wasn't typically exclusive, I also wasn't fooling around with anyone else. And while I was a man of many needs, I wanted Emme for now.

Hot date? The question was bitter to type, but as long as we played these awkward word games, it was my only response. I already knew what my reaction would be if she answered with another yes.

Sore throat.

I choked at the thought.

And a headache.

I laughed. Not like I hadn't heard that excuse before, although it had been a long time since that happened.

Good excuse. I guffawed to myself, bitterly.

It's true. I get migraines once a month.

I stared at the words: once a month. Well, this was no good. Emme was out of commission, if it was that time of the month. Not that I was opposed to that experience, but we didn't have anywhere near that comfort level.

Okay. Well, hope you feel better soon.

When the only response was a smile emoji, I felt less than stellar. I called my brother instead.

Finding ourselves at Bruno's late on a Tuesday night was dangerous. The Cubs were on, and the place was packed. Marshall was in rare form, hitting on anything with two long legs even though Bridget was having his baby. It reminded me of when I was still young, and foolish, and didn't know better. Marshall wasn't a youngster, though. He needed to get his head out of his ass and marry the girl. Pissed off in my own right, for no apparent reason, I picked at Marshall.

"What the fuck you doing, man?" He'd just tugged a girl onto his lap. "You're going to be a father."

The girl looked over her shoulder at Marshall and cooed. "You're going to be a daddy? That's so sweet." She was wasted and had no idea what she was saying.

"I'll be your daddy for the night," he slurred, and the brunette giggled.

"I mean, a real father, dickhead." I sucked back my beer, briefly glancing at the game on the large screen.

"Like you're a real father?" He barked back over the uproar of the bar when the Cubs scored. My eyes narrowed at him.

"I don't need this shit tonight," I said, standing abruptly, brushing back my chair.

"Sit down. I didn't mean it." Keeping his eyes on me, he placed a kiss on the neck of the girl.

"What did you mean, then?"

"Nothing. What's your problem tonight?" He nudged the girl to shift to his other thigh.

"You've got a girl who loves you. She's having your baby, and you're out here dicking around."

The expression of Lap-girl shifted. Her eyes lowered, and she picked at the label on Marshall's beer bottle.

"Dicking around is what we do," Marshall laughed, jostling the girl up and down on his knee.

"Why?" Lap-girl and I asked at the same time.

"Because your heart broke once and it's safer." Marshall arched an eyebrow. Lap-girl nodded as if she was part of our conversation.

"Then what's your excuse?" I snapped. Marshall only glared at me across the table. Bridget loved him, I was certain of it. She'd loved him since we were kids, only she married some asshole and had three kids with him before my brother paid attention. Now, he dipped in the honey pot, stirred up the bees, and he was going to get stung, if he wasn't careful. I knew. I had the history to prove it.

The bar crowd cheered again at another hit by the Cubs, but I wasn't in the festive mood. In fact, ever since Emme used the headache and monthly-bill excuse on me, I'd been down right pissed off.

Before Marshall could answer my question, another girl sauntered up to the table. Late twenties. Size C cup. Narrow hips. Size four. Blonde hair. Not fake. I played this game with myself, sizing up the possibilities for a night then shared the skill with Marshall in a drunken stupor when he was twenty-one. We'd bet on it. Then it was tell-all once we had our hands on those breasts and our dick between those thighs. We were on the honor system to share details. No fudging the results. My stomach soured at the thought of this game, that we hadn't played in years.

When the woman stopped at our table, she helped herself to the spare chair.

"Judy, whatcha doing?" she asked Lap-girl, still perched on Marshall's lap.

"I'm going home with my new daddy." She giggled then swung an arm to wrap around Marshall's neck. Only it knocked him in the nose, and he cursed while tears filled his eyes. She peppered him with kisses, murmuring words to soothe him.

"Oh, for fuck's sake," I muttered, standing again. "I'm headed home." I hadn't gotten very far before I sensed someone behind me. Glancing over my shoulder, I noticed I was followed by the blonde.

"Hey," she called out. "Looks like Judy's tied up with your friend. Mind giving me a ride?"

I laughed at the irony of her question but kept walking.

"I bet you'd like a lift," I snipped under my breath.

"Actually, from the likes of you, I bet the lift would be pretty amazing."

She bumped into me as I spun on her. Her young form saddled against mine and my hands instinctively settled on her hips. An arm draped around my neck, and I leaned forward. Whiffing a strong scent of citrus and bar smoke and something else, I froze. The fragrance was wrong. This wasn't what I wanted. While I typically didn't care who I drove home, tonight I didn't want to give anyone else a ride, but Emme.

My hands gently pressed Blondie away from me.

"I can't tonight." I paused. "I have a headache."

Chapter 20
In Sickness

[M.E.]

I was sick. It was more than a headache, and blast it, if I didn't have my period, too. I ached all over. A summer cold, and I blamed the combination of air-conditioning and college students I encountered at the university. The day was gorgeous outside, but I tossed and turned in bed. Merek clearly didn't care for my excuse, which was not an excuse. Moments like this reminded me of Nate. As a mother, I wasn't allowed to get sick. When my daughters were little, I worked through my own fevers, sore throats, and earaches. There was no one to take care of me. Nate was the worst. He still expected dinner on the table when my girls were young, and I was a stay-at-home-mom. He had no sympathy for a headache and forget about the pain of a period. It was all an excuse, he would say. People wondered why I married Nate and some days, I did, too.

When a knock came on my front door, I ignored it. *Nobody's home*, I cried in my head. It was only me. The girls were at work, and I was slightly grateful I had the house to myself. No one would take care of me anyway. Being sick brought out the Debbie Downer in me, and I hated it. I acted like a baby. Melancholy and illness certainly did commiserate.

Emme? My phone pinged.

I stared at my name on the screen. It was rare for Merek to text me early in the day. Even more rare was the fact that it was actually the day after his last text.

Hey, I typed weakly. I didn't have the energy for Merek at the moment. Contributing to my headache were wayward thoughts about him, his lack of kissing, and his sexual history. I hadn't thought about it before, but if I didn't fulfill his needs last night, had he found someone who did? The weight on my chest was as heavy as the ache in my lower back and I sighed audibly in my empty bedroom.

Open the door, he replied, and I heard a knock again. I shot upright. The pressure on my head forced me to wrap my hands around my forehead. He couldn't possibly be at my house. He didn't know where I lived. He didn't care that I was sick. He wouldn't want to see me looking like I did: unshowered, sick-smelling, greasy haired.

I'm not home, I responded.

Your van's here. I remember it.

Damn it, I sighed. I didn't have the energy to play Merek's games.

I'm sick, Merek. You don't want to see me like this.

Yes, I do...want to see you.

This can't be happening, I thought as I slowly pulled myself from the bed. I snuck to the bathroom first, able to see Merek's truck parked in the street before my home. Hastily, I brushed my teeth and straightened my crooked ponytail. I gripped the railing as I descended the stairs, each step hurting my head as my body quivered from lack of food. I dreaded the next move, but I opened the front door and found a vision of health standing on my front step. Not only was he holding a bouquet of meadow flowers, but a grocery bag dangled from his hand and a huge smile framed his face.

"Hey." My voice was weak.

"Hey. You don't look so good." He blinked, his smile fading a bit.

"Yeah, well, I've been better. What are you doing here?"

"House call," he said, and reached for the handle of the screen door. I stepped back while he helped himself inside without invitation.

"You need to get back in bed," he teased, and his flirtatious grin wasn't lost to me.

"Wouldn't you like that?" I snipped, my tone harsher than I intended.

"I would." His lips twisted. "But not today."

My legs wobbled, and I had to sit down. I hit the landing with a thud. Merek set the flowers on the floor along with his grocery bag and reached out for me.

"I can walk," I said, but he was already hoisting me upward. An arm wrapped around my back and another scooped under my knees. I was suddenly carried up the stairs as if Merek knew where he was going.

"How did you know where I lived?" I asked.

"I have my sources." He winked. Sensing his struggle to carry me up the set of stairs, I offered once again to walk, but he ignored me.

Pointing right at the top of the staircase, Merek carried me all the way to my bed. I settled back, propping up my pillows then looked up to notice his eyes roving my body.

"What are you wearing?" he groaned

"A nightgown." It wasn't an old-fashion, long sleeve, high collar outfit. This was not my grandmother's get-up. This was an elongated tank top, hugging my body, currently minus a bra, and falling mid-thigh. It was cool and comfortable. Nate never liked them; said they reminded him of his mother, but after his death, I began wearing them again. It seemed rather slinky to wear all alone, but I liked it. Merek looked a bit appreciative of it, too.

Shaking his head, he said he'd be right back, and I slipped lower on the bed. Sitting upright wasn't helping the pounding in my head, and I couldn't take more meds for another two hours. My eyes tried to focus on the silent screen of the television. It was on, but I wasn't listening to any sound. I'd tried to read earlier, but I didn't have the strength to focus on words. I could hear Merek opening and closing cabinets, then my refrigerator and I smiled in spite of myself to think of all he learned about me from my household appliances. I wasn't much of a cook and my bare cabinets proved it.

He returned to my room with the flowers in a vase and a wine glass.

"Here," he offered.

"What's this?"

"Water."

"You brought me water in a wine glass?"

"I figured it would make you feel better, drinking it out of something fancy." His eyes didn't have to roam far to see the plastic cup of water resting on the floor near the bed. It was slightly out of reach, and he picked it up after setting the wine glass on my nightstand.

"When was the last time you ate?"

I actually couldn't remember. I'd come home from class around noon and took a nap. I told the girls to fend for themselves regarding dinner. It was almost eleven the next day, and I hadn't had breakfast…

"A while."

"Feel sick to your stomach?"

Actually, I did. Migraines did this to me, but I also knew if I ate something or had some caffeine, it normally helped despite the lack of hunger.

"Eggs or soup?"

"Ugh..." I groaned, and his eyebrows pinched in concern. "How about some toast first?"

I nodded, and he disappeared. Returning with a small plate, he'd decoratively spread triangle cut pieces of toast around some scrambled eggs. I had to smile. If nothing else, his presentation skills were commendable.

"So, this is your room?" he asked, slipping his hands into the pockets of his shorts and taking in the space. I had a king size bed with one side still made. There was no point to mess up what used to be Nate's side. In fact, I considered getting a smaller bed, but the girls would occasionally crawl in with me to watch television, and for that reason alone, I kept the bigger one. Merek slowly turned, noting the lamp, a jewelry box and the television on the long dresser. Clothes were piled on a chair in the corner. Framed photographs stood on Nate's dresser. Our wedding photograph stood at the back of the collection.

"Mind if I sit?" he asked, already removing his shoes and climbing over me. He plopped back on the extra pillows and faced the television. Eventually, he rolled his head in my direction, taking in my exposed neck and sagging breasts.

"You didn't have to get all dolled up for me." His gaze scanned the nightgown again.

"I didn't know you were coming," I reminded him.

"Not coming yet," he muttered, and I groaned.

"You didn't just say that," I laughed. He smiled weakly in return. We stared at one another for a long moment. I suddenly felt exposed. My mind wandered to what he'd done without me, when I didn't take up his invitation last night. My mouth couldn't filter my thoughts.

"How does it work?" I asked quietly.

"Excuse me?" he stuttered, his eyes blinking.

"If you call, and I can't...I mean...what do you do? Call someone else? Or do you have standing appointments? Like Wednesday is Wendy, and Tuesday is Tiffany."

"Emme," he warned softly, looking away from me and settling his eyes on the television again. I continued to stare at his profile. He was such a good-looking man. His salt and pepper scruff only heightened his looks. Despite the crinkles by his eyes, his face was young, and his body, good Lord, his body was built like none I'd seen in person. To fill the awkward silence, I had to speak.

"That's what your call was, right? A booty call? You wanted sex, but I couldn't. So, what did you do?" I tried my hardest to keep my voice from sounding accusatory or even condemning.

He rolled his head back to face me and ran a hand down his face. "Jesus, where do you come up with this shit?"

"I read. A lot."

He stared at me. "I called my brother," he sighed. "We went to the bar." He paused, and I sensed there was more. Merek was often evasive, and while I was easily distracted by his body, I didn't miss that he didn't share about himself personally.

"I didn't know you had a brother."

"He's younger than me by seven years. He was considered their miracle baby, as my parents didn't think they could have more after me and my sister. She had been two years older than me, but she died when I was three." His voice faded as he spoke of her. My hand reached out to touch his forearm. While he didn't flinch, he didn't seem to notice either.

"I'm so sorry, Merek."

He shrugged. "It was a long, long time ago."

"Still, it must have been hard for your parents, and growing up as a young child."

I couldn't imagine the loss of a child. I didn't want to imagine it. The pressure on his parents. The way they either smothered him or stepped away from him with their loss. Then another child came along.

"So, what did you and your brother do last night?" Attempting to shift the conversation, I realized I might have been drifting into another discussion I didn't wish to have.

"My brother's…he's having a difficult time, but his head is so far up his ass, he's making a fool of himself. He's about to lose everything because of it." The anger in Merek's voice surprised me.

"What kind of difficulty?"

"He got a girl pregnant. Although she isn't a girl, and he isn't a kid, either. He's thirty-five and needs to grow up." Merek's tone had turned to irritation. He turned to face me again.

"Hey, I didn't come over to share my brother's life with you." His tone lowered, but his eyes were tender. I continued to stare at him.

"Why did you come over here then?" In answer to my question, he reached out for my forehead. My eyes closed as he began a slow circular motion at my temples. The thick pads of his thumbs rubbed over my brows while his index fingers continued to circle near my eyes. Tender lips met one temple and then the other. The kiss was sweet, and his lips brushed my nose before I opened my eyes again.

"Where else does it hurt?" he asked softly, and I muttered, "My back."

"Roll over," he prompted, and I twisted so my back was to him. His expert hands started with my lower back, as if he knew exactly where to touch. As if he knew exactly what I needed. Like he knew the first night. Like he knew the other night. I should have cared that his hands worked on something similar to an inner tube, but the soothing sensation mesmerized me. He massaged over the thin cotton of my nightgown before pulling up the material to get at my skin.

Sweet lips met my spine and trailed downward. He shifted to my lower back and alternated between tender massage and searing kisses. He turned me on even when I had no intention of following through with the seduction.

"I went out with Rod again," I blurted, and his hands stilled, his mouth resting against my lower vertebrae. I waited a beat before continuing. I wasn't certain why I told him. Maybe it was because I wanted to hurt him for being evasive about what he did last night. Knowing it wouldn't hurt him, that reason seemed childish. I said it for honesty. I wanted him to know what I'd done. "But I don't plan to see him again."

His hands returned their attention to the thick muscles of my back. My hand stilled his.

"I can't fool around, Merek, if that's why you're here." I couldn't face him as I spoke. I didn't want to stop him, but I didn't wish to proceed either. There was no way I was having sex while I was sick or while I had my period.

"That's not why I'm here," he replied, and I noted again he hadn't told me the reason he was at my home. "What happened on your date?"

"He kissed me." Merek's fingers dug into tender flesh for a second, and I flinched as it tickled, although that wasn't his intention. "I didn't like it. And I'm only telling you to be truthful." I didn't want to add that I didn't like secrets. We were each going to have our own, if all we were sharing was sex. But I also didn't want to lie.

"Why didn't you like it?" His sultry voice and demanding lips traced over each blade waiting out my answer. "Tell me."

"It didn't feel right," I whispered.

"Do you want to be kissed?" His mouth rose to meet my shoulder.

"Yes," I breathed softly.

"But not by him?" His lips were at my neck and his tongue snuck out to lick from my shoulder to below my ear.

"No." I didn't know why we were having this conversation. It wasn't like Merek was going to kiss me. He made it clear he didn't want to, and while I thought it strange, I also strangely understood his reason. A kiss was personal. My kiss with Rod had been impersonal enough for me to know I didn't want to do it again. To my surprise, Merek nipped the juncture of my neck and shoulder.

"Did his kiss feel like this?" His gravelly tone was low as his mouth continued its travels under my ear.

"No."

"Did his kiss feel like the other night?" That seductive tone made my body tremble. "When I came at you from behind?" His body shifted and the warmth of him pressed against me. I couldn't believe I was turned on by his voice, distracting me from how I physically felt otherwise.

"No," I exhaled.

"I plan to do that again. And again," he muttered into my ear between gentle nips of my lobe. While my head should have been in the seduction he was attempting, my mind flipped back to my original question. The pressure of my headache overruled the slow building desire of my body.

"What if you call me and I'm not in the mood, and I tell you *no*. Do you make the offer to someone else? Is that how booty calls work?"

The loss of him was immediate. He released my side and rolled away from me. I didn't turn to look at him, feeling safer in asking my questions while I couldn't see his face. We remained silent and I expected him to leave. I really believed that's what he was about to do. He'd made a house call, booty call, and he wasn't going to get what he came for.

"No, it's not how it works. Or maybe it does work that way for others." Shifting behind me, his hands returned to my lower back.

"Is that what happened last night?" I couldn't let it go. I had to know if he'd been with someone else when I turned him down. In my heart, it would be a deal breaker. I'd have to move on.

"Emme," he exhaled into my neck and slipped his arm over my side. He pulled his body flush to mine again. "No, that's not what happened last night." He sighed. "And as long as we are being honest, if I call, and you said no, I'd just keep calling back."

I smiled to myself and let my arm cover his. He tugged me closer to him, and I gave into the steady breathing of him behind me.

Chapter 21
In Health

[M.E. 2]

I woke with a start at 3:30 p.m. I don't know what made me wake, but it took a moment to realize where I was: wrapped around Emme. In her bed. It felt strange, and yet, holding her didn't. It seemed strange to snuggle, such a girly word, but I liked the feeling of it. The pressure of her leaning into me, like I protected her. It made me feel…important. I wasn't one to cuddle, and I typically didn't fall asleep with women. In fact, I couldn't remember the last time I had slept holding a woman. The usual result was present. I was hard and ready for Emme, but she slept soundly, her body limp and relaxed against mine.

Her questions upset me. *"How does it work?"* She was digging for answers, and I didn't want to lie. When she offered her honesty, it felt safer to admit the truth. I would keep calling her. But if she continually told me no, I'd want an explanation. Why she had a change of heart. Then again, she hadn't wanted matters of the heart to be involved. She wanted sex, so that's what we had done on two occasions. That was the deal.

Knowing her girls would be home soon from their summer jobs, I had to get out of her house.

"Emme, darlin', I need to leave."

"Mmmm…" she purred and wiggled her behind into me. My dick strained against my zipper. Why did she have to be sick? And why did she have to make this harder on me? I kissed her shoulder as I slipped my hand over her hip. She hardly stirred as I balanced upward. She rolled to her back just as my leg hitched over her to exit the bed. Our eyes caught as I straddled her.

"Where are you going?" Her scrunched brow questioned.

"How's your head?"

"Better," she exhaled, rubbing a hand over her forehead.

"I need to go," I whispered. She nodded. Slipping off of her, her hand caught the pocket of my shorts as I bent to pick up my shoes.

"Thank you." The tenderness of her tone pinched my heart. The way she looked at me, like I was her hero, made my heart jump in my chest. My mouth watered to taste her sweet mouth, but I settled for a kiss to that crinkled forehead and let myself out of her house.

I called her on Thursday. It had been a full week from the time in her van, and I was ready to burst at just the thought of entering her. She was hardly through the apartment door, and I had her pinned against the wall, my mouth devouring her neck and making its way down to her breasts. Her hands slid over my hair, and tugged gently, guiding my destination. I slipped the cup of her bra under her large breast and sucked deeply, falling to my knees before her. My mouth watered with the fullness as I laved and nipped at her peaked nipple. Her responding moans and rolling hips told me she was desperate for me, too.

My hands slid up her dress and gently removed her underwear while my mouth moved to her other breast. Her fingers tenderly scrapped against my scalp, and each prickle sent sparks to my already straining length. My fingers slipped up her thigh and entered her quickly.

"So wet," I moaned against her warm breast. "So ready for me." Surrounded in warmth, her muscles clenched around two fingers, holding me inside her.

"Merek," she groaned, while her hips rocked forward, sucking me deeper inside her. My thumb circled the pearl of pleasure outside her entrance and her knees bent. Her back supported by the door, I forced her upright as I continued my attention to her breast and her clit. My mouth sucked harder, my fingers dove deeper, and then the tell-tale sign I'd quickly memorized about Emme happened. Her legs stiffened. Her thighs clamped together, holding me inside her, and she hissed my name in pleasing wonder.

"Oh my God, that was fast." She anxiously laughed, as the orgasm slowed, and my fingers released from her. "Well, I guess I can go now," she teased, but I stood quickly, framing her in with my body.

"Oh, I'm not nearly done with you yet," I murmured, returning to her neck, pecking a trail up to her jaw. My mouth watered again. What would it be like to kiss her? Would it be so wrong? Was Marshall right, my heart had been so broken in the past I didn't wish to get close to anyone again? That scar had been made long ago. I'd found the means to move on, but before me was someone I might want to take one more step forward with.

I released her as my prisoner, letting my hands drift down her arms to circle her wrists. Stepping back, I tugged her toward the bedroom.

"What, no plying me with wine first?" she teased. I stopped in my tracks.

"We can drink after," I suggested, wondering where the suggestion came from as well as noting it implied she should stay awhile. She smiled in response, and I began walking backward again.

"I'm sorry you always need to come here," I said for no particular reason. While I wanted to have sex with her at her house, I understood the reason why we didn't. I didn't want to take her to a hotel. I had long since stopped doing those kinds of rendez-vous.

"I don't mind," she said. "Although it does make me feel like a hussy."

She stumbled into me by my abrupt stop.

"Why?"

"I feel like you call, and I follow. I come to you, booty call." She shrugged like it didn't matter, but it was clear that it did. Based on all her questions the other day, it was obvious that Emme wasn't going to be able to remain in this mindset of casual sex for long. She was a woman who would need a little bit more and I was going to be sorry if that day came soon.

When we entered the bedroom, she placed her hands on my shoulders, forcing me to sit down on the edge of the bed. Her mouth came to my forehead, then my cheek. She dipped below my ear and nipped the lobe, causing me to shiver.

"What are you doing, you vixen?" I laughed, but she ignored me. Her hands tugged my shirt, and I raised my arms, allowing her to take it over my head. Paying close attention, her fingers mapped my body, starting at my shoulders, and travelling down each arm. She lowered her body to kneel between my thighs, and I swallowed hard at the idea of where she headed. A fingernail traced over the artwork on each bicep. Looking left, then right, she covered the outline of tribal bands, and fire symbols, and an Irish trinity.

"CFD?" she asked softly. My eyes closed, having memorized the date under the bold styled letters.

"My father was a fireman. He died in a blaze when I was in my late twenties." I swallowed the lump in my throat after the explanation. Her eyes didn't move from the tattoo and her lips covered the symbol of my father's death with tender kisses. Her mouth took its time down my arm, sucking at cool skin, and nipping in places, sparking a sensation unlike any I'd known before. It was tender and tempting, and when she reached my wrist, her tongue flicked a design around it. When those lips covered my index finger, and sucked it deep inside her warm mouth, I had to loosen my shorts, the tension was too tight.

"Emme," I whispered on a groan. Her fingers unzipped my shorts and I sat up enough to tug them down to my knees. Her mouth moved on to another finger, building the anticipation of what she'd do to another part of me.

"I'm not terribly good at this," she prefaced, wrapping her hand around me and stroking. Under her tender touch, I flinched, and my dick pulsed within her grasp. Delicate fingers circled me, dragging over each ridge of silky skin, tugging firmly over my erection. Her tongue hesitated as it licked over my head, and I sprang forward with the contact. Moisture seeped out the tip, and she smoothed it over my tight shaft before diving forward and sucking me deep into her warm mouth. The sensation was clearly unique, as she tugged me to the back of her throat. One hand cupped my balls, squeezing tenderly while her hot mouth covered me.

My fingers briefly slipped into her hair. Not wanting to take control and do to her mouth what I longed to do to another part of her, I fell back on my elbows to watch the show. She was on her knees, but she rose higher, pulling me deeper. Her tongue worked harder as it wrapped around me, circling and sucking the veined ridge of me.

"Emme, you're gonna make me come, beautiful," One hand returned to her hair to still her. While I enjoyed each lick and suck of her mouth, I wanted to be deep inside her.

"Emme, come here." Tugging her upward, I smiled to see her lips moistened by her attention to me.

"I wasn't doing it well, was I?" Her face fell, and I had a sick feeling it was another thing her dead husband hadn't appreciated about her.

"Emme, it was incredible, but when I come, I want to be deep inside you." I stood to my full height, stepping out of my shorts, and taking her dress with me over her head. My eyes roamed her body, while my palm flattened and dragged down her body. Something was different. Her breasts sat higher. Her panties were lower. The material was lacy and thin.

"Are these new?" I fingered the fabric with an eager finger. "Did you buy this for me?"

"I bought them for me," she sassed, but as I reached behind her, and unclasped her bra, she admitted the rest. "To wear with you." I smiled into her shoulder before kissing it and slipped the new bra down her arms. Next were the panties. We stood naked and ready, and my hands skimmed over her cool skin. She shivered, but it wasn't the air conditioning.

I sat back on the bed, scooting backward toward the pillows. Emme followed over me like a cat on the chase of her prey, and I willed her to catch me. She straddled me and I reached under the pillow where I already had condoms waiting. Her eyebrow rose in question, but her lip twitched into a smile. While I fiddled with the wrapper, she covered me. Hot, wet folds spread over my heavy dick, and she dragged herself slowly up and down the firm length.

"Emme," I warned, as her body undulated, her hips rocked. My hand came to her hip, and she shook her head. She was finding the friction she needed, and her pace increased.

"Let me get the condom on, darlin'." She dragged back only enough to allow me a quick second to cover myself. Her wet heat slid over my balls, and I lost my train of thought, pausing mid-roll of latex as she circled the tender sack.

"Fuck, Emme," I groaned, softly. My attention to the condom complete, she pushed my hands out of the way to ride over me again. Her thighs clamped, and her heat swelled. I watched in wonder as Emme took control. Placing the tip of me at her entrance, she rose up on her knees only enough to balance on the precipice of my head

"Now, Emme." My hands gripped her hips, and she forced herself downward, impaling herself. Her hands rested on my chest as she took me deep and stilled. Her hips swiveled and then she rose again, dragging up to the tip, keeping me just inside, but not enough. My temptress, not nearly deep enough. Then she slammed down on me again and I bucked up, my pelvis colliding with her thighs.

She repeated this motion several times before remaining sheathed over me, rocking rapidly, forcing that nub of pleasure to rub in the right way against me.

"So close, baby," she whispered, clearly lost in pleasure, and my heart swelled at the endearment. "So close." Her breath caught. Her fingernails lightly brushing over my pecs, teasing my nipples and playing with the slight V of hair on my chest. I'd considered shaving it off as the gray hairs filtered in that area, but I noticed Emme rub her fingers through it the first time, marveling at the curls. She seemed to like it.

Suddenly, she tightened. Her muscles clamped over me. Her rapid rolls stalled to circling curls of her hips, and she sucked me deep inside of her. She stilled, her mouth slightly open. Her face flushed. Watching her come, and feeling the warmth surround me, pushed me over the edge. I'd been holding out all week for her, and the orgasm was so intense that I saw stars. I held her hips, forcing her down as I spilled forth, filling the condom, but wishing I filled her.

Emme fell forward, her hair tickling my neck, her mouth finding my shoulder.

"Thank you," she whispered, and I chuckled at the sensation of her words on my skin.

"For what?" I laughed.

"That was amazing." She smiled into my neck. Covering me, her breasts flattened against my chest and my fingers tickled up and down her back. Her breathing slowed as she melted against me.

"I like you, Emme."

"I like you, too," she muttered, giving me another smile against damp skin. "But I thought that wasn't allowed," she mumbled, pulling back, a tease to her tone. Understanding her meaning, I thought of the proposal.

"It isn't, I guess."

"Too bad," she said, quietly, shifting to release me, and lay to my side. I didn't like the empty feeling that followed the loss of her. One leg still draped over mine, but her body angled to the side of me. The moment was shifting for us.

"Why?" I questioned, attempting to look in her eyes, which followed her finger, tracing over my chest and teasing through that V of hair.

"Because everyone could use a friend."

"Yes, but if we were friends, we'd be friends with benefits, not fuck buddies," I joked. Emme's finger stilled. Her eyebrows pinched at my attempt for humor. Her expression shifted while she tried not to betray her hurt.

"I guess," she muttered, removing her hand from my chest and slipping her leg off mine. I reached out to stop her thigh, but her momentum kept her moving. She lay on her back, looking up at the ceiling and I balanced on my side. She refused to look at me. I had turned an incredible moment to dust. *Fuck.*

Chapter 22
Bike Rides

[M.E.]

To say I was surprised when Merek texted me the next day and asked if I wanted to take a bike ride was an understatement. I first thought it was a euphemism until he explained it was another bona fide offer. After his crass comment about friends with benefits being slightly better than fuck buddies, I wasn't certain how I felt. My body felt amazing, and I felt wanton, and wanted, the second Merek had me pinned to the wall. But my heart withered with this arrangement. He'd been so sweet to help me when I was sick, and tender as we had sex. Then he said what he said when we were finished. My stomach roiled at his words, and I left shortly after he'd ruined the moment. I refused the offer of wine and decided to go home with hardly any dignity remaining in my new bra and matching panties.

Want to take a ride? His text asked.

My answer wasn't immediate. I wasn't certain I could continue with whatever it was Merek and I were doing. We'd been together three times and I knew nothing about him. Children? Job? Ex-wife? Hidden body parts in a freezer in his garage? I mean, what did I know? He gave me incredible orgasms, yet he wouldn't kiss me.

But I took the time to struggle with a bike in the garage, pulling it out from the clutter surrounding it, and filling the tires with a handheld pump. I hadn't had that kind of workout in a while, and I was a sweating mess when I finished. I wrestled the bike into the back of the van, and then showered. I went casual, in shorts and a tank top, not certain what all a bike ride would entail. It was a beautiful summer day and Merek said to meet him at Irving Park by the lake. I was familiar with the large parking lot, as we had parked there for Cubs' games years ago. The thought brought back memories of fighting with Nate about directions, and then his refusal to spend money at the park on hotdogs or drinks for the girls. He was tight like that. It was one reason I always had popcorn at movies when I went with the girls as children. He had refused the purchase when we were on a date.

As I parked near the tennis courts, where Merek had suggested, I noticed a man in a biking outfit standing next to a black truck. Spandex shorts hugged his ass. A loose-fitting bike shirt hung over his midsection. Helmet, gloves and narrow shoes completed the outfit of a man ready to race the lakeside. I parked near him as he fiddled with something on his fancy bike. Exiting the van, I came around the back, and struggled to remove my own bike.

"Beautiful day for a bike ride," I huffed, as I hopped into the back and worked the twisted handlebar.

"Yes, beautiful." My rear end pointed outward, and I glanced over my shoulder at what sounded like a familiar voice. Standing at the end of the van was the man covered in biking gear, his face hidden by aviator sunglasses. His lip twitched in that telling grin and I realized it was Merek. Stunned, I stopped fumbling with the bike and turned awkwardly to face him. My tank top dangled forward and Merek seductively lowered his glasses to get a better view.

"What do you have on?" He asked breathily.

"What do you have on?" I barked with a laugh. Oh my God, we couldn't have been more opposite with him in his sporting gear and me in my ragged shorts and a ribbed tank top. I walked hunched over to exit the van and he reached up to help me out. His hands were covered by the elaborate riding gloves.

"Clearly, I've misunderstood what you meant when you said bike ride," I gasped, taking in his full apparel again.

"Clearly, I misunderstood," he said, looking into the back of the van at the Target special, mountain bike, that looked like it came from a dumpster compared to his thin racing bike.

I exhaled deeply and sighed in embarrassment. There was no way I could keep up with him if his idea of a bike ride was for exercise or speed. I just assumed he meant a stroll along the lakefront. It confirmed what I already knew—Merek and I thought differently. And I was not in his league.

"I guess…I guess…I misunderstood," I said again, rubbing at my forehead and trying to fill the awkward silence as Merek removed his riding glove. "I mean, you're dressed for a race," I laughed, nervously. "And I...am not."

"Where's your helmet, at least?"

"I don't have one." As if that decided things, I turned to close the van. "I think I'll just go. You go have fun. This was my mistake." My humiliation mingled with irritation. His sleek bike and riding outfit was another reminder Merek was very physically fit, and I was not. It also was a reminder of the young girl he cornered at the club. It made sense that he preferred younger, more active women. As I slammed shut the van door, Merek's hand came to my arm.

"Just wait." He paused.

My chest rose heavily with the exertion of climbing in and out of the van, then shutting the heavy back door.

"Give me a second. I'll change." His lips twisted. "No peeking." He opened the door of his truck and slipped inside. I remained next to his large vehicle, confused. Stepping out of his truck, he now wore sport shorts. His feet were covered in regular gym shoes. He wasn't wearing a shirt.

"We'll just rent the blue bikes," he offered. "We can ride where we want and park them when we're done." He dragged a t-shirt over his head, covering those tattoos and firm abs. I stared at him in wonder.

"Emme, you with me?" He smirked. He reached out his hand and I took it, letting the warmth wrap around me and drag me over to the blue bike display. He paid for two bikes and then told me we were headed south toward the city.

The Chicago lakefront bike trail is an active place. The majestic lake with a backdrop of the city is a juxtaposition of nature and industry. It's gorgeous. The trail was difficult to ride side by side and Merek let me lead, setting the pace as we passed runners, walkers, and intense bike riders. We followed the curve around North Avenue Beach and continued on until we reached Navy Pier. The ride was peaceful despite the bustle of traffic to the right and pedestrians to the left. The time allowed for thought instead of conversation and after the awkwardness of our first meeting this morning, I relished the silence.

Merek and I were different in so many ways. I often wondered what I possibly did for him, as I knew what he did for me. He taught me to use my body to seek pleasure, and I was more than satiated after my yearlong dry spell. Could I go back to being alone? Probably not. Did I feel more confident to seek out others? Possibly a little. Could I move on from Merek? My first thought was absolutely not, but when I questioned again what I did for him, the answer had to shift to a maybe.

I'd already had twenty years of ups and downs, with mediocre sex, and Merek had taught me there was more to the experience. What I also realized was that I wanted more than just the experience of sex. I wanted a relationship. I wanted the emotion behind sex. I didn't have to have marriage, but someone committed to me, who wanted only me, didn't seem like too much to ask. Thoughts like these forced my mind to the horrible parts of my marriage. The parts I swore I'd never take but did. I shook my head to rid the thoughts, pulling myself back to the beautiful day. Merek rode up next to me and reached out for my handlebars.

"Hey," I laughed as we almost collided. "You're going to wreck us." His hand remained on my handlebar, but he balanced in a way that we were parallel to one another.

"I don't want to ever do that," he said, and my head swung to look at him. The tone of his voice hinted at something more.

"Let's stop up here." He nodded at Navy Pier. "We can take a cab back to Lincoln Park." I nodded, sad to see the ride end, but we had gone a great distance, and I didn't know if I could cycle back the miles we had covered. We parked the blue bikes in another rack and crossed the street to hail a cab. When Merek ignored the busy pier, I decided he was done for the day, and this was his polite way of ending our trip. He'd compromised to ride the city bike instead of his racer, and he had missed out on a workout.

Entering the cab, Merek told the driver to take us to 2056 Lincoln Park West. I assumed this was an address near Irving Park, although I couldn't be certain. It seemed easier to specify the park.

"Hungry?" He turned to me, and my eyebrows pinched in confusion.

"I'm starving." A smile passed over his face and his hand covered my thigh. Dragging his thumb slowly over damp, warm skin, a pulse beat at my core. We pulled up to a restaurant I hadn't been to in years. R.J. Grunts was a burger joint across from Lincoln Park Zoo. The place was packed, and I waited outside while Merek went in to give his name. Returning outside, he walked into my space, hovering before me as he brushed back loose hairs from my sloppy ponytail.

"Where'd you go when we were riding?"

"What do you mean?"

He tapped my forehead. "In here. Where did you go?"

"Nowhere," I lied. Hoping to change the subject, I said, "I thought we rode too far, and you were done with me." I tried to tease.

It was his turn to be surprised. His hands brushed up and down my sticky arms.

"I'm not sure I can be done with you, Emme." His tone was serious a moment as he brushed at a wayward hair by my ear. "But I was tired of being behind you. I mean, I liked looking at your ass, but I wanted to talk to you, and it was hard to be side by side on the trail."

I stared at this man, who was a constant conundrum to me.

"What did you want to talk about?"

"The Lake, the people, anything. I just…" His voice trailed off as the buzzer for our table vibrated in his pocket. He pointed for me to lead the way and I inhaled the glorious scent of cheeseburger heaven, the conversation forgotten for the moment. I didn't need a menu to know exactly what I was ordering, but I picked it up all the same.

"You aren't going to be one of those women who order only salad, then eat half of it, are you?" He laughed looking at me over the menu.

"Do I look like I eat only salad?" I joked. His menu dropped to the table.

"I hate when you talk like that." His voice serious again.

"I…"

"I think you're beautiful, and I like your body. A lot. So, I wish you'd stop."

"I…I'm sorry." I didn't even know if an apology was the right response. I wasn't used to compliments at all. Nate was similar to Merek in that he worked out constantly. But his comments about my body were quite the opposite. His remarks at the potential for improvement only left me self-conscious. Instead of motivating me to work out like him, it often discouraged the desire to change my body. I'd never been perfectly slim, and having children changed my shape entirely.

The Sex Education of M.E.

Merek stared at me across the table and my nervousness made me reach for the glass of water before me. His hand shot out to cover mine and water spilled over the rim a little.

"Hey, don't do that." His voice was firm, his grip hard as I balanced the glass between us. His eyes narrowed. "Why do I feel that this has to do with someone other than me?"

"I guess because it does." Merek released my hand and I set the water down, no longer interested in my thirst. He glanced out the window at his side before he responded, "No disrespect to the dead, but he seems like a douche bag."

I was silent. Could I disrespect the dead? Could I share secrets of Nate that I swore I'd take to my grave? It didn't seem appropriate to tell Merek, and yet, Merek seemed like exactly the right person to hear my story.

"Nate wasn't perfect. He was a good man in many ways, but he certainly wasn't a saint. I can't say when things changed, when we went from this spontaneous combustion to a fizzled flame, but it happened. Maybe it wasn't how I remembered, and it was always just a slow burn with no spark. Maybe it was having kids. Maybe it was me. It was certainly him." I paused to take a sip of water after all.

"At some point, he didn't want to be a father anymore. He didn't want to be a husband. He had an affair." I swallowed hard. "Most women swear they'd leave a man who did that. They wouldn't take that shit, but I had two small kids and I wasn't working. I didn't know what to do." Merek's eyes focused on the table.

"I took his apology and his promises, and I let him come home. Then I went to work, and we were happy." I swallowed deep. "No, not happy. That's not the word. Content. We coasted. He wasn't a gentleman any longer, and I told myself I was okay with it. When he died, I was lost, but not for reasons people would think." Merek looked up at me, and it was my turn to look away. I sounded pathetic to myself. I was an educated woman and yet I hadn't made an intelligent decision. I made an emotional one. If he wasn't interested in my tale, he'd hear it anyway. I didn't have the strength to stop.

"I was lost because I felt like I'd given up so much time. I'd lost me along the way. I regained it a little when I went to work. The girls were too young to know the difference of who I was and who I am. Pieces of me were missing for so long. When he died, I felt empty, but not for him. For me."

I decided I needed to be finished. I'd just shared too much information, and Merek clearly wasn't interested. I turned to look out the window and noticed a group of college girls sitting on the fence rail, waiting to enter RJ Grunts. My thoughts sank, just like my heart. I'd spilled so much of my history, and assumed Merek wasn't listening, just like Nate.

"I'm sorry. That was kind of heavy. Forget I said all that," I said, with a dismissive wave.

"I'm glad you told me. It explains a lot." He shifted back in his seat as the waitress approached, and we ordered burgers, as if I hadn't said a thing. The direction of our conversation shifted to more casual conversation, like my work and the girls. Nerves made me talk too much. Merek wasn't interrupting me, but he wasn't offering anything about himself, either. While it seemed the natural course of conversation would allow for Merek to speak next, he didn't. In fact, he was very vague about his work, saying he worked for the city, which could be any number of jobs. He never talked of old loves or even current flings, and it left me wondering again about his kissing denial. He didn't mention children.

When we finished our lunch, he reached for my hand, and we walked toward Lincoln Park Zoo. Stopping inside the gates, he sheepishly asked if I'd like to walk around the zoo, not just through it.

"Like a date?" I blurted out, startling myself.

"I…"

"Oh my gosh, forget I said that," I laughed. Of course, it wasn't a date. It was a bike ride that turned into lunch, and now a walk through the zoo. It wasn't a date. We weren't even friends. We were fuck buddies, but I was suddenly confused. My eyebrows pinched in question, and then I shook my head.

"I'd love to walk around the zoo," I said, attempting to brush off my awkward reaction. "I haven't been here in years."

"Yeah?"

"Yeah." I smiled and Merek placed his hand on the small of my back, leading me through the landmark city zoo. We watched the lion yawn, the tigers pace, and the gorillas scratch one another. We circled the llamas and the zebras, doubling back to see the seals and find the polar bear. It wasn't a terribly large zoo, but I remembered days of visiting with the girls, nights of summer concerts, and even a Zoolights visit one Christmas. That was all a distant memory.

Merek was attentive as we walked, alternating between holding my hand or rubbing my back. In fact, he was in constant contact with my body, and I enjoyed each touch. Subtle and tender, it was a slow burn to greater possibilities with him, and I treasured the day. I also prayed I'd get another night with him.

The girls wouldn't be home until four, but Merek said he had a thing that evening. It was almost three, and it didn't appear there was time to head to his place. In broad daylight, we couldn't use the van, and I was too shy to suggest such a thing, regardless of my growing sexual bravado. Last night I'd certainly taken what I wanted, and Merek let me. The thought warmed me. I suddenly wanted him. Like immediately.

Chapter 23
Afternoon Delight

[M.E. 2]

"Do you need to be home when the girls get home?" I asked, brushing back a stray hair, like I'd done all day. A soft gasp would escape her, similar to when we were joined together, letting me know she liked the tender touches. I liked how she leaned into each caress, like she didn't want it to end, or didn't want me to let her go.

"I could text Mitzi and say I'd be home a little later, but I thought you had something to do?"

I had work, but I was willing to be late. The need for her had been growing all day and when she told me about her husband, whose ass I wanted to kick despite his death, I wasn't ready to let her go. When she discussed feeling lost, like pieces of her were missing, it sparked a flame long extinguished inside me. My heart flickered. I understood what she meant.

"I do have something, but I could be a little late, too." I stroked down her neck as we stood in the late afternoon sunlight. "Emme, can I ask you to come to the apartment?"

Her breath hitched in that way she had, and it was the ignition to my dick, which had been standing at attention on and off all day. Watching her ass while she pedaled her bike, then hearing her sad story, and finally, touching her throughout the walk in the zoo, sent me into all kinds of overdrive. I wasn't going to be able to wait a few nights to be inside her again. I wanted her. Now.

She nodded slowly, letting my hand continue to caress the nape of her neck, and my thumb rub up her throat.

"I'd love for us to ride together," I said. "But it's best that you follow me, okay?"

She nodded again, breathless, and I felt her swallow under my fingers. My mouth wanted to take hers, but it didn't seem right. I'd held off for so long. I wasn't giving in, even though I wanted her. She'd been hurt, and I didn't want to lead her in a direction I couldn't go. We couldn't be any more than we were, and yet, we were becoming friends. It frightened me. It would make things all the harder if we got too close, and I decided right then and there that I'd take one more afternoon. Then I'd end things. Her confession about her husband was a cry for something more, and I didn't have it in me to give.

She followed my directions and pulled up behind the garage in the alley instead of trying to find a space on the street out front. We walked through the backyard and up the back-porch stairs to the second floor. Entering the apartment, I was ready to take her against the wall like I had wanted the other night, but I stalled when I noticed the suitcase just inside the door.

"Marshall," I called out, dropping Emme's hand.

"Dude, clean up after your—" Marshall stopped in his tracks as he entered the kitchen where Emme and I stood just inside the backdoor. Marshall held Emme's light blue panties in his hand.

"I thought you'd be gone," I said, pissed that he was still home, and I'd been caught bringing Emme here. I snatched her undies from his twirling finger.

"I'm leaving now, but *hellllooo...*" Marshall's eyes rolled up and down the length of Emme. This pissed me off more and I stepped in front of her.

"Is this—" Marshall paused, raising his eyebrow in recognition.

"Mary Elizabeth Peters." I introduced her. Marshall leaned forward, reaching out his hand while Emme stepped around me.

"Emme," she offered as they shook. Of course, Marshall lingered a bit too long.

"Okay, Casanova, let her go."

"How can you?" he responded, insinuating what I'd already planned to do. I couldn't be committed to someone. I'd already tried before. Marshall's appreciative smile continued to fuel my growing anger. He was such a flirt, and with obvious intention. He would steal Emme from me, if he thought he could. As I watched her blush sweetly, I realized she would fall for someone like Marshall, suave, ridiculously rich, and unable to commit to a woman. Hello, pot calling the kettle black.

"Here for a little afternoon delight?" Marshall asked, crudely, lifting his eyebrows up and down suggestively.

"Don't you have a cab waiting for you?"

Marshall glanced at his expensive watch and clapped his hands once before reaching for his suitcase.

"Too bad, I do. I'd love a three-way."

That was all it took. I stepped forward ready to clock my brother, like I had so many times when we were punk kids.

"Fuck off, Marshall."

"That's enough," Emme said, reaching for my elbow, attempting to drag me back. Marshall smirked.

"That's what I thought," he said, smug, his brow rising in a knowing fashion. I don't know what he thought he knew, but I wanted him to leave. His demeanor changed, and he straightened up with his suitcase in hand. "I apologize, Emme. It was a pleasure to meet you." He nodded in my direction, but I didn't miss the twist of his lip, like he knew a secret.

"Oh, and Merek, I'll take front row bleacher seats. September will be the perfect month. Go Cubbies." He winked at me, and again, the temptation to deck him rippled through me.

After I heard the soft click of the front door, I turned to Emme, whose eyes were wide.

"You're going to a Cubs game?" Her eyes alight with surprise. Ignoring her question and my brother's implication of our bet, I changed the subject.

"I'm sorry about that. He just killed it, didn't he?"

"Killed what?" she said, smiling softly, and I reached for her. My hands cupped her cheek, and my mouth came close to hers.

"Kiss me," she demanded sweetly.

"Make love to me," I countered. Her soft gasp was all the answer I needed before I dragged her to the bedroom. Our clothes were removed in haste, but once I laid her down, I took my time to draw over her skin, which smelled of sunshine and sweat. She was salty from our bike ride and walk in the heat of the zoo, but I savored each lick of her. From neck to clit, I sucked her clean, then entered her slowly. I worshipped her like I thought she deserved, dragging out the lazy pleasure of sex. It wasn't fast or frantic, and her sweet sighs encouraged me to linger. I pulled to the entrance of her, then pressed forward, one ridge at a time. Her wet channel welcomed me, as her thighs spread wide, and her ankles wrapped around my lower back. Her hands stretched above her head like a sluggish cat, and she gripped the headboard, holding tight. She let me glide in and out of her. Preventing herself from touching me intensified the longing, and she opened enough that I filled her to the hilt. Taking it slow, she held me tight, and her inner muscles clenched around me, drawing me deeper.

"Emme," I strained. She felt so amazing wrapped around me, delaying the release. "Emme, I can't last." I warned. She removed one hand from the headboard and dragged it down her body. My eyes watched the path she drew. She paused at the mound of dark hair, her fingers hesitantly twirling through it.

"Touch yourself," I whispered, willing her to take the risk. I sucked in a breath as her fingers glossed over herself while I entered her.

"That's…so hot," I gasped, watching her touch herself while I slipped inside her. I was so fucking hard, I needed to burst, but I wasn't going to until she went, especially when she was doing what I asked her to do.

"Merek," her voice hitched. "Merek," she cried out again. "Merek!" she screamed, and I slammed into her, feeling my release the instant she squeezed around me. Despite the daylight, I saw stars and collapsed on top of her, trapping her arm between us.

"Emme, I…" I didn't know what to say. Marshall's words haunted me. *How could I let her go?*

"I know," she said. "You need to go, don't you?" I did, but it wasn't what she thought. I suddenly wanted to tell her everything like she'd been open with me this afternoon, but there wasn't time. I pulled out of her and saw her shut down before me. It was a reminder that I needed to walk away, when I didn't know how.

Chapter 24
Loose Hose

[M.E.]

It had been over a week since my day with Merek. I couldn't call it a date. *It can't be considered a date when he doesn't call, right?* I didn't have the heart to tell Gia that I'd failed. I'd failed at upkeeping the relationship of not having a relationship. I told him too much, and I scared him away. It was that simple. I hadn't dated in twenty plus years, and I still recognized when too much was shared.

"Gia, he isn't going to call," I told her on the phone. "It's fine." I lied. *Fine*, a word he didn't allow to describe how things were between us. It hadn't ever been fine, it had been amazing, eye-opening, enlightening. I'd never experienced anything like it, especially the last time we were together. The way he took his time. The way he dragged it out. It was lazy and raw, and on some deeper level, I thought we connected. It wasn't how much he filled me, as much as I thought he *felt* me. He felt my insides: the beat of my heart, the warmth of me holding him, the oxygen I breathed. But that was me, reading too many books about romance, which didn't exist in real life.

"I said too many things," I added.

Her breath caught. "Oh my God, did you tell him you loved him?" I could picture her covering her mouth in horror.

"What? No," I gasped. "No, of course not."

"Okay," her voice lowered then hitched again. "You told him he had a small penis." The horror again.

"No," I laughed despite not feeling jovial. "No, nothing like that, either."

"He has a huge one, doesn't he?" she teased.

"Gia…" I warned, not wishing to share my intelligence about the size of his private parts.

"Okay, okay. Don't worry. He's going to call. Maybe … maybe he just has something going on," she stuttered, recognizing the truth. She'd been with enough men to know the signs. A week without contact was too long.

"Did you try to text him?" she suggested, but I didn't have the courage, and she knew that. While I'd been the first to make contact, in jest, I hadn't been the one to initiate any other dates. Arrangements. Oh, whatever, they were called.

"I can't, Gia. I just can't do this to myself." I sighed into the phone.

"Em, I'm really sorry. I thought ... I thought it would be different, honey."

What did she think would be different? I was about to ask when something caught my attention. I balanced the phone as I walked to the basement. It wasn't a glamorous part of my home. A finished room had been made for the girls to collect their millions of toys but our laundry room off to the side was still cement block walls and a cold cement floor minus the rug area in front of the washer and dryer. Entering my laundry room, I took a whiff of air.

Sniff, sniff. What the heck?

"Emme, don't cry," Gia sighed.

"I'm not crying." *Sniff, sniff.* "Something doesn't smell right in my laundry room."

"Try doing it," Gia laughed.

"Ha, ha. Very funny. Seriously, it smells ... like natural gas or something in here. Really gassy." Examining the tube behind the dryer, I noticed the dryer had shifted forward compared to the washing machine. The girls must have been doing laundry again, overfilling the machine.

"Gia, I gotta go. I can't get a look at this while I'm holding the phone."

"Em, don't play around. Maybe you should call 911. It could be a gas leak."

"I don't know. I don't see anything, but the smell is strong. Really strong."

"Is your carbon monoxide detector going off?"

"What carbon monoxide detector?" I laughed, knowing the smoke/carbon monoxide detector laid on the ledge heading down to the basement. It was there because the last time I cooked it went off and I had to take it down to stop it from beeping.

"That's not funny. I'm calling the fire department for you."

"No, Gia, I'm fi—" The line went dead. I stepped away from the dryer and headed back upstairs. The smell lingered, and I opened the front door for air. I heard the sirens long before I saw any trucks and I shook my head in embarrassment. I'm certain it was just a loose hose, or the dryer vent had disconnected. I needed to call a gas repairman, not the fire department.

When the truck pulled up in front of my house, a second truck, more like an SUV, pulled up behind it. I was mortified at the amount of men who came toward me, one of which was suited up despite the heat.

"What seems to be the trouble?" the first fireman asked.

"I guess a gas leak or something. It's coming from the basement," I said, pointing in the direction of the front door. When I turned around, Merek stood before me. Dressed in uniform blue, his status showed on his shirt.

"Commander, gas leak," the fireman told Merek, who hadn't moved.

"I'll show you where," I suggested, stepping forward, but Merek's hand wrapped around my arm.

"No, you won't. Murtaugh, head in." His voice commanded.

The man in gear and another fireman entered the front door, making their way to the basement on their own. Merek and I were left to stare at one another on my front lawn.

"You work for the fire department?" The tattoo hidden under his sleeve should have tipped me off. It didn't only represent the death of his father, it was a symbol of him. Merek didn't respond.

"Why was that such a secret?" I questioned.

Merek still didn't answer. "Are you all right?"

"Am I ... no, honestly, I'm not."

Merek's eyes finally met mine full on. That familiar darkness was missing their flecks of gold, despite the sunshine.

"What's wrong?" he asked, stepping forward, but I stepped back.

"You haven't called," I muttered, and he stopped.

"I know...I..."

I raised my hand to stop him. "I'm not stupid, Merek. I might have been foolish, but I'm not dumb. I get the hint."

"Emme...it was..."

"Fun while it lasted?" I suggested, spitefully. *Did men still use that line?*

"It was a loose hose," the man in full gear blurted, exiting my front door. "We tightened it up, but you might want to open a window down there. The gas was pretty strong. No working smoke detector or carbon monoxide detector. Want me to write her up, Commander?"

Merek's eyes widened.

"I'm not a good cook," I said to the man in gear. "I took it down."

Merek's eyes opened wider.

"That's a city violation, ma'am. Commander, ticket her?" he suggested.

"No," Merek smirked. "Don't ticket her." Looking at me, he said, "You could have died, if that was unattended."

Like you'd care was on the tip of my tongue, but I bit back the words. Bit them back hard.

"Is it safe to go inside now?" I addressed the second fireman, ignoring Merek.

"All clear," he offered.

"Fine. Thank you, gentlemen. Sorry for the inconvenience."

"No, inconvenience, ma'am, just doing our job," gear-boy said.

"Just doing a job," I repeated spitefully, glancing at Merek. His eyes shifted away from mine, and I had all the answers I needed.

Later that night, the girls told me they were headed to Jake's to swim. The day was extraordinarily warm. I didn't know who this Jake kid was, other than a new teenager in the neighborhood. The girls left while it was still daylight, and I headed to my porch for some fresh air and a good book. The heat of the day lingered as I sat on the glider, rocking to and fro. My eyes were trained on my Kindle, but they weren't focused on any words.

Why hadn't Merek told me he was a fireman? Why did he keep secrets from me? Innocent secrets, like who he worked for, or what he did. My assumption had been he was a businessman. The first time I'd seen him in the grocery store, he had on a suit. Any other time, he'd been casually dressed as it had been evening, and I again assumed, it was after work hours for him. Of course, he worked at The Square as security and that certainly clashed with being a businessman. Had I been so blinded by lust I hadn't asked enough questions? But I wasn't about to let myself take the blame. I had been a willing participant, and Merek didn't need to hide these facts from me.

As I rocked on the glider, the doorbell rang. I didn't feel like answering the door, too busy nursing my wine and my broken heart, but the front door was still open for air, and I couldn't pretend I wasn't home.

"Commander Elliott," I snapped.

"Emme," he nodded. "I wanted to check the hose."

"I didn't realize firemen made house calls."

"Emme," he said, reaching for the handle of the screen door. "Let me in." He paused, waiting for my consent. I pushed open the screen door then turned for the basement stairs. Hearing his heavy footsteps were my only sign that he had followed me down into the cooler region of my home. I entered the laundry room and stood before the washer. I kept my back to him.

"The loose hose was here, but your men fixed it," I pointed to the dryer vent and the gas valve positioned upward behind the machines without looking at Merek. Immediately, I was pressed forward against the washer. Thick hands roughly caressed up my back before sliding down my arms and pinning my hands to the top of the machine. His chest brushed my back.

"Emme, I'm sorry." His words were tempting, his voice low and gravelly.

"For not telling me the truth, or not calling me?" His answer didn't matter as I had lost all train of thought. The firm length of him met my backside. God forgive me, I curled back against him. He hissed, "Both."

"Why the big secret, Merek?"

"I just don't share my personal life with…"

"With what, Merek? With your friends with benefits? Oh wait, we weren't that, we were…"

"Don't say it," he growled behind me, letting his hands glide up my side, drawing dangerously close to my breasts. "It wasn't like that with you."

My hips lurched back as his hands came just below my breasts, and his nose nuzzled the back of my neck.

"What was it like, then, Merek?" I groaned as he pressed forward. Cursing the moisture pooling between my thighs, I arched back against him, my body taking control as I was clearly losing it.

"It was like this, Emme. Hot." His hands slid to my hips, and he tugged me toward him, the force of his erection thrusting toward me. My hands gripped the washer as I arched my back, forcing my rear against him.

"God, I've missed you," he sighed, letting his hand rove to my lower abdomen. Could I do this? Could I let things get out of control? Could I *fuck* him, like he wanted things to be between us?

"Are you wet for me, dirty girl?" he muttered as kisses washed over my neck. The irony of where we stood wasn't lost on me.

"Stop it," I hissed, allowing the kisses to continue.

"Really?" He paused.

"No," I whispered.

In answer to those thoughts about fucking him; surprising myself, the answer was yes.

His hand delved into my shorts, and I let out a long moan as his fingers parted me.

"Shit, you are wet," he growled. I didn't respond, as my hips rolled forward, and his hand cupped me in a way that his fingers entered easily. My knees hit the washer as I rocked into the invasion of his fingers. His other hand released my hip, and I heard the heavy unbuckling of his belt and the sharp unzipping of his uniform pants. Whoever says "lusting over a man in a uniform" doesn't know the half of it, until that man is behind you, ready to enter you in the most primal way.

"Get down on your knees, Emme," he barked, quietly, and I followed his command. His fingers never left me, except to remove my shorts to my ankles. He followed me down onto the laundry room rug.

L.B. Dunbar

On my knees, ass in the air, my elbows braced me. Anticipation built as he worked that pleasure spot then dragged his length to meet his fingers. Withdrawing only briefly, he entered me with one heavy thrust, pushing me forward.

"Emme," he cried out as I pressed back with equal force, eagerly drawing him in. His fingers still played the instrument of my desire while he entered me repeatedly with an increasing tempo. The feeling was unlike the first time in my van. This was animalistic, raw, and rapid. The tension built quickly, and I clenched hard, holding fast with each thrust as his fingers played me. With hasty vigor, I burst over Merek and he stilled behind me. Pulsing deep inside me, while I came around him, I was filled with the strangest sensation. I groaned while I arched back, holding him deep within me.

We remained like this, on hands and knees. Ragged breaths slowed. His head fell to my back, the length of him still buried inside me.

"Emme, I…that was…" He couldn't finish his thoughts. A trickle of moisture slid down my leg and reality hit me.

"You didn't have on a condom," I squeaked, twisting out from under him and standing awkwardly while moisture dribbled down my thigh. Reaching for a towel in the laundry basket on the floor, Merek quickly swiped up my leg.

"You caught me off guard. I didn't expect this to happen," he said, still on his knees, then slowing rising. He tugged his pants up, but his eyes shifted to my face. He must have read the horror on it because he stopped tucking himself back in and reached for my cheeks. Without another breath, his mouth crushed mine. Warm lips sucked hard, nipping the lower lip between the eager ones of his. Not releasing me, he pressed forward forcing me against the washing machine. His mouth covered mine, molding, melting into my lips before his tongue snaked out and stole across the seam of our joining. I opened with a sigh of blissful relief, and his tongue eagerly met mine. Tangling for control, my body was pulled against him, as our mouths discovered each other. My hands, ready to push him away, wrapped around his neck, desperate to hold him closer. His arms crossed behind my back, holding me against him. Connecting in a more intimate way than the primitive joining on our knees, I lingered in the heavenly experience of kissing Merek Elliott.

The Sex Education of M.E.

"Mom?" The cry was faint but growing. "Mom, are you down there?"

Merek pulled back quickly, hastily righting his pants and tucking in his shirt. My shorts had already been pulled up, and I tugged at my shirt to straighten it. Merek looked up at me with a devious smile while I called out, "I'll be right up." His mouth returned to mine too briefly before we heard a footstep on the top step.

"Lead the way," he whispered, and I walked around him to exit the laundry room.

Chapter 25
Coming Clean…and Not Just in The Laundry Room

[M.E. 2]

"Mr. Whittington?" The young girl's voice nearly slapped me in the face as we climbed the staircase. "Mom, what is Mr. Whittington doing here?"

Emme stopped cold, one foot landing on the stair above her other. She slowly turned toward me, then returned her attention to her daughter. The resemblance to this girl was nonexistent. Dark hair and dark eyes could only be the trademark of her father.

"This is Fire Commander Elliott. He came to check a loose hose," she choked on the last words.

"Mom," the girl eyed me. "That's Mr. Whittington, Jake's dad."

I remained frozen on the stairs, slow to recognize that she might have been one of many girls in the neighborhood to visit our new home.

"Mr. Whittington," Emme whispered. Regaining her composure, she took another step upward.

"Mitzi, let us through," she snapped at her daughter. As Emme entered the kitchen at the top of the stairs, another girl, who was clearly her daughter, met my gaze. Blonde hair and bright blue eyes matched her mother's perfectly.

Emme didn't stop, however. She continued to march toward her front door and stormed out it onto her front stoop. I followed behind, bracing for what was to come.

"You have forty-two seconds."

"Why forty-two?" I laughed, attempting to ease the tension. Her arms crossed. There was no humor in her expression.

"My name is Merek Elliott *Whittington*, fire commander of Station 119. I go by the name Merek Elliott, like it's all one name, but Elliott is my middle name. It was my mother's maiden name."

She waited for me to continue, not needing to spell out the questions I knew she would ask.

"I have a son, Jake. He's seventeen, and we just moved to the neighborhood."

"Wait, you live here?" she blurted, unfolding her arms, leaning forward astonished.

"I bought the old MacAllister home. The one with a pool." Even though I was the new owner, the home was deemed the MacAllister house, named for the previous owners of over forty years. Its trademark was the in-ground pool.

"So, you don't live in that apartment," she gasped when realization hit her. "What is it? Some place to…to…fuck people?" she hiss-whispered.

"It's my brother's apartment. Marshall. He travels a lot, and for obvious reasons, I took you there."

"Obvious reasons?" she choked.

"Yeah, you have kids at your house. I have kids at mine. It's neutral."

"How…how many…" her voice nearly sobbed. The implication was clear.

"I've never, ever taken anyone there beside you, Emme. You have to believe me."

"How can I believe you?" Her eyes filled with liquid as she questioned mine. "I know nothing about you." She paused. "You lied to me." Her tone was bitter.

"We were pretending," I stated, straightening in my defense.

"I wasn't pretending," she gasped, running a hand through her messy hair. "I never lied about me. You…you did." Her voice grew shaky.

"I didn't lie to you. Absolutely did not lie."

"You didn't tell all the truth," she stated, completely flabbergasted with me as her hand lowered and slapped at her thigh.

"I…" I didn't know what more to say. "Don't lump me with him," I snapped.

"How dare you!"

"You did dare me, Emme. Sex, remember? That's what you wanted. But I'm telling you everything right now. I work for the Chicago Fire

Department. I live three blocks away. I'm a single father to Jake and Cassie."

"Who's Cassie?" She blinked. A sliver of liquid rolled from her eye.

"My daughter. The girl at the bar. She just turned twenty-one and I didn't want her there. The Square is filled with old horny men and desperate women, and Cassie's too young to be there." Something struck in her expression, and she stood taller, pulling back against my hands that gripped her arms for attention.

"Desperate. Women," she choked.

"Not you, Emme," I assured, but it wasn't reassuring. She broke my hold by stepping back.

"I'm such a fool," she muttered under her breath, shaking her head vigorously back and forth.

"Emme, I . . ."

"Just stop," she barked. "Just stop right there." A hand came up to still me, putting space between us. "I'm…I've just…oh my God, what did I just do with you . . ." Her voice caught as she covered her mouth holding in the sob, threatening to escape. Her body shook, and in desperation, I reached for her, prepared to envelop her in my arms, and apologize for holding it all back from her. But she broke free of me, before I even had a grasp of her. Darting up her front steps, she yanked open the screen door, and from the angle where I stood, I saw her run up to her second floor. Her blonde teenage daughter stood inside the doorway, staring me down with eyes that matched her mother's. Then she slowly closed the door on me.

Chapter 26
Fine

[M.E.]

"Did you know?" I yelled into the phone.

"I might have had an inkling..." Gia answered, sheepishly, guiltily.

"He's your damn neighbor, Gia. He lives next door. Did you...did you set this up?" The pause was telling.

"I might have worked your phone, then hinted that you'd be interested, then told him some ways to win your heart."

"Win my heart," I choked. "He used my body."

"You wanted to use his," she reminded me, bluntly. "He was a willing participant."

"Because he's done this often," I retorted. "Oh my God, Gia, did you have sex with him, too?"

"Because we're friends, and you're in shock right now, I'm going to ignore the insinuation," Gia stated, fighting her own anger at my tone. "He did not come onto me, and I did not come onto him. He lives next door and I saw the perfect opportunity to help you."

"Help me?" I sobbed. "He's wrecked me."

"How?" she stated, firmly.

"He lied to me. Did you know he had children?

"You didn't?" Her stunned tone told she thought I knew.

"He never talked about them. Not his job. Not his ex-wife. Please tell me he's not still married," I nearly shrieked and my skin crawled.

"He's not married, and as far as I know I don't think he ever has been."

"He lied." My voice faded, and my hand gripped back my hair, ready to pull it off my own head.

"Did he? Or did he not tell you the whole truth?"

"What in the hell is the difference?" I huffed.

"The difference is, maybe he wanted to pretend, too. He's a single father of teenage children, and maybe he wanted a little identity freedom, just like you."

"But I told him what I did, where I lived…I…wait, he knew where I lived because of you," I clarified.

"Yes, when he mentioned that you had a headache, I explained that you suffered migraines."

"Gia, that's personal."

"Did he come to take care of you?"

"Obviously only because you told him to," I snorted, feeling more the fool with each new discovery. "So, the bike ride, the lunch, the zoo…" I drifted off afraid to mention all the different ways he'd touched my body.

"I know nothing of those things."

"Gia!" I groaned.

"I'm serious. If you had a real date, he did that all on his own."

"Sounds like everything else he did was at your direction," I snipped.

"He did no such thing. He was interested. You were interested. I was simply a guiding light."

"You knew he was a fireman, didn't you? You called him specifically today."

"I won't deny it," she chuckled. While Gia seemed to be enjoying her matchmaking skills, she failed to see that she'd failed. Dismally.

"I don't plan to ever see him again," I stated defiantly.

"That would be impossible, as he lives next door to me."

"Well, I don't plan to ever visit you either," I assured her.

"Emme, honey, that's not true."

I remained silent to emphasize my point.

"Look, I adore you," she started. "And you wanted this. You needed it. You deserved it," she emphasized. "And I just wanted to see it happen for you. Nate Peters was a perfectly respectable guy, and he wasn't for you. You need to be wild and carefree, and Merek was your chance."

"Well, that chance is over," I snorted.

"Don't say that. Cool down, give it time. He liked you. He did, and he wasn't fooling around with other women."

"How do you know that? He took me to his brother's apartment. He could have had days of the week scheduled out."

"Emme, stop it. He didn't do that, and you know it. He called you each night he was free, and the other nights he was at the firehouse."

"How can you be so sure?" But I knew the answer. Merek didn't make a move without Gia knowing, Gia orchestrating everything.

"He didn't even like me, did he?" I whispered. "He did it all because you asked him to, but why?"

"Of course, he liked you, honey. What's not to like? He did it because he feels like you. He just wanted to have sex."

"But he had it all the time."

"People change," she responded, her voice exasperated. "Maybe he wanted something new?"

"Oh, right. Forty-two-year-old hot guy seeking widowed, round lady. Very plausible."

"Emme, stop it. He found you attractive. He wouldn't have slept with you, if he didn't."

"Do not tell me you know his sexual history?" My head banged back against the wall. Rolling it back and forth, I couldn't believe the details she knew.

"I don't. But let's be realistic, he wouldn't have slept with you, if he didn't find you attractive."

"He might."

"A man that looks like him isn't desperate, honey. He did it because he wanted to."

What did that say about a woman like me? Was I so desperate? Then again, he was an attractive man, so at least I was lucky in that aspect. His body and his features were overly pleasing.

"Emme, don't overthink this. You're forty-two years old. You're still young, beautiful, and vibrant. You have life in you. Live it. Take charge. Take what you want. You wanted to have fun. Wasn't it fun? He was good, right? You needed this. He was the ice-breaker. The transition man. Now, you're ready."

Ready? I wanted to scream. I couldn't go through any of this ever again. The reality was I'd never have sex again because I'd never be able to keep my emotions separate from the action. As much as I wanted that sexual freedom to be with Merek, or any man, it wasn't going to happen for me. I wasn't built to be a fuck buddy. I wasn't made to be friends with benefits. I was me, and I needed more of an emotional attachment. I wanted a relationship. The sob escaped me as reality took over.

"Gia, I need to go," I said through a covered mouth. I clicked off the phone before I could hear her response.

"Mom." A tentative knock jiggled the door.

"I'll be out in a few minutes." Trying to sound cheerful, I gave up quickly. Sometimes a mom just needs a moment in the bathroom to cry. Curling into myself, I sobbed, the second Mitzi cleared the door. Deep, wracking tears of stupidity and heartbreak were muffled as best I could with double coverage of hands over my mouth. *I just needed a few seconds*, I told myself. *I'll be fine, in a minute.*

Chapter 27
Bedtime Stories

[M.E.]

Two nights later, I curled up on my bed, attempting to read. Some nights, I was tired of all the romance in romance novels. It wasn't ever going to be like it was in books. On the other hand, some stories were so hot I couldn't help myself. If Christian Grey was the best sex I'd have, I'd take it. I'd read the book before, so tonight I skimmed for review.

Mitzi entered my room. Summer camp was over. Summer session courses were finished for me. It was August, and we had a few weeks' reprieve before the cycle started again. School. Work.

"You're reading that smut again?" she laughed.

"Well…" I didn't have an intelligent answer.

"Bree's watching Harry Potter again." She rolled her eyes. She didn't understand the love of characters as much as Bree and I did. That strong connection one could feel to someone fictional. I nodded, sensing she had something more she wanted to tell me. She crawled over me, then untucked her father's side of the bed. Pulling the covers up to her neck, she smiled up at me. For a brief flash, I saw the child in her at eighteen. The little girl who wanted to sleep with Mom and Dad after a bad dream. She swooshed her legs under the sheets for a second, slicing back and forth under the tight tuck.

"It's cold on this side," she mumbled. Her words struck me. Nate hadn't been a cold man, but I would not have considered him overly affectionate either. We didn't hold hands. We hardly ever hugged. We didn't greet each other with kisses like I'd seen other couples do. We were good in bed. Good. Not incredible.

Mitzi looked up at me after tussling the blanket.

"You liked him, didn't you?"

"Who?"

"Mom."

"What?" I grinned, despite myself.

"Mr. Whittington. You liked him."

"What's not to like? He's new to the neighborhood and he came here to check on the gas leak in the basement."

"It seemed like you knew him a little more than as the new neighbor."

"I didn't." It was the truth. I didn't know him as the neighbor. I didn't know him as anyone. I wouldn't have even guessed he worked for the fire department, if he hadn't arrived in the CFD truck. He was a liar.

It surprised me how quickly the old feelings of Nate's infidelity rushed back to me. The insecurity of being told one thing, to discover later the truth was completely different. I tried to justify that Merek and I weren't in a relationship. He owed me nothing, and yet, I believed that common human decency allowed for some honesty from him.

"Jake is really cute," Mitzi said, a little noncommittal.

"What about Kevin?" Her boyfriend had hardly been around this summer. We usually spent time discussing him at length, but this summer, things seemed quieter in regard to him.

"Mom, Jake's a junior."

"Oh." *Heaven forbid,* a budding senior be interested in a boy a year younger.

"I think Bree likes him, but she makes a fool of herself every time she's near him. Her friends all giggle and act silly. So sophomore."

Rolling my eyes, I nodded as if I understood. Ah, the difference between eighteen and sixteen. *So worldly.*

"Jake's fun, but he's kind of serious, too. I guess his mom left after he was born. She didn't want to be a mom, or something like that. His older sister Cassie is so cool. She's twenty-one."

Mitzi looked over at me.

"She's going to be a junior at North East next year, did you know that?"

No, I wanted to quip. I knew nothing about Merek Elliott Whittington or his family. Mitzi continued.

"I guess she didn't like Iowa State, so she decided to come home. If I had to guess, I bet she partied too much. Her dad is kind of intense sometimes. Cassie says he's really strict."

"Strict how?" The words edged out.

"He doesn't let her go out. I mean, she's twenty-one. Shouldn't she be able to go where she wants, when she wants? She says it's because he's worried she'll turn into her mom. Drink too much. Sleep around."

"Mitzi, that's a terrible thing to say." My eyebrows pinched in disapproval of her speaking in such a way about someone's mom.

"Those aren't my words, Mom. Those are Cassie's. She says they hardly ever see her. She had some kind of breakdown a few years back and moved to the suburbs."

Mitzi paused briefly.

"Cassie's very determined not to be like her mom. Her mom had her when she was eighteen. Can you imagine?" Mitzi shuddered at the thought. "Anyway, she said when her dad decided to buy a new house, she decided to come home. Her grandmother died last year. They used to live with her. She thinks her dad wanted a fresh start. Plus, she said she'd finally have a big room."

My eyes were pointed at my open book, but my mind wandered through all I was learning.

"You seem to know a lot about Cassie."

"Yeah, she's cool. We hang out when I go to Jake's. Their pool is so amazing."

I wanted to remind her that a twenty-one-year-old wouldn't think an eighteen-year-old was so cool, as she referenced her age difference with Jake. But then again, Mitzi was an easygoing girl, with an open mind and a gentle heart. She got along with everyone.

"How's Kevin?" I asked, hoping to change the subject.

"I don't know," she answered, shrugging and looking away from me.

"What's going on?"

"I like him. I do. He's really great, but I just...I don't know, you know?" Brown eyes that matched her father's looked over at me. I had to giggle when I recognized I didn't need to be part of the conversation she was having with herself. I waited for her to continue before I spoke.

"That's what dating is all about, Mitzi. You don't have to marry him. You're trying him on, seeing if you like him. What you like. What you don't."

She nodded, quietly staring at the television that was off.

"I just feel bad because there's nothing wrong with him. I just don't think he's for me."

"Why? Did something happen?"

She wasn't looking at me when she answered, "I just don't think we want the same things. I feel like I have things all planned out and he doesn't have any idea what he wants to do in life." Mitzi already knew she wanted to study to be a nurse. Helping others was in her nature. Kevin wasn't even certain he wanted to go to college.

Ah, the wisdom again of eighteen.

"Life will change," I stated. Mitzi rolled her head to look at me.

"I know. But I don't think my feelings will."

I stared down at this miracle that came from me, realizing that there *was* wisdom in that eighteen-year-old brain. While I willed my feelings about Merek to change, they actually hadn't. I missed him when I didn't want to, because I liked him, when I shouldn't have.

"Sometimes it's just that people change," I offered, hoping to sound positive. But isn't that what Gia has said to me. People change. Maybe Merek wanted a change, she suggested. Could I be that change for him? My thoughts wandered back to the almighty question of *why lie*?

"Sometimes they do," she sighed. "Can you fall out of love as easily as you can fall into it?"

Sighing heavily, my heart ached. I didn't have an exact answer. I wouldn't say I fell out of love with Nate, but my love certainly shifted with the betrayal of our marriage. The man I married, and thought I'd love for the rest of my life, was not the same man twenty years later. I believed love came in many forms. Without my answering, Mitzi continued.

"I mean, you loved Daddy, but you could love someone else, right? Like, if Kevin died, I would love someone else."

"Oh, honey. It's different. Daddy and I were married. You and Kevin are dating. You're so young. If Kevin died, and let's hope he doesn't, you would definitely love again."

"Well, I don't think you're really that old, Mom. Couldn't it happen for you, too?"

Mitzi turned on the television shortly after that comment and I closed the chapter on Christian Grey. Could I love again? I didn't want

The Sex Education of M.E.
to think of it as *again*, as if I was repeating what I'd already done. It would have to be loving *anew*, meaning something different, something unlike what I'd had before. Either way, loving meant being involved with another. It meant commitment and dedication and honesty. I didn't have those things from Merek. Hell, I'd hardly had them with Nate. My heart ached, as did my head, at the thought that love like I imagined might not be a part of my life story.

Chapter 28
Liberal Libations

[M.E. 2]

Our block hosted an end of the summer party. Unlike the 4th of July festivities a few blocks over, which included fireworks and tricycles with flags, this was more of a traditional party where people gathered their dinner and shared it outside with the neighbors. An open grill was available when neighbors were ready to cook. Coolers were filled with ice, and drinks could be dropped in to share. Children ran up and down the street playing tag. I warned Jake the pool was off limits with the little ones around. Our compromise was a bonfire for teens after nine.

While the party was mainly for our block, Gia told me other neighbors sauntered over and the street would be packed by six. She wasn't lying. We'd only been living in the house since May, and I knew most of the people up and down the block, especially the nosy ones, but I didn't recognize half the other people milling about. One person I did note was Todd Swanker.

He had no boundaries, no filter, and his comments were inappropriate, his mannerisms immature despite being in his thirties. He was the type of guy that gave the fire department a bad name and he fit the *muchacho* stereotype of being an asshole in uniform. I didn't care for him although we were on friendly terms within the department. I especially didn't care for him having his hands all over the back of Emme.

Gia warned me she might be attending. Warned isn't the correct word. She hinted, hopeful, suggested that Emme would possibly be present. It had been over a week. I didn't call when I knew I should. I didn't know how to explain myself, and at first, I didn't think I had to. I had already determined I wasn't going to see her again after our bike date. *Day*. Not date. Then we made love in that lazy afternoon. I steeled myself to let her go, before the inevitable, before she could leave me.

When Gia called the firehouse, telling me about the gas smell in Emme's house, my natural fireman instincts took over. *I could do this*, I

The Sex Education of M.E.

pep-talked myself. I could see her, and not react. This was a routine visit, for a basic call. No emergency. No need for the commander to attend, and yet, I couldn't keep myself away. I was concerned for her. Then I went back for the second torture. What happened against the washer made the machine want to rinse itself. As always, Emme was ready for me, and when she arched into me, basic instincts took over. I needed to be inside of her. I wasn't even thinking about protection. It was a natural attraction.

The instant I entered her, I recognized the difference. It had been years since I'd been bare with a woman. Years. The way Emme melted over me, drawing me into her. I'd never been so hard in my life. She was drenched, sucking me deep within. Coming at her from behind was a totally different sensation: intense, animal, and incredible. After realizing what we'd done, her frightened eyes scared me, and my mouth did what I hadn't done in years either. It kissed her. My God, that kiss. It crawled to my toes and back up my legs, priming me for another round with her. Her mouth was heaven and years of pent-up denial washed out of me, as I took what I wanted from her. Connection. Emme was solid. She was real, and I was ready for what came next.

Only there was no next. The revelation of who I was, so unpredictably shared by her daughter, sent things into a tailspin. I hadn't been honest, but I hadn't outright lied. My children weren't something I intentionally hid. I just didn't wish to share that I had them. I didn't need the sympathy some women offered; that knowing look of pity for the single father. Or that hopeful gleam of *I can be the next Mrs.*, though there had never been a first one. I didn't want to go through the whole explanation of Janice. I just didn't want to share all the painful parts of my past with her, when all I suddenly saw was the future. If anything, I thought Emme would understand. She's the one who mentioned not feeling whole and wanting to escape. She's the one who no longer wanted to be defined by her children, but as her.

My mind raced as I slowly stood and neared Emme. Gia saw me approaching over Todd's shoulder, warning me with her eyes to tread lightly. I understood Emme's misgivings. I was scared, too. I hadn't been committed to one woman in almost two decades, while she had spent twenty years devoted to one man. She looked for relief, and I wanted to satisfy her. I wanted to loosen up the tight wall surrounding her, only I never planned on her breaking through mine.

Todd shifted, glancing over his shoulder.

"Chief," he called out, letting his hand rub down Emme's back. She flinched out of his touch. I was a commander now, but he'd known me from before, when I was a chief. She stepped forward, clearly uncomfortable with his groping. "Emme was just sharing her adventures in singlehood with us."

Scoffing awkwardly, she retorted, "I was not."

"She was describing her nefarious ways of luring men into her bedroom and taking advantage of them."

"Pretty sure, it was the other way around," she muttered, side-eying me and then looked away.

"I was just about to share some of my tricks with her. See if she could put the master's tactics to practice." He winked at me. Emme continued to shake her head. Gia shuddered.

"Oh, God," Gia laughed.

"That's what she says," Todd guffawed, and Emme choked.

"Okay, I'm stepping away now. The student will never surpass the master here," she joked, swirling a hand between herself and Todd.

"Are you admitting I'm a master in the bedroom?" Todd stilled.

"I wouldn't know any such thing!" Emme shrieked.

"Thank God," I sighed.

"That's what she said," Emme muttered, and we both broke out in laughter. Running its course, the tension rebuilt, and Emme pulled away from the group, on the guise of getting a drink. I followed her to a cooler.

"How are you?" I asked, offering her a beer.

"Okay." She shrugged. "And you?" It was painfully awkward. All I wanted to do was reach for her and pull her toward me.

In reply I asked, "Have you ever been in the MacAllister house?"

"Their children were older," she replied, shaking her head. "I heard it's unusually laid out."

"I'd love to show it to you," I offered, and it was the truth. I hadn't ever brought women to my brother's apartment, my parents' old home where we lived until recently, or to the new house. I hadn't wanted to share the personal side of me, until now. I was too vulnerable. The whole

The Sex Education of M.E.
Janice experience gutted me as an impressionable young man and I refused to place myself in a similar situation, especially with the added risk of children involved. The only love I had was for my children, until now.

Following my lead, Emme entered through the side door. The house was on a narrow piece of property, set the long way; meaning, it was a deep structure with a small front entrance and a larger one on the side of the home. The kitchen had been modernized, although it was long and galley-like. The dining room was next to this unique kitchen space and the official center of the home. With a sharp gable roof line, and its dark brick, it looked like something from an ancient time. The interior design appeared as if the original architect was uncertain which direction he intended to take. Additions and updates seamlessly connected the quirky layout. This neighborhood had a slightly eclectic feel to it, anyway. The houses weren't rows upon rows of Chicago bungalows, like my parents' old neighborhood. There was more space between houses, and more diversity in structures.

"We don't have much furniture yet. I'm waiting for Cassie to pick some things out for me." The living room was in the front, the family space in the back overlooking the pool.

"It isn't legal to have an in-ground pool in Chicago anymore. Any pool built after 1979 was considered an ornamental pond and could be no deeper than five feet. The pool was grandfathered into this property, and it was one of the buying points for me." I rambled my pool history lesson to fill the silence between us.

"I wanted something that would keep my children coming home, even if we could only use it three months of the year. More so, I hoped to keep Jake out of trouble. My old neighborhood held too many temptations for a teenage boy, especially after the loss of my mother, who helped me tremendously. It was time for a change. Not to mention, I wanted Cassie closer. Her failing grades pulled the trigger on college out of state. Her new, larger bedroom was enticement to return home." I babbled on.

We paused at the bottom of the stairs, and I hesitated only slightly before leading her upward. The house was old, so the stairwell was narrow and steep. Cassie's room was to the front of the house, Jacob's to the left over the garage, and mine was in the back. The décor was similar to my room at Marshall's, blacks and grays. It was a reminder of where we'd been together, and I longed to tug her down on the duvet, to beg her for understanding.

"It looks familiar," she snipped under her breath, stepping back to the hall. I stepped left to block her retreat.

"Let me explain," I plead, raising an arm to prevent her running down the stairs. "I don't share my past because it's painful. I just wanted it to be us. Only us. No looking back." I brushed at a loose hair by her cheek. "I'll tell you anything you want to know, but it won't change anything. It won't take away the hurt, the mistakes, the poor decisions. I can't change that, and it took me a long time to accept that fact. I learned long ago to only look ahead." My hand cupped her cheek. "I've missed you."

"Don't do this," she whispered.

"Why?"

"Because I'm weak," she exhaled, her eyes closing under my touch.

"I want to kiss you."

"You didn't before," she bit.

"Emme, please." My mouth watered as I drew closer to her lips, my hands framing her face. Her shoulders sagged. A hand tentatively came to my waist. Closing the distance, I took her lips gently with mine. I'd kissed her quickly, harsh and hot in the heat of the moment a week ago, but this moment, I wanted to savor. I wanted to drink in her sigh and swallow her sound. My lips moved over hers, hesitantly exploring. Slowly, I outlined the curve of her bottom lip and sipped the bow of the top. My tongue pressed the seam of our joining and she opened. Lazy, like the love we'd made, our tongues looped around one another, tangling tenderly. She was sweetness and spice, and I wanted more.

My body pressed forward, pinning her to the wall, the steel length of me erect and ready against her lower abdomen. Her hands gripped my sides, bunching up my t-shirt. My mind begged her to remove my clothes.

"What are we doing?" she muttered against my lips which refused to release her.

The Sex Education of M.E.

"It's called messing around," I teased, as I redirected her mouth with mine, sucking her tongue into me.

"I don't want..." I cut her off with another searing kiss. "...to just mess around," she gasped against my mouth. "I want to get messy with someone."

"Get messy, with me," I begged, continuing my attention on those amazing lips. The connection between us was a wick deep within my chest and a fuse to my dick. I was full to bursting, ready to explode, and I wanted her to light the cord.

"I can't be a fu..." My mouth cut off the words. I didn't want to hear her label us.

"You aren't," I muttered after another deep kiss.

"I can't be friends with benefits."

"I want to be more than friends."

She practically climbed me after that. Her arms wrapped around my neck, and she hoisted her body upward, hitching a leg around my hip, drawing me against her. Minus the clothing, I'd be buried inside her. I needed to be inside her, to feel the connection and prove that opening up to her wouldn't push her away. After all the years it took to find someone like her, I didn't want to lose her.

Chapter 29
Exs and Uh-ohs

[M.E.]

Our hallway make-out session was stopped in the nick of time, as I was two seconds from stripping him, and tackling him to the hardwood floor. His son's voice calling from the lower level was a warning to cool down. We were at a community block party, and there were things to discuss before anymore nakedness occurred. Merek pulled back from me.

"We'll be right down." The implication of a *we* was not lost to me, neither was the fact that I hadn't met his son, and Merek just implied someone was upstairs with him. He brushed back my wayward hair and kissed me one final time before straightening his shirt. He was the epitome of casual sexy in his untucked dress shirt and khaki shorts. His short, peppered hair was slightly mussed from my fingers and his smile sparkled to match his eyes. He looked like he'd just gotten away with mischief.

Taking my hand, he guided me down the stairs, but dropped it instantly upon finding his kitchen filled with teenagers, including my own two daughters.

"Mom," Bree said gleefully, ignorantly blissful of how I appeared. She reached out to hug me. Mitzi stood near a girl that I could only assume was Cassie, as I recognized her from The Square. She was a beautiful girl with eyes matching Merek's, but she had a slinky young body.

"Mom, this is Cassie." My daughter had a girl crush on Cassie. She wasn't into girls like that, but it was obvious she was smitten with the attention from an older girl. Cassie waved shyly at me and reached for a red plastic cup.

"What's in that?" Merek snapped behind me and Cassie tipped the cup toward him.

"Coke," she sighed. Merek exhaled.

"Sorry, Cass," he muttered, but a subtle tension spun through the room.

"Bonfire?" Mitzi suggested pleasantly, and I thanked heaven for such an easy-going girl.

"Bonfire," a young man agreed, and he reached above the refrigerator for a box of matches.

"Not too close to the house," Merek warned.

"Dad, stop being a fireman for five seconds," the boy scoffed, and I realized as he looked over at his father, this was Jake. Young Merek Elliott stood before me, a mirror image of his father from twenty-five years ago.

"Uncanny, I know," Merek said, breaking my stare. There wasn't a trace of anything but Merek in the boy. The teens exited through the side door, and Merek and I remained in the kitchen.

"You okay with this?" he said, pointing over his shoulder.

"Are you?" I laughed, nervously.

"Baptism by fire," he said, and we laughed together. Taking my hand, he led me out the door.

The blaze lit up the surrounding patio space. The glistening water shimmered within the pool. My mind raced with images of Merek and me naked. Our kiss upstairs wasn't enough. The barrier had been broken, and I wanted the wall to crumble around him. We sat in silence as the teens around us joked easily, clearly unabashed at two adults present. In many ways, listening to their banter and the freedom of flirtation, I was reminded of my own youth. How innocent and carefree the youth deserve to be, because life gets progressively harder.

I longed to touch Merek's hand, hold it as if we were young, too, but my own reserve prevented me from reaching out for him. The feel of his lips lingered on mine and I caught him seductively tracing over his bottom lip. His playful eyes often met mine, and if I ever thought I could read minds, this would be the time. He wanted me.

"Come here, I want to show you something." He stood abruptly and sauntered to a dark corner of his yard near a shed.

"Where am I going?" I laughed.

"Just follow me," he said, waving his hand like he tempted a child to candy. Once he'd sensed we'd gone far enough, he tugged me forward and I fell against him. Blocked by the shed, he kissed me. Hard. There was desire and longing and a promise of things to come in that kiss. His mouth controlled mine. Lips and tongue colliding. He pressed me into the side of the shed.

"I couldn't wait any longer," he sighed against my mouth.

"We can't do this here," I mumbled.

The slamming sound of the front gate brought our mini make-out session to an end. Metal against metal startled me out of my reverie of lust and drew my attention to a thin woman who entered the backyard as Merek and I cleared the darkness of the back corner.

"Janice?" Merek choked, dropping my hand, and Cassie's head spun.

"Mom!" Her voice broke.

"Hey baby," she purred, stepping closer to the circle of friends. Cassie untangled herself from her Adirondack chair and walked into outstretched arms. Even in the dim light of fire, I saw a stunning woman in her late thirties. Her hair still dark, her body slim like it had never known the struggle of bearing children. She held Cassie tight against her, and then pushed her back to look her up and down. Their figures were remarkably similar. The two could have been sisters instead of mother and daughter.

My eyes drifted to Jake, who hadn't moved from his spot. He didn't greet Janice or acknowledge her. His expression was hard, and it matched his father's. The irritation on his face could have set the delicate fire pit flame to a raging blaze.

"Janice," Merek commanded, stepping closer to the fire. "What are you doing here?"

"I heard there was a party and I wanted to see the new house."

Merek stared at his daughter, who had the decency to hang her head.

"It's a private party," Merek replied. Janice tossed her hair over her shoulder, nodding toward the active street. "Seems rather public to me."

"It's not," Jake snapped.

"Jacob," Merek warned. His tone clearly set Jake off, as he abruptly stood and stalked to the house.

"Cassie, why don't you introduce me to your friends?" Her mother's overly enthusiastic voice was nails on a chalkboard. Sugar sweet, high-pitched, and too friendly. Initially, I couldn't move. On second thought, I needed to get out of this awkward situation.

"Merek," I said lightly, my hand reaching out tentatively for his arm. He bristled when I touched him, staring down at my fingers.

"Merek, shouldn't you go after Jake?" I offered. His dark eyes lit with sparks as he looked up at mine.

"He'll be okay."

"Will you?" I asked, hesitantly.

"And who might you be?" That sugar tone addressed me. "I'm Janice Whittington." Before me stood a woman of model proportions, extending a well-manicured hand. The only imperfection I noticed was the slight sway to her stance.

"I'm Mary Elizabeth Peters." Shaking her slender hand, I noted her cold fingers. Her touch was like dangling a dirty dish rag.

"And you're one of the neighbors?" she implied.

"Yes," I answered quickly, not feeling the need to further commit details. The woman before me staggered back and Merek reached forward to steady the sway of her body.

"Have you been drinking?" he hissed, drawing closer to her.

"It's a party, Merek. Lighten up." Her gaze fell to him, and I watched her lick her lips. He turned his face like she slapped him. The tension between him and his ex was so thick I couldn't decide if it was pure hatred or lusty attraction. My inadequacy hit hard, and I excused myself. I hadn't made it to the front gate before my waist was encircled and I was tugged against a firm chest.

"Don't go," he whispered behind me.

"Merek, there's clearly an issue here."

"I'll get her to leave. Just give me a few minutes." His lips brushed my neck, sucking lightly. "We need to talk. You and me." I nodded in agreement. "But let me talk to her first."

I twisted in his arms and hugged him for assurance, uncertain if the need for comfort was from me or needed *for* me. I wanted to be understanding. We were adults. These things were going to happen. Even though I marveled at the youth around the fire pit, life had tolled forward, and we weren't young anymore. Kids. Homes. Exes. This was messy. These were going to be the norm of any man I met after Nate. I had to be compassionate. He kissed my cheek and led me back to the bonfire. Embarrassed at my attempt to leave, I avoided looking at my girls. Only

Mitzi's eyes were on me. Bree had disappeared, most likely to follow Jake. Merek's voice was the sharpest I've ever heard as he called out his ex-wife's name and nodded toward the house. For the briefest second, I almost felt sorry for her. The seconds passed quickly, but time seemed to stand still.

The minutes rolled over slowly while I waited for Merek's return. At the twenty-minute mark, I stood to excuse myself again. It was obvious that Merek and Janice needed more time and waiting made me edgy. After I passed the side door, I heard it open. I shouldn't have looked.

Turning I saw Janice exit the house followed immediately by Merek. He buttoned up his shirt. She smoothed a hand through her hair.

"As always Merek, it's a pleasure to see you." Her voice rolled over the *-ure* and my stomach roiled. She placed her hands beneath her breasts and pushed them upward as if adjusting them.

"Janice." His chin dipped dismissively as he completed buttoning his dress shirt. I stood still, unable to draw my eyes away.

Janice leaned forward and kissed his cheek, then intentionally turned in my direction. Her sharp blue eyes set my feet in motion, and I yanked the gate free of the latch. I didn't stop as I raced for the sanctuary of Gia's home. Gia followed me, as I cursed myself internally. I'm too old for this shit. Why am I running to Gia's? The truth was I couldn't have made it home fast enough. Gia's was a safe haven, and she wouldn't let Merek step one foot into her house with her children nearby. Unfortunately, her children ran wild in the streets.

"Just don't say anything to me," I blurted as I slammed her bathroom door. I'd trapped myself. I was a rational, educated woman and I'd locked myself in my best friend's bathroom, hoping that the night would just end. Sliding down to the floor, my back braced against the door, my head fell forward, and I slipped my hands into my hair. I closed my eyes but instantly opened them after picturing Merek in compromising positions with his ex-wife. I'd read about this — relationships that continued despite divorce. The chemistry was still present. Their history built a familiarity. Shared hatred for one another actually flamed the passion.

My head thudded back, and the door rattled.

"Emme, let me in."

My head shook back and forth, regardless of the fact he couldn't see me.

"Emme, I can explain."

Are there any worse words?

Emme, I can explain, Nate's voice drifted into my thoughts. Oh, Nate. I shook my head again. Even the apologetic tone of Merek was similar. Merek could explain. *Men can always explain*, my mother would say sarcastically.

Fool me once, shame on you. Fool me twice, shame on me. This was my own undoing. I couldn't keep my legs clamped shut. *You wanted this.* The words of Gia rang in my ears. Not this. Not this rollercoaster of a ride. Not this feeling of unworthiness. Not this sense of being pathetic.

I didn't move. I would ride out the night on the floor of Gia's powder room if I had to, but I wasn't opening the door.

"Emme, I gotta pee." Gia's son Sam's little voice whined through the wood. *Thud, thud, thud* went my head against the door.

"Go upstairs, Sammy," I muttered.

"I can't. Mommy says Sarah's up there."

Damn, Gia. She'd stop at nothing, using her kids to pry me out of her bathroom.

"I really gotta go, Emme." His voice whimpered. Standing slowly, I opened the door to see Merek hand Sammy a dollar. He was quick. Ready to slam the door again, he pushed it open and entered the small space with me.

"We need to talk."

The lipstick on his collar said it all to me.

Chapter 30
Listen With Your Heart Before Other Body Parts

[M.E. 2]

Women. Damn it, they were impossible to figure out. This is why I didn't date. This is why I didn't do relationships. Women were complicated.

I wanted to break Janice's neck regardless of her being the mother of my children. Then I was going to wring Emme's for jumping to conclusions. With a shaky hand dragging over my face, I took a deep breath. It was a mistake. In the tight confines of the bathroom, all I inhaled was Emme. Summer and bonfire. She filled my head.

"Look, just let me explain."

"That's never a good start."

The comparison to her dead husband was present between us. A history that didn't involve me. The avoidance of her eyes let me know I was correct.

"I'm not him," I stated, and her head snapped in my direction.

"No, you aren't." Her eyes roamed over me, and what should have made me feel dirty, only turned me on. I wanted to take her on top of the pedestal sink. I wanted to bury myself inside her until she saw reason. She was for me.

"Janice is not Janice *Whittington*."

"Oh my God," Emme sucked in a breath. "This just gets worse."

"Yeah, well, welcome to my life. Janice is Cassie and Jake's mother, but we never married." I had her attention suddenly.

"When I was twenty-one, and stupid, I came home from college, got drunk, and fucked a girl from the neighborhood. A one-night stand produced a baby, and I didn't want to run from my responsibilities. She was only eighteen. A high school graduate fresh out of school. I was fucking stupid."

Rubbing a hand over my head, I took another breath. Emme's eyes were aimed at the floor, but she listened.

"My dad got me in the department before you had to have a degree as a requirement. At twenty-one, I was a newbie and a father with a woman who didn't love me. I tried to make it work. I was willing to marry her. She refused, but she lived with me. It was a nightmare, not a dream come true. We fought constantly. She drank. She ran around. I was nothing but faithful to her, for the sake of our baby. One night we had a huge fight. I threatened to leave and take Cassie with me. She begged me to stay. She promised to change. When she got pregnant with Jake, God forgive me, I wasn't even certain he was mine. Then I saw those eyes. My eyes peered back at me, and I knew I couldn't continue the way we were. She left me before Jacob was one."

Emme sighed, her eyebrows pinching in that curious way.

"Twenty-two years that woman has tormented me. She fooled around. Got drunk. Had a nervous breakdown. And I tried to take her back, but I reached a breaking point myself. The women started when I was twenty-six. It was easiest to have one-night stands and walk away. I couldn't risk the kids getting close to another woman. I didn't want to risk myself either. Fucking MatchMe."

"Random women were getting old. MatchMe was organized but women were looking for the love of their life. That was their tag line: *We'll match you for life.* I didn't need that. I decided I'd find my own way. Everything was fine. Fine," I spat.

"But you came along, all bright-eyed and I-just-want-to-have-sex, and I didn't want you to be doing that miserable random hook-up shit and wading through all the creeps on MatchMe who care nothing about a life match." I reached out for her, resting my hand on her neck. "You wanted the ride and I wanted to be the driver."

"So it's my fault?" she questioned softly.

"Yeah, it's your fault," I laughed. "No whips. No chains. Jesus, Emme, I just wanted to tie you up right then and have my way with you, and then you let me. You came to me, willingly, and I reacted to you like none other. Once wasn't enough. It wasn't going to be enough."

"What about tonight?" she interrupted.

"Nothing happened. She wrapped around me, kissed my neck and started unbuttoning my shirt. She does this shit when she's drunk. She'll disappear and the kids will be a wreck. I thought I'd be done with this crap when we moved. Damn Cassie, for calling her." My hand came down on the pedestal sink behind Emme and she flinched. Our bodies were close, my arm trapping her, but we were a million miles apart. I could see in her eyes that she wanted to trust me, but she couldn't. And while it hadn't been my fault that she didn't trust, I couldn't change her mind. Some wounds go deep. I knew. I wanted to love Janice. It's what I thought I should do. The honorable thing to do, considering I'd knocked her up. Janice threw that in my face. As if it was my fault alone. She didn't even try to work at a marriage. She fooled around. She carved out my heart and crushed it. It took years of random hook-ups before I came across the first person to revive me.

"That's a lot of baggage," she commented.

"Well, I just unpacked everything for you."

She remained silent, and it was the exact reason I didn't share all this shit with women. It was too much. Single father jilted by woman he never loved but tried to. Man with two kids who he'd throw his life in front of the L for, if their mother tried to take them. Only one more year before Jacob was legal and I could finally rest easy. As adults, they could make up their own minds. Jacob already had, but Cassie, she still struggled. She couldn't come to terms any more than I could with the fact her mother didn't want to be her mother. It was always best to just keep all this private.

With other women, I could pretend I wasn't who I was. They were never going to get close enough to know me. I didn't date. I hooked up. Maybe a few crossed the line into fuck buddy status, but none went further. No one became a friend with benefits. It only complicated things. Life complicated things. With Emme remaining silent, I'd reached the end of my fuse.

"This is why I don't get involved. It's too messy."

"Earlier you said you wanted to get messy with me," she said, finally looking up at me.

"I do. But...but maybe it's not worth it. I told you everything. There's nothing between us now. You need to listen to your heart for a while, not your body." I pushed off the sink. Her brows pinched with hurt.

"Because inside that amazing body is a heart that's beating for more than just sex. I know it, and you know it. My heart," I pounded my chest. "It's finally beating again. And I'm ready for more, but not like this. Not

The Sex Education of M.E.

with hesitation and speculation and distrust. I've already been there, and so have you."

Her head whipped back, and she blinked.

"Listen to the pulse of your heart." My finger tip-tapped her chest over her left breast. "Before you listen to any other part of your body."

Too often I'd listened to the wrong part of mine, and her silence proved, I'd done it again.

Chapter 31
Breakfast Dates Are Better

[M.E.]

Merek's words stung, but they were true. My heart could not close off what my body yearned for it to. Whether the emotion was unadulterated lust or just magnetic attraction, the fact was, my body wanted Merek's. But so did my heart. He left me standing alone, uncertain of everything. When I finally had the courage to leave the powder room, I found Gia and excused myself. The walk home was only a few blocks, and I needed the solitude.

There's a certain peace at night, sort-of like grocery shopping after ten p.m. The world is quieter. The streets emptier. My thoughts were rabid though. All I had wanted was sex, a thing you can't do alone. The concept of masturbation doesn't qualify. It isn't the connection you get when you are physically intimate with another person. Gia would say some women prefer to get off alone. I didn't understand that belief. It wasn't that I couldn't be alone. It was that I didn't *want* to be. I wanted to feel the thrill of a man entering me. I longed for the touch of another's fingers, the discovery of what I liked. I enjoyed the sensation of a warm tongue opening me. I couldn't do any of those things on my own.

Then there was the deeper connection. Not the idea of being joined as one, but the simple things. Holding hands. Tender touches. Hugging. You can't do any of those things alone either. It's a natural need for contact with another person. It wasn't in my nature to *not* be affectionate, but for too long my affection had gone to my children. I embraced them. I held their hands. I tickled their necks. But that was never the same, *never*, as the link between a man and a woman.

Merek was correct. As much as I denied wanting deeper intimacy, I lied to myself. I craved it. It was easier to brush off the need, because my husband was dead. What other man was going to give me those things? Who would want to hold my hand? Who would touch me tenderly? Who would hug me late at night? My own husband hardly did those things. Why would another man? My self-pity did not run deep, but my self-deprecation did. It had been conditioned over years of not receiving such kindnesses.

Any person can have sex with another person. I wasn't fool enough to dismiss that idea. A primal need for that satisfaction could be fulfilled with any man and an imaginative mind. Fantasy is a great escape. But those baser needs were not fictional. They were a reality unreceived, and while I felt ancient, *damn it*, I was still young enough that I deserved such attention. I'd put in my time. Twenty years. I was ready to take back the person I truly was, for no other reason than that I deserved it.

The next morning, I woke up completely renewed. As a professor, years don't run cyclical, but by school calendar. August was my January and I determined to begin this year anew. The first step was exercise. While I didn't faithfully follow it—who was I kidding, I didn't follow it at all—I decided I would walk at least three days a week. I could do this. Preferring the outside, I'd do it as long as I could before I was forced to use the indoor track at the university.

Donning my gym shoes, a work-out skort and a t-shirt, I hit the forest preserve trail by my home, and turned up the tunes on my iPhone. The brisk pace refreshed me, and I was in a good groove under the cover of full trees when I saw a man running in the opposite direction. I knew how I'd respond. I'd smile politely, say good morning and continue on with my day. But as the man drew closer, there was a familiarity about him that I couldn't ignore.

Merek.

My pace slowed. There was no way to avoid him. We were the only two on the trail and he'd spotted me. I could run for the trees, but that would be silly, not to mention, my shirt was hot pink, and I'd stand out wherever I tried to hide. Merek stopped abruptly and walked the few steps that separated us. He had sweat rolling off his body. It should have been disgusting, but it was strangely hot. Jealous of a bead that caressed down the side of his face, I swallowed back the ache inside me.

"Good morning."

"Hey," he replied. We stood for a moment in silence, awkward, and unfamiliar, as if we were strangers.

"I didn't know you ran. I mean, of course, you run. Look at you. I mean, I've looked at you, but..." Closing my eyes, I inhaled. Could the verbal vomit not start? I was nervous, when I shouldn't be. I'd seen this man naked, but that's what made me nervous. We'd hardly spend time together clothed.

"Do you walk here often?"

I laughed. "That sounds like a pick-up line."

"I wasn't trying to pick you up," he deadpanned, and my heart fell to my feet.

"Oh…I…" I brushed a piece of hair behind my ear.

"Where are you headed?" he asked

"Just to the end of the trail and back," I offered, my finger working harder on that wayward piece of hair.

"Mind if I walk with you?"

"Weren't you going the other way?" I paused. "You're clearly trying to get in a work-out and I'm not a runner."

"Emme, if you don't want me to walk with you, just say no." He dropped his tone. His hands came to his hips as he looked away.

"I …" Yes. No. Maybe so. "I'd like that."

He lifted the edge of his shirt and wiped away the heavy sweat on his forehead. He twisted to face my direction and we fell into step next to one another.

Is it strange that I'm okay with silence? I typically am, but the need to speak gnawed at me.

"What are you listening to?" His head inclined to the phone.

"Oh, Sam Hunt. My kids are trying to convert me to country artists."

"Ever been line dancing?" he laughed.

"Merek, you know I don't dance," I stated. My breath caught after the comment.

"Maybe we need to change that," he said quietly. His eyes forward and his jaw clenched; my heart leapt with hope. As we neared the end of the trail, Merek noted that a coffee shop was up the street.

"I don't drink coffee."

"What?" He nearly shrieked like a teenage girl. "That is sacrilegious. I can never see you again, if you don't like coffee, woman."

"I didn't realize you were going to see me again," I offered, teasingly.

"One can only hope." We fell silent waiting for the crosswalk. Cross the street or stop. A metaphor flashed in my mind.

"I could still walk with you, if you want to grab a cup." I nodded in the direction of the coffee shop, and Merek held out his hand to lead the way.

He sipped the black brew slowly as we retraced our steps back through the forest preserve. We chatted minimally, ignoring topics like his ex-wife and my deceased husband. He mentioned Cassie enrolling at NEU for the next semester. I mentioned Mitzi would be starting her senior year, and we'd begin the college decision-making process.

"Ah, to be young again," he sighed. I smiled in return.

"If only I'd met you sooner," he shrugged. We neared the end of the path, and I ached at the thought of walking away. Our time together seemed rather final.

"If you met me earlier, you'd never be interested in a girl like me." My brush-off-giggle attempted to lighten the moment.

"Why not?"

"I had commitment written all over me, and you, my friend, are a player." It was his turn to smile sheepishly.

"I might not have been, had I met the right woman."

"Well, it still probably wouldn't have been me. Straight-laced, buttoned up tight, you wouldn't have noticed the wallflower."

"Maybe. But then again, the quiet ones always have a secret, wild side." His eyebrows wiggled deviously up and down. I had to laugh, if for no other reason than the truth of his words. He did make me a little out of control when we were physically together. I would miss that part of him and me.

"I guess I did it all backwards with you," I shrugged, trying to play off what I was about to say next. "I mean, I had sex with you first, when typically, you date first, then have sex. Who wants to climb uphill when you start at the top, right?" I huff-laughed.

"Emme," he paused as we reached the crossroad again. His house was straight ahead. "I feel like I should ask you to dinner. Like a real date, but I have to work the next two shifts."

"Oh." I waved dismissively. "I don't want you to feel like you have to do me favors. You already did, right?" I laughed again, the sound faltering. I wasn't bitter. It was true. Merek Elliott had slept with me when I wanted someone to have sex with me. With the light of a new day, I tried to face the reality.

"Emme, that's not what I meant."

"I know, but I don't really need dinner," I said, stepping away from him in the direction of my home. "I think breakfast dates are better." My smile hinted. His head tilted to the side.

"Breakfast dates?" he questioned, his brows pinching.

"Yeah, no one ever has breakfast dates. Eggs, bacon…coffee, too, I suppose. It sounds much better than a stuffy dinner."

"Breakfast dates?" The curve of his lip exposed that damn dimple. We lingered in the side street for a moment. I wasn't ready to say those final two words. I slowly sauntered away from him, stepping backward while I faced him. Almost across the street from him, I turned for home.

"How about Thursday morning?" He called out to me. "I know the perfect place nearby." I turned back to face him and signaled the direction of his house with his head.

"What are we doing?" I laughed, shaking my head.

"We're making a date. For breakfast."

Chapter 32
Fire Alarm Bells

[M.E.]

For a week straight, we met. We walked together, and I looked forward to each date, as he called them. I missed the touch of him, and he didn't reach for me, but we talked. He shared anecdotes of the firehouse and how he really wanted to be an architect. I knew the reasons why he wasn't. He told me about his parents who had both died: his father from complications during a fire, his mother from cancer over a year ago. He'd lived with them while he raised his children, and he told me his family was everything to him. His younger brother was his best friend, even though he was upset that Marshall wasn't taking his future fatherhood seriously.

Not wanting to bog him down with tales of Nate, I shared with him how I loved reading and dabbled with writing. I always wanted to write the great American novel, emphasized by air quotes. He said I was smart enough and I laughed. Smart was never something I'd heard from Nate. He didn't believe in that dream of mine, and after his first negative comment in regard to writing in general, I held that dream a secret. Merek knew I taught literature and it turned out Cassie was in my sophomore level course on short stories in the new semester. She needed to make up a credit or three before she was fully admitted to junior status.

I enjoyed our time together, but each day I felt a little emptier when we parted. There was no hint anything else would happen between us. Merek and I were clearly becoming friends, and as I had said to him one day, everyone could use new friends. However, friendship wasn't the only thing I wanted with him, and I realized it was time to either take action or walk away. The problem was, I had no clues from Merek which direction he wanted things to go. He was honest and direct, if he had to work at the club, or if he had a shift. He didn't mention dates, or arrangements, or any other sexual innuendo, and I could only hope he wasn't with other women.

L.B. Dunbar

On a Monday, we were supposed to meet once again, and for the first time, Merek didn't show. I waited patiently for fifteen minutes. I still had his number, but I didn't want to use it, not wanting to appear needy. Need passed to concern, and at the fifteen-minute mark, I texted him.

You coming?

It sounded so suggestive, and I laughed out loud, literally. Hopeful he'd find it humorous as well, I panicked when he didn't respond after two minutes. I took one more final look toward his street, and decided I needed to walk off the steam building inside me. I'd been stood up.

The forest preserve trail, throughout Chicago, twisted and curved through sections of woods scattered among the city neighborhoods. For some reason, Robert Frost's poem, "A Road Not Taken," filtered into my mind, and I focused over and over on the concept of two roads and divergence. I'd been on one path my whole life. I married my college sweetheart. We had the two kids, the perfect home, and the appearance of an ideal life, but I can't say I was ever happy. I should have been. God forgive me, I should have been. The road was well traveled in the direction I paced. And even with the bump of Nate's affair, I still stayed on the path. But I was ready to diverge.

Merek might not be the man for me, but he had sparked something long-repressed. He was the opposite of all that I had known. His fireman status, colorful tattoos, and player mentality were very different from Nate's clean cut, business suit, accountant ways. I wanted to veer off on the road less traveled, which was scary and unknown, but thrilling. While I loved learning about Merek as a person, I could not deny, I loved what his body had done to me weeks ago. I was the road less traveled; hardly noticeable, but still present under the decay of years. And like the great poem, either path might result in the same destination, but it was the journey I needed to enjoy.

I returned home a bit somber from my walk and noticed I had three missed calls from Gia. I didn't understand how I could miss them as the phone was in my hand, but I was still considered technologically incapacitated when it came to all functions of the phone.

Clicking into the first voice mail, Gia's voice was calm but adamant: Call me.

The second sounded a bit frantic: Emme, have you heard anything? The final one, complete panic: OMG! Call me immediately.

Pressing her contact, I didn't hear one ring before she answered.

"Holy horses, where's the fire?" I laughed.

"You haven't heard?"

"Heard what?" My voice lowered. My heart rate increased.

"There's a five-alarm fire off on Northwest Highway. A lumberyard caught fire last night and the blaze has been going strong through the night. Merek's unit is there."

"How do you know this?" I exhaled.

"I watch the news."

"Not that, about Merek."

"Jacob's home alone. I went to check on him."

"Where's Cassie?"

"Jacob doesn't know."

"Oh my God. This is terrible. And Merek?"

"He's been part of the team on the scene. He was interviewed at some point, and he was on the news. But Emme, the building collapsed, and some men are unaccounted for at the moment."

"Dear God," I whispered. The reality of Merek's job caught up to me. He mentioned the training and the strength needed to battle a blaze. Physical upkeep was important for jobs like his.

"What should I do?"

"Text Merek, although I doubt he'll answer."

I hung up and texted immediately.

Are you okay?

I didn't have Jake's cell phone number, and like most modern people, Merek didn't have a landline phone. Sometimes, I hated modern technology. Hours passed, and I heard nothing. What should I do? I wondered. What would I do if he were injured? Easy, go to the hospital. What if it were worse? I refused to think that way but thoughts of Nate's heart attack and death tapped at my brain. I couldn't lose Merek. We'd just started forging a new path with each other. I wanted to see where the trail would take us. I wasn't ready to lose him.

By noon, I couldn't take the unknown and I drove over to Merek's house, my heart hammering in my chest. Jacob answered the door.

"Hey." His surprised voice turned to a smile.

"Hey. How are you?"

"I'm good. Everything's good. My dad's upstairs." My shoulders sagged in relief.

"Is he…is he okay?"

"Yeah, he's always fine, he says." Jacob shrugged. I imagined this was common reassurance from father to son, so he wouldn't worry about the dangerous jobs.

"He's making me go to school," he said, hitching up the strap of his backpack. The local high schools already started, but my college courses didn't begin for another week. "But you can come in and wait, if you'd like. He's in the shower."

"Well, I just…"

"I know he'll want to see you," Jake smirked, like a teenager would. He held the door open wider for me, and I stepped inside the cool front hall. "Cassie isn't home," Jake offered, then walked out the front door. This seemed like odd information to share with me. Standing in the entry way, I didn't know what to do with myself. Should I make myself at home, as the saying goes? I didn't want to startle Merek. I figured the kitchen might be a good waiting spot, or maybe his family room, where he could see me from his descent down the stairs. After a few minutes of awkward pacing, I decided waiting wasn't an option. The road less traveled was instead.

I climbed the stairs slowly, but my heart beat rapidly increased. Reaching the top landing, I heard the steady sound of a shower in the direction of Merek's room. I entered hesitantly, calling out his name, but my voice squeaked quietly. My hands shook as I knocked on the bathroom door.

"Merek," I said, still too low.

"I can't hear you, come in here." My head whipped upward. He couldn't have meant me. He must have thought I was one of his kids.

"Merek," I called out, as I gently pressed forward the door. He hadn't answered me, and my breath caught. A plopping noise came from the tub, as if he rinsed out his hair.

"Merek," I said louder, and the curtain slid open. That breath I held, I swallowed it whole and choked. Before me stood a god of a man with streams of water gracing his body in all manner of direction.

Can't breathe, my brain shouted.

Need to touch, my hands twitched.

"Emme," he struggled, wiping water from his face.

"I…" My thumb pointed over my shoulder, but it was the only motion I made. I couldn't speak. I couldn't draw air. I could only stare at toned muscles teeming with rivulets of water. I was so thirsty, so, so thirsty.

He leaned forward. The spray still hitting his back. His hands reached forward and gripped the front of my shirt. Instantly, my chest was soaked, and my mouth crushed. He was already taller than me but standing in the tub made him even taller. He bent his knees to scoop up my behind and drag me upward. I balanced on the edge of the tub, not breaking the connection of our lips and tongue.

"Oh God, are you a vision," he muttered.

"My God, you are," I mumbled, still keeping his lips underneath mine. My arms wrapped around his neck. The front of me soaked through from his wet body pressing against me. I kicked off my flip flops while his hands maneuvered my damp shirt over my head. He tugged me into the shower and slid the curtain closed.

"I was so worried about you," I said, brushing back tendrils of his hair which stood out all wet and wild.

"You were?"

"Yes." I nodded vigorously before his mouth crushed mine briefly. "You could have been injured. Or worst. And then you'd be lost to me, and I couldn't live without…" His mouth stopped my ramblings.

"I'm fine," he muttered over and over. "I'm okay."

I nodded, continuing to rub my hands over his body, affirming his presence.

"How worried were you?" His tone teased while his hands deftly unbuttoned my shorts and he pushed them toward the tub.

"Very, very," I eagerly replied, before taking his mouth back with mine.

"You're very, very wet," he teased.

"Yes, I am," I answered breathlessly. "Yes, I am."

He laughed knowingly.

"You're kind of a horny woman, Emme."

My hold released, and I stared up at him.

"Is that bad?" I asked, sheepishly.

"Are you crazy?" he laughed, placing his hands on either side of my face, and taking my lips once again.

Within minutes, the remainder of my soaked clothes were removed, and his hands roved over my body. Our palms rediscovered one another and I didn't shy away from the slow drag of his fingers over my curves. Those fingers found the place longing for him and my own wrapped tightly around him. Solid, velvet steel rested in my palm, ready to take me, and yet, he dragged out the foreplay, until I nearly fell over.

"Let's step out." He reached for the faucet and turned off the water. We stood in his bathroom only briefly facing each other before he spun me in the direction of the large mirror over his sink.

"See that," he said, pointing my attention to the naked reflection in the glass. "That is a beautiful woman."

I smiled despite myself, and his mouth nipped the juncture of my shoulder and neck. Sucking on me, my knees buckled, and I gripped the sink counter. His hands remapped my body until his fingers found a home and I came so quickly I screamed.

"I'm so tired," he said, "but I don't want to move. I want to watch you like this." Understanding his meaning, I leaned forward, letting the length of him drag over my backside. I wasn't as tall as him, and I lifted a knee to the counter to level with his height. He slipped into me instantly, and we groaned in unison at the long-awaited connection.

"Mother of all things holy," he moaned as he hammered in and out of me. The position allowed him to hit something deep inside me, but when his fingers returned to the achy nub of pleasure, I thought I'd take too long to crash again.

"No, I'm okay," I said brushing away his hand, and wanting him to take his own pleasure from me.

"I want two," he muttered, forcing his hand back to my center.

"I can't," I grunted as he filled me.

"You will." He teased, he toyed, and I gave in. The orgasm washed away my fears of his safety and our status. He joined me, filling me as he pulsed deep inside, matching the rhythm of my heart.

Chapter 33
Slow Burn

[M.E. 2]

We tumbled to my bed, replete from the bathroom acrobatics. I couldn't believe her flexibility at times. I couldn't believe she still wanted me. Opening the curtain, I thought I was dreaming. Her standing there all wide eyed, like she can be. How I wished I could read her mind. The wheels were always spinning inside her. But I instantly realized she'd come to me, and she stood in my bathroom full of concern for me, while I remained naked and wet, which was exactly how I wanted her to be.

She didn't deny me, and I was so thankful to have her in my arms, and in my shower. Making love to Emme was the last thing on my mind when I went to work the day before. In fact, the thing on my mind was the slow burn sparking between us. We'd done things backward like she said. We started with the fire but needed to step back from the blaze. Only from the moment I met her, there had been a spark. These days of walking and talking and breakfast dates were only increasing the flame, but I wasn't getting a sense of direction from her.

She was reserved while she teased. She'd make comments and retract them so quickly I didn't know what she meant. But here she lay in my arms, on my bed, in my home.

"Oh my God, where's Jacob?" I blurted, completely forgetting for a short time that I had children.

"He left for school. He told me to wait for you and he let me in," she said, twisting back her damp hair.

"What about Cassie?" I swallowed hard, recalling the fight Cassie and I had before I went to work last night.

"Jacob said she's out."

The mundane conversation seemed so real, so natural, like she was my wife, and I was getting a rundown of my children. The thought threw me off and I fell back on my pillow, staring up at the ceiling.

"You okay?" she whispered, bracing herself on her side, propping her head up with a hand.

The Sex Education of M.E.

"Yeah."

"Want to tell me about the fire?"

"It was your typical blaze that got out of control. More departments were called in and we were one of them. I..." I stopped. Explaining the ins and outs of my job seemed surreal, too. She was naked in my bed, and she asked about my day. The concept was so refreshing. I'd never had this before. I rolled my head to face her.

"What's happening here?" I asked, narrowing my eyes at her.

"I'm asking you about your day, and..."

"No. I mean us. What just happened? You here now. What is going on?"

"Well, I... I was worried, and I came over to see if you were home. Then I saw you in the shower and one thing led to another." She smiled, but it slowly disappeared from her face as her eyes lowered and her fingers played with the coarse hairs on my chest.

"One thing led to another?" I stated, shifting to my side to face her. "I like you, that's what happened." I brushed back a wet strand of her hair.

"I like you, too."

I waited for her line, but it didn't happen.

"Is this allowed?" I asked, smiling slowly.

"I hope so," she whispered, those blue eyes opened wide.

"Friends?" I nodded.

"With benefits?" she added, twisting her lips before they broke into a smile.

"How about the benefit is being your friend," I said.

"What about the rest?" Her eyes dipped to the hair she tickled on my chest.

"Maybe we could not define it for now. No labels. Just let it be."

She nodded slowly, her face falling in question, but I leaned forward and kissed her. Our mouths meshed, and her body twisted against mine.

"You seem insatiable," I said, pulling back from her as her body started to squirm against mine.

"Do you need to invest in those drugs? You know the ones *to put you in the mood or for erectile*—"

I cut her off with my mouth before pulling back. "I don't think I'll have any issue being in the mood for you. And as for the other thing, I'll show you how well it functions."

My body covered hers instantly, and her thighs opened wide, allowing me to prove myself to her. Yes, we were definitely more than friends with benefits.

Chapter 34
Teenage Boys

[M.E. 2]

"Where's Dad?" I heard Jacob ask Cassie while I prepared dinner for the three of us. Grilled steak was on the menu for this evening. I'd been outside but came back in the house to grab some tongs.

"He's outside, why?" Cassie answered.

"Don't you think it's strange he's having more sex than me?" My path to the utensil drawer stilled and I held my breath.

"He should be having more sex than you, Jake. He's an adult. Plus, we already know he's had tons of girlfriends." Cassie's voice hushed, and I strained to listen.

"Not girlfriends. Just friends." I could picture Jake in my head using air quotes to emphasis the friends of my past.

"Well, either way, you're only seventeen," she stated, sounding like the mother hen she could be toward Jake, despite her rebellious behavior toward me. Cassie definitely took on a second-in-command attitude with Jake, ranking her motherly position after my mother, who was the best example either of my kids had.

"Yeah, well, when will I have it like him?"

"Never, I hope," she snorted. "Old love is so…eww." I turned away from the drawer and crept closer to the kitchen entrance to the dining room. *What the hell was old love? And who was in love anyway?*

"I mean, when will I know when I've found the right girl? You know, the one I give it up to?" I paused, holding my breath in anticipation of Cassie's answer.

"You just know, Jake. It's just a feeling that it's the right person to share the experience. But you should definitely wait." I smiled to myself at the motherly wisdom.

"Why wait if it feels right, right now?" he asked. I twisted to lean against the door jamb, my arms folded as I listened.

"Who does it feel right with, Jake?" Cassie asked and when he didn't answer, she responded, "That's what I thought."

"But it will happen, right? I mean, I'll recognize the feeling?" he questioned so innocently.

"Yeah, Jake. I think it will just feel so different from any other person you've been with that you'll just know she's the one. The one you want to share time with, share yourself with. You'll know inside your heart, that you love her."

How did my Cassie get so wise? My mind slowly swirled with her words. *You'll know inside that you love her.* At one point, I thought I loved Janice. I thought love was just that hard, difficult, and painful. Then I realized what had been a moment of foolish lust became a nightmare of time spent trying to give what I didn't have, and she couldn't offer in return. I didn't know what love was, any more than my son. I only knew what it wasn't.

"Who told you all this? Did Dad in all his, Emme this and Emme that?" Jacob mocked. While my first thought was *I do not talk like that*, I worried that maybe I did, and the kids didn't like her.

"Grandma," Cassie stated, startling me, and I shivered. My mother, she had been a saint, raising two more children after her grown child effed up.

"Think Dad loved Mom?" Jake snorted.

"I don't know. Maybe he did."

"But she didn't," Jake said, softening his tone.

"No, I don't think Mom did," Cassie replied. They were silent for a second before Cassie spoke again. "Isn't it sad? Two people who don't love each other produced us. It's pathetic." I imagined Cassie shaking her head, with that famous look of disgust on her face I saw all too often lately.

"It's sad, that Mom didn't love us," Jake replied.

"Oh Jake, Mom loves us. She does. In her own way." They were silent again.

"Guess Dad gave it up to the wrong girl, huh?" Jake attempted to laugh.

"Well, I'm guessing Dad gave it up long before Mom, but…ew…let's not talk about that," Cassie teased.

"Think Emme is the right woman? I mean, I think he's giving it to her, a lot," Jacob emphasized the last word, and I was ready to intervene. Disrespecting Emme wasn't acceptable to me.

"I think Emme could be the right woman for Dad, if he let her in. He's been alone a long time, Jake. I don't know if Dad knows how to love like that."

And out of the mouths of teens, my sad life was summed up.

"Like what?" Jake asked.

"Date. Wine and dine. Meet the family."

"We've met her," Jake said.

"Yeah, but she's still a secret. He talks about her, but we don't know her."

"Do we need to know her?"

"If he's going to marry her, we should."

Whoa, whoa, whoa. First, they were talking love, now they're talking marriage. This had definitely gotten out of hand.

"I don't think Dad will marry her," Jake said. "He's not the marrying type."

Cassie laughed. "You sound like a woman. What's the marrying type?"

"You know, commitment and all that," Jake replied. Totally enthralled with their conversation about dear ole dad, I nearly fell through the kitchen and dining room opening.

"Jake, there's no one more committed to something than Dad, but love is different."

"Which leads us back to my initial question? How do you know?"

Cassie sighed, and I smothered a chuckle.

"Jake, you're just going to know, okay? You'll just know."

I stood taller now behind the entrance. The comment lingered with me. Would I know? It had been so long, and what I had with Janice hadn't been anything compared to how I felt with Emme. While I stood in my stupor, unclear if I could define love, Cassie's head peered around the corner.

"Did you hear it all?" she asked, sarcastic. Without thought, I reached out and pulled her toward me. It had been a long time since I hugged my daughter, but my love for her was something I definitely recognized.

Chapter 35
Rain Delays

[M.E.]

Merek and I lay entwined. My leg rested over his hip. His arm dangling over my waist. We were breathless, and still joined as one even though the moment had passed.

"Listen to that rain," I mumbled.

"Hmmm...I like the sound."

"I wish I didn't have to go," I said, risking sounding desperate and clingy. We'd continued to meet at his brother's place when we could. It was difficult to find alone time at our own homes, and Merek refused to pay for a hotel room, making what we had seem cheap.

"We'll keep using the apartment," he said, offering the use of his brother's place as if he owned it. But each night, we still had houses to return to, and children to attend. After years of sleeping, literally, with Nate, I'd gotten used to being alone in a bed, even with a partner. I missed snuggling and cuddling from years long ago. Nate wasn't a cuddler. Merek might not be either, but I risked my desire, nonetheless. I wanted to stay all night with him.

"Keeping the apartment sounds so clandestine." I laughed in response.

"It's so *Fifty Shades*," he replied.

"How do you know anything about *Fifty Shades of Grey*?" I laughed.

"I read. A lot," he said, stealing my line.

"That is not true." I lightly laughed again.

"Okay, someone told me."

The response immediately put me on edge. The only person who would mention such a thing would be another woman, and one rather familiar with the storyline. My mind raced, thinking this meant Merek knew more than just the apartment situation about a book famous for the BDSM lifestyle.

"Who?" I blurted out.

"Just someone." He shrugged to dismiss it, but I couldn't let it go.

"Am I enough for you?" I asked, letting my leg fall away from him. One of our phones binged a text notice in the background, but I ignored it.

"Emme," he warned.

"I mean it. Maybe this isn't enough for you. I mean, you're used to several different women in what, a week? And I have no idea the variety of things you've done, so maybe I seem kind of plain or tame compared to others. Not to mention, you've probably done it all sorts of places and we keep meeting here, like some sordid affair."

"Emme," his voice grew in agitation.

"I mean, what if you are into whips and chains, floggers and flexibility, ties and such."

He rolled away from me to lie on his back and stare at the ceiling. "Are you serious?"

"Yes." We remained silent for several minutes, letting the patter of rain mix with our thoughts. Lightning crashed in the distance.

"I don't like the idea of you driving home in this. I don't like the idea of you leaving me each night to go home alone. Emme, I haven't felt that way about anyone before. In the past, I wanted to leave when I was done. With you, it's not like that, so can we please stop with the comparisons."

"I'm sorry," I mumbled, and he rolled his head to look at me. He twisted his naked body to the side and reached for my face. Tender kisses sparked flickers of excitement. I turned into him and wrapped a leg over his hip.

"Again," he muttered as I ground against him. "I've created a monster." He laughed, but I pulled back.

"Too much?" In many ways, I questioned what was wrong with me. Why did I want him so much? Why didn't I feel like I'd had enough of him each time?

"Never. I like that you're insatiable," he said, letting the back of his fingers coast down my neck and brush lightly over one breast. My back arched, chasing the caress.

"If you don't want to…" My voice faltered as his knuckles continued down my center and rubbed back and forth over my waist.

In the distance, a phone binged again.

"Ignore it," he said. His fingers spread as he covered the mound of curls at the top of my legs. Fingertips tickled through the coarse hairs, then dragged lazily over sensitive folds. My hand went to his wrist, guiding him where I wanted him to go.

"Want to take over?" His rough voice croaked. "I'll gladly watch the show." The low tone sent a shiver through me, but the answer was no. I wanted his touch on me. My other hand trailed down his chest, but he stopped me.

"You're becoming too much for me," he said softly, and I thought he meant he couldn't go another round. He raised his fingers to his mouth, sucking them deep for a second, then returned to my center. Cool, moist digits entered me. He told me to hold onto the headboard. My other hand fanned out to my side and gripped the sheet.

"Take a deep breath," he said. "Now let it out slowly." I did as he said, concentrating on each motion. Air in, air out. Finger in, finger out.

"Close your eyes," he demanded softly. "Feel each sensation." His touch was so tender, my folds already sensitive from him being inside me. His fingers were lazy. Each movement exaggerated. The flutter began in my toes, crept up my legs and burst forth. Literally coming off the bed, I gripped the sheet and headboard, calling out his name. It had to be a record. I had three orgasms in a couple hours. That had never happened to me before.

I fell back so replete I didn't think I'd move for a week. The rain beat the window and my heart lowered to match the steady rhythm. My eyes drifted shut, and I breathed deep. A phone beeped again. Not moving in response, I sensed Merek rolling from the bed and fumbling through his jeans.

"Emme, pick up your phone."

My eyes flew open at the command in his tone. Ironically, he sat holding his own phone. I twisted lazily, reaching for mine on the nightstand.

Mom. I've been in an accident.

Chapter 36
Derailed

[M.E.]

We dressed in silence, rushing with our own thoughts. All we knew was Mitzi and Cassie had been together and they'd been in a car accident. Merek wanted me to ride with him, but then I'd have to come back for my car. I wanted control and driving my own vehicle was some small semblance of it.

Merek followed me, but I didn't look back. I raced for my first born, holding my breath as the text said nothing else. It was Merek who discovered which hospital they were taken to. I'd called Bree, who only knew that Cassie picked Mitzi up hours ago and they had not returned.

Entering Lutheran General, I rushed to the registration station, not waiting for Merek.

"Mitzi Peters," I blurted. Considered an adult to the hospital, as she was eighteen, I had to prove I was family. I followed the nurse's directions, going left at the nurse's station, then right to the third curtained area. My breath hitched as I stepped around the orange and yellow striped material.

"Mitzi?" My voice was hardly above a whisper as the swollen face of my daughter made me briefly question if I was in the correct place.

"Mom?" Her head rolled in my direction, but I sensed she couldn't see me clearly. I stepped forward and reached for her hand. "Oh, Mom." The tears fell instantly from two eyes already blackening.

"What happened?" I asked. I prided myself on always asking *are you all right* first. But it was clear she was not all right, so on to question number two.

"Cassie and I were at a party."

"On a school night?"

Ignoring my response, she continued.

"I told Cassie I needed to get home before you."

The silence hung.

"And?"

"We got in an accident." Her voice hesitated.

"Mitzi?" I asked softly.

"She only had one drink."

"Mitzi," I nearly shrieked. The tears streamed down her face, telling me now was not the time for the lecture that instantly came to my lips. She was only eighteen, and Cassie was too old to hang out with her, and on a school night, no less.

"I thought we'd be home before you ever knew," she muttered between sobs, as if getting caught was worse than the danger she'd been in. The air bag had done most of the damage to her, thankfully, but the thought of something worse, much, much worse, sent me into my own set of tears. I held Mitzi to me, afraid to let her go.

Doctors came and went. Tests were done. Mitzi was sent for x-rays. Taking a deep breath, I went in search of Merek. When I found him outside a curtained area a few beds down, I paused. He looked as old as I felt suddenly. His graying hair was a sign of his age; the worry he endured raising two children on his own. He'd lost his parents eventually, who had been his support system, and the mother of his children had given him the ride of a lifetime. None of it excused how I felt about his daughter at the moment.

"How's Cassie?" I asked. Merek stood with his arms crossed over his chest, one hand raised upward to cover his face. He stepped toward me, but I stepped back. His eyes shifted, questioning mine.

"She's getting examined by another doctor." His voice was cold. His eyes suddenly distant.

"What will happen?"

"What do you mean, what will happen?"

"She was drinking and driving. She endangered the life of a minor. She…"

"Endangered the life of a minor might be a bit strong." Merek's eyes narrowed on me. I hadn't witnessed this side of him before.

"Mitzi is barely eighteen." My defensive mama-bear claws were about to scratch.

"And she made the decision to go with Cassie." Merek stared at me, his expression incredulous. He had a point; I just couldn't see it clearly.

"Who should not have been taking her anywhere on a school night," I retorted.

"Cassie did not intentionally harm Mitzi." His tone changed. He practically growled.

"I didn't say she did it on purpose, but she's twenty-one, and Mitzi is not. She's a college student and Mitzi is not. She shouldn't have been drinking and driving."

"You don't think I know these things?" he snapped.

"I do. I just..." The words struggled to be released.

"You just what, Emme? Say it." His voice rose, and I looked around me to see if people were watching us. I don't know what I intended to say. I just didn't want this to be happening to my daughter, that's all. And for that fact, I didn't want it to be happening to his. Our girls were each hurting and arguing with each other wasn't going to stop their pain.

"I wasn't going to say anything else," I replied, lowering my tone and my eyes.

"But you want to, don't you? You want to tell me I'm a bad father. You want to say that if I had been home, this wouldn't have happened? Well, if I recall, you were with me," he barked. If we hadn't been at the apartment, fulfilling my fantasies of sex, he would have been home, and so would I. Would it have stopped the accident from happening? Maybe. Could it have happened at any other time? Quite possibly. I wasn't thinking clearly, though. I couldn't focus on the what-ifs or could-haves because the fact was, it had happened.

"Don't. Don't you dare say that to me. If it wasn't me, it would have been someone else." My lips clamped shut. Funny thing about words. Once they are out there, you can't take them back. A million sorrys and a thousand apologies do not reverse those things once released. I knew this to be true from all the little things Nate had said, and didn't say, over our twenty years together. You cannot take words back.

"I think it's best if we each deal with our own child tonight." He turned away from me.

"Me too," I agreed, even though I disagreed. Merek had come to mean a great deal to me, and while I was mad at the result of the accident, I wanted his support. I was upset that my daughter had been in an accident. I wanted someone to hold me, tell me she would be okay, and

I wanted it to be him. Biting my tongue, literally, I spun away from him and returned to Mitzi's curtain. It was only then that it hit me, he never asked about Mitzi. My head shook in disappointment. Maybe I was wrong about Merek, after all. Maybe it was just sex.

Chapter 37
Children Are a Hard Limit

[M.E.]

"I think children are a hard limit for me," I said to Gia three nights later, as she sat on my back deck in the cool, fall evening. Mitzi returned to school for half a day, and she was exhausted. I was paranoid as the reality of the accident hit me. She could have died. I could have lost another family member and I would have never forgiven myself for not being home. My guilt cup ran over, flooded the floor, and drained me.

"Honey, this could have happened at any time. You could have been home, and she could have said they were going to the mall, and then not gone," Gia chastised, recalling the ways of teenagers. A parent never gets the full truth of where they go.

"I'd just like to think that Mitzi knew better," I sighed.

"Mitzi knew you wouldn't like her going out with Cassie, to a college party, on a school night," Gia looked down the bridge of her nose at me, as if she wore glasses. "She's not stupid. She's responsible. But she's also young and foolish and things happen."

"Well, this could have cost her life," I admonished.

"It could have, but it didn't," Gia said, looking away from me. "How long are you going to hold it against her? And him for that fact?"

"What do you mean?" I asked, spinning to face her direction.

"You haven't returned his calls, have you?" Gia questioned.

"I hate that you know every move he makes."

"I don't know if he is or isn't calling you. What I know is you and I bet he is calling, and you aren't answering." She gave me her scolding look again. "And that fact that you hate I might know more about him than you, proves you care about him. You're interested."

Damn it. I hated that she was right. Merek had been calling me, and I hadn't responded to his calls. I was filled with disappointment at his lack of concern for Mitzi, when I had been interested in Cassie. I was disappointed that he hadn't agreed with my initial assessment: Cassie was in the wrong taking Mitzi to a party and drinking when she was underage. But mostly, I was disappointed in myself that I wanted one more orgasm from a sexy man, and I'd ignored my phone when my child needed me.

I exhaled deeply.

"If I date a man with children, how do I get past the difference in parenting beliefs? Parenting skills? Opinions?"

"You don't get past them; you accept them for what they are. Differences in opinion and skill."

"What if I don't love his children? What if I don't like them, even? What if they don't like me?" My voice rose with each question.

"Emme, who cares? Are you dating the child? No. Are you marrying the man?" She paused for effect. "I didn't think so. You're dating. You're trying each other out. Some things you'll agree on. Some you won't. You have to decide which ones you can live with and which ones you can't."

"Children are a hard limit. I can't live with ones who will be reckless with my child." I reached for my glass of wine and gulped the sweet fall taste of the red. I loved the change in season, which meant a change in temperature, clothing choices, and specialty flavors.

"Was Merek reckless with Mitzi?" She paused again. She was right. It wasn't Merek who caused the accident.

"Let's back up for a second. What if it wasn't Cassie? What if it was Kevin, her boyfriend?"

I snorted in doubt.

"Just hear me out," she continued. "The point is this was an accident. A senseless, risky accident, that could have been worse, but thankfully wasn't." She crossed herself. "And it could happen again, but God willing, it won't. Mitzi is a smart girl. She won't make the mistake of getting in a car with someone she questions has been drinking twice. She also won't try to go to a college party on a school night again. Or she might. She's eighteen, Emme. She's growing up."

Gia was right. In every word she sputtered was the truth, but I had trouble shaking my own guilt and the fear of what could have happened. My phone buzzed on the patio table, and I quickly reacted by flipping it to glance at the screen. Merek Elliott. I hit ignore.

"Stop ignoring him," Gia bit, irritated at my hasty action. "I've never known you to be like this."

"Be like what?" I snapped.

"Judgmental. He's trying to talk to you and you're shutting him out. Don't you think he's hurting, too? His child was in that accident. His child caused it. You want comfort and sympathy for what happened to Mitzi? Maybe he needs it for Cassie. You said he has fears she'll be like her mother. This is confirmation of his greatest fear, if she's drinking and driving and acting irresponsible. And he can't control her any more than you can control Mitzi. They are maturing adults that don't always have the judgment necessary to make good decisions."

I stared at my dark-haired friend, who was flirty and fun, and loved life more than anyone I knew.

"How did you get so wise?" I inquired. Her children weren't as old as mine.

"I remember being young," she remarked. I stared at her. Had I forgotten? Merek popped into my head; he certainly reminded me what it was like. The copious sex, the subtle attention, and the surprising compatibility was so refreshing, I felt young again. Was I making myself new? Yes, by living my life and taking the risk to be with Merek, but just like sex, this newness took two. Merek had been the key instrument to helping me experience what I wanted to experience in order to be young again. I couldn't lose him. I didn't want to let him go.

In front of Gia, I clicked on Merek's number. My eyes didn't leave hers as I stared her down and waited for the line to ring through to him.

Five. Six. Seven rings. I was ready to hang up when a breathy "hello" crossed the line.

"Merek," I said softly.

"Emme," he exhaled. The line remained silent after that, as if saying each other's name in recognition was all we had left to say to one another.

"How's Mitzi?" he asked, and the simple question chipped away at my hardened heart.

"She's sore but doing better. I made her go to school, so she doesn't get too far behind. She's exhausted. Maybe I pushed her too hard," I sighed, squinting up at the fading evening light. "How's Cassie?"

"She's grounded for life," he attempted to joke, but I didn't laugh in response. He choked through the phone. "She's sorry for what happened." Silence filled the line again. "I'm sorry, too," he breathed.

I sighed softly, my shoulders sagging. "Me, too," I whispered.

"Why are you sorry?" he asked, with a surprised tone.

"I said too much in my anger. In my fear." I paused and twisted my lips. I didn't know what else to say. Gia's eyes weighed on me, and when I gazed sideways at her, her lips tweaked into a small smile.

"Are you home?" he asked.

"Yeah, Gia's here."

"Can we come over?"

My eyes shot up to Gia. "Who's *we*?"

"Cassie and me. She has something to say. I'd appreciate it, if you'd hear her out."

My heart thudded in my chest. My eyes still connected with Gia's as she questioned me, mouthing: *What?*

He wants to come over with Cassie, I mouthed back. Her smile deepened as she sat back in the chair with a thud. She slowly shook her head in disbelief as she stared out into my yard.

"Okay."

They arrived roughly ten minutes later. Cassie moved with slow, exaggerated steps and the second she saw the black and blue marks on Mitzi, she burst into tears. Reaching out for Mitzi, they hugged like long lost friends. Cassie muttered her apology over and over into Mitzi's shoulder and Mitzi stroked Cassie's hair. My heart shattered at the sorrow. I had to believe the accident scared Cassie as much as it frightened Mitzi.

When the girls pulled apart, Cassie glanced at her dad before facing me. Tears still slipped down her face as she took a deep breath.

"I wanted to say how sorry I am for what happened. It was stupid. I should have never been drinking and attempting to drive home. Mitzi was so worried she'd get in trouble, and I didn't want her to be late. I wasn't thinking." She gazed over at her dad.

"Please, don't be mad at my dad," she started.

Merek's mouth popped open. "Cassie," he warned.

"It's not his fault. It's mine. I know it. It was my mistake, so please don't take it out on him."

"Cassie," Merek choked.

"I haven't ever seen him like this. He smiles all the time. He's always talking about you. He's…happy. Don't be mad at him," she pleaded.

"Cassie," Merek stammered again then interrupted her plea. "This isn't why we came here," he addressed me, his voice full of confusion. We stared at one another. My eyes noticed the dark circles under his and the addition of wrinkles around them. Worry was written on his face and the irritation with Cassie's outburst etched over his forehead. He rubbed it, shaking his head in frustration. Suddenly, his head snapped upward.

"Cassie wanted to apologize," he said. "I wanted to see that Mitzi was doing better."

In all the time they'd been there, I hadn't said a word. It was as if my mouth couldn't form a syllable. I didn't know what to say to either of them.

"I'm feeling better," Mitzi offered, a tear slipping from her eye. "I'm sore and I'm tired, but I'm doing better," she said to Cassie and Merek before looking over at me. We still stood just inside my living room, hardly out of the front entrance.

"Cassie's license has been suspended. She's enrolling in therapy," Merek added.

"Dad," Cassie admonished, her eyes lowering at the mention. Merek's lids closed in defeat.

"I think it's very brave of you to face your issues," I said to Cassie, surprising us all. Merek's eyes shot open. Cassie's head popped up. Mitzi's face softened. "It's very hard to face our fears, sometimes. It's even harder to admit we have them," I said, glancing in the direction of Merek, but afraid to meet his eyes. "Sometimes we just have to plow forward, to work past the past."

Cassie stared at me, her head slowly nodding. I didn't know what else to do, but to reach forward and hug her to me. She was stiff at first, arms dangling at her side. I only intended a quick embrace, but when I pulled back, her arms encircled my waist and she held me to her. My hand dropped to rub up and down her back, and I felt the words more than I heard them whispered: "I'm sorry."

I glanced at Merek over his daughter's head.

Thank you, his tear-filled eyes spoke to me.

Chapter 38
Hostile Takeover

[M.E. 2]

On Friday night, I didn't have to work. I looked forward to some long overdue sleep. Emme had forgiven Cassie, but she wasn't exactly forthcoming in mending the fences with me. She answered my calls, but the conversation was stilted and brief. I didn't like it. I didn't know how we'd work through it. This was the messy part I wanted to avoid. Even if Cassie and Mitzi hadn't been in the accident together, there could have been something else. Something that exposed my children, my biggest vulnerability. When Emme hugged Cassie, I knew how I felt about her. The realization hit me like a wave. I could love her. She was a good woman, with a compassionate heart, and I wanted to feel that daily.

But she hadn't forgiven me.

"Dad, let's go out for dinner," Jake surprised me. Friday was the night I ordered pizza and watched whatever game was available while my children enjoyed a social life. Later, I'd find my brother at Bruno's and, in the past, find a woman to bury myself in before returning home. I lived a dual life. It had been easier when I lived with my mother, and Jake was taken care of in my absence. Living in our new home, without another adult, I slowly became more conscious of how and when I did things. After hearing Jake and Cassie's discussion a few weeks ago, it was clear to me that they knew more than I realized.

"Where do you want to go?" I asked, staring at the television. I'd been home more often than not, finding things to do around our new home, attempting anything to keep myself busy and my mind free of Emme.

"Dad," Cassie snapped, "change your clothes. Put on your dark jeans and that plaid shirt you like so much." I stared in disbelief at the recommendation. Cassie hated my purple plaid shirt with the white button snaps. She said it made me look like a hillbilly biker dude. Jake glared at Cassie while she smiled at me.

"What's going on?" I leaned over the arm of the leather lounger.

"Just get dressed," Cassie said again, holding her smile a little too firmly. "Don't forget your cowboy boots."

Jake's eyes closed and he shook his head. His hand came to his forehead in this way he had when he was flabbergasted with his sister's ignorance. He looked up at me, continuing to shake his head.

"I knew this wouldn't work." His eyes focused on mine.

"What are you two up to?" I laughed, sitting forward in the chair, twisting to face them both.

"Hostile takeover," Jake stated. Cassie glared at him. My questioning glance shifted from one to the other of my children.

"Just get dressed, Dad," Cassie demanded softly. "Dark jeans, purple plaid and cowboy boots. Don't ask questions." The tone of her voice reminded me of my mother when she'd tell the kids to do something. I chuckled at the similarity. I'd missed my parents greatly this week, especially my mom, who was more of a mother to Cassie and Jake than their own. I stood and followed directions.

Fifteen minutes later, we pulled up in front of Emme's house. Jake drove my truck and the two of them eagerly exited. They walked confidently up to her front door and rang the bell.

"Pizza," Jake called out, knocking on the door. Emme's daughter, Bree, opened it. I followed slowly behind, not certain why we were here.

"She's not cooperating," Bree flapped her arms as she spoke when I reached the top of the front stoop. I entered their front hall feeling shaky and highly nervous.

"What is going on?" I asked, more gruffly than I intended. Emme rounded the corner of her living room, stopping short when she saw me. Her hair was pulled up in a messy twist. She wore a heavy sweatshirt with shorts. Her make-up was minimal. She looked beautiful.

"Merek?" she questioned. "What's going on here?" She looked from one to the other of us. My shoulders shrugged; I was just as clueless as her.

"Kidnapping," Jake stated.

"Surprise," Mitzi interjected, a smile beaming from her still off-colored, bruised face.

"Now, get freaking dressed," Bree said, slapping her hands on her thighs, clearly frustrated with her mother. Emme stared at me, questioningly.

"I have no idea." I held up my hands in surrender.

"You two are going out," Cassie stated. "Rowdy's."

My head shot up. "How do you know about Rowdy's?" Concern that Cassie had been to the famous country bar in Wrigleyville was evident in my tone. Known for their line dancing and beer specials throughout Cub season, Rowdy's was a place I'd frequented a while ago.

"It's one of your favorite places for country music," Cassie shuddered.

"I love country music," Mitzi added. "Everyone knows about Rowdy's."

"I don't dance," Emme stated, crossing her arms over her chest.

"First time for everything," Mitzi stated. "Like going on a real date," she leaned in conspiratorially toward her mother. Emme stared at her oldest, and then slowly glanced around the room with an exasperated expression of defeat on her face.

"I don't think this is a good idea," she stated.

It was my turn to stare. I wasn't taking her out, if she didn't want to go anywhere with me.

"I think I better..." I started.

"Stay right there," Cassie demanded.

"Because she's getting dressed," Mitzi commanded, placing an arm around her mother and pushing her toward the staircase.

"I think..." Emme said.

"This is a great idea," Jake and Bree interjected. We all stilled, and then burst into laughter. The tension was thick and awkward, and even the laughter stifled a little, but it was helping.

"Fine," Emme said, like a petulant child, and I cringed at the word. She shook off her daughter and headed for the staircase.

Fifteen minutes later, her hair was down. She wore a floral print dress covered by a jean jacket and a pair of flip flops.

"You can't dance in those," I said, slowly rising from the couch where I'd been waiting. I felt like a schoolboy on my first date. Eyes on the boy, worried he'd attack the girl. I wanted to attack. I wanted to kiss that look of distrust off her face, then pin her to the wall and screw some sense into her. I wanted her, period.

"I don't have cowboy boots."

"I have the perfect pair," Bree offered and ran up the stairs, returning immediately with a worn brown pair with turquoise designs. Emme slipped them on and stood upright, flipping back her hair.

"I look ridiculous," she stated.

"You look beautiful," I muttered, and all eyes were suddenly on me. Emme bit her lip, and the awkward tension returned to the room.

"Okay, kids," Jake said, clapping his hands. "No shenanigans. Don't stay out too late. I want her home at a respectable time. Keep distance between you when you dance. And no fraternizing with the patron."

I rolled my eyes.

"That didn't even make sense," Bree laughed.

"Okay," Mitzi interjected. "Have fun."

Forget it, this was more awkward then being a teenage boy meeting the parents. The scrutiny of children had to be twenty times worse.

"What are you going to do?" Emme asked, narrowing her eyes at Mitzi.

"We are going to stay right here," Cassie offered, wrapping an arm around Mitzi. "Pizza is coming in thirty minutes. Jake has his Chrome device. We aren't going anywhere."

Emme needed that reassurance because her shoulders relaxed. She nodded her head at Cassie and turned to face me. Doubt and concern were written on her face, and my heart crumbled at the apprehensive vibe radiating from her body.

Chapter 39
Line Dancing or Crossing the Line

[M.E.]

The ride to Rowdy's was tense. The radio low, the music was a sultry country tune. I didn't recognize any of the lyrics. Merek asked a sporadic stream of questions about Mitzi, and about the new semester. I'd wanted to take days off to sit with her, but I couldn't start the semester already missing classes. Those first days set the tone. Gia had been a lifesaver, as she came to my home after her kids went to school. Her shift rotated at the hospital, and she only had the one course at the university. We worked out a schedule to monitor Mitzi for days.

Cassie was in my sophomore level English class, and while I initially thought it would be a conflict of interest, the way things were going with Merek, I changed my opinion. She hadn't been present the first week of class anyway, and I excused her, assuming she was still recovering like Mitzi.

As we drove closer to Lake Shore Drive, Merek gave up on conversation. Not forthcoming in offering information, I wasn't asking any questions in return. When we hit the Drive, I just enjoyed the ride. Lake Shore Drive lines the shore of Lake Michigan, splitting the coastline from the cityscape. Its peaceful rhythm in the growing darkness mesmerized. City lights lined the drive, as we drew closer to the towering structures, but off to the side rolled the subtle, dark waves of the lake.

"If you really don't want to do this, I can turn around," Merek finally said, breaking into my empty thoughts. "But I'd feel guilty if we were back too early. They seemed to have put some thought into this." Collectively, our four children had plotted this fiasco of an evening. I was already in my comfy clothes, ready for a date night with a book and a large glass of wine.

"They were only trying to be nice," Merek said, running a hand over his wrist, where he wore a small, beaded bracelet. Gazing sideways at him, he was the epitome of country masculine. He only missed a baseball cap or a cowboy hat, and the look would have screamed country superstar. He looked so good. My heart raced while I risked glances at him as he drove. That plaid shirt hugged his solid form. His jeans were snug on his thighs. He looked calm, while I was a bundle of nerves. I wanted to relax, and yet I couldn't seem to let go.

"I know," I said, softly, looking away from him. I had to look away. Looking at him brought on a wave of regret. Not at what we'd done, but at what we didn't have. I missed him. I missed his smile. His laugh. His hand in mine. His touch.

"Look, how about if we go for an hour. That's plenty of time to fool them, and then we can go back." His proposition was so straightforward, like he'd been considering it the whole time we rode. He didn't want to be with me, and my shoulders sagged. I wanted to turn back time, but I didn't know how. I didn't know how to wipe away the absence of days from him and the tension over Cassie and Mitzi. Although she'd apologized, I didn't know how to let the situation go. I didn't really need to forgive Merek, as Gia said. He hadn't done anything wrong. I just didn't know how to let go of the past.

We parked at a firehouse a few blocks away and walked to the bar. Merek's stride was long and quick, like he was racing, attempting to speed up time and end this misery. He practically stormed down the busy street, and I struggled to keep up, skipping at times to catch up to him. We drew near the corner of Addison and Clark, and the historic Cubs' stadium was lit up for a night game. Merek reached for my hand, holding it firmly as our pace slowed and we wove through the fan crowd. We neared Rowdy's, a bar I'd never even heard of before tonight, and Merek moved to the front of the line.

"Merek Elliott," the bodyguard acknowledged, slapping hands with Merek before pulling him forward for a guy hug. Merek smacked the back of the burly man.

"Let us in?" Merek questioned. He reached for my hand again. The burly man's eyebrow rose in surprise.

"It's crowded in there," he stated, his eyes widening, as if he was trying to tell Merek something.

"We'll be okay," he said, drawing me forward, and securing me before him. He moved his hands to my hips and nudged me toward the door. It opened with a firm pull, and the music nearly slapped me in the face. Loud, twangy sounds filled the red backlit bar. The place pulsed with a youthful, bouncy sound and the dance floor moved like a rhythmic, living organism. It shifted forward and back, then swung to the side and repeated a synchronized motion. Merek still had my hips and maneuvered me to the bar.

"Merek," the bartender called over the crowd, and Merek released his hold on me to reach over the bar and high-five the young man behind the large wooden structure. He nodded toward me.

Merek yelled, "Emme." I looked from Merek to the bartender, who winked at me.

"How about something stronger than white zinfandel?" His lips lowered to my ear so he could be heard over the music.

"Sure. Margarita, on the rocks with salt," I suggested. I had no idea what to order. A country bar screamed buy-a-beer, but I wasn't a beer drinker.

"Rita on the rocks and a whiskey straight up," Merek yelled over the heads of people leaning on the bar. His hands returned to my hips. While we waited for our drinks, my eyes observed the wood décor, red haze, and country vibe of the place. It was rather addicting, and the beat of the music was slowly loosening me up. I took my margarita and Merek knocked my glass with his. He swallowed the shot in one gulp while I took a hefty sip of my tart and salty drink.

"Let's dance," he said, ignoring the fact that my margarita had a long way to go before it was finished. He removed my drink from my grasp and handed it back to the bartender. Taking my hand, he led me to the floor. My discomfort built.

"Merek, you know I don't dance. I don't know how to do any of this." I tugged back on his hand. He stopped.

"Emme, there comes a point where you have to trust me." His tone was serious, the implication clear that he meant more than dancing. "I'm not going to lead you astray or do anything to embarrass you. Just take my hand and follow my lead. Take a chance." His eyes were intense as he stared back at me. He still held my hand, and I squeezed his fingers in acceptance. He guided me to the back of the line.

"Just follow what everyone is doing. Don't worry if you mess up. Just go with it."

The Sex Education of M.E.

I nodded, suddenly more frightened of this bar and dancing in public than I was with my propositioning Merek about sex. Sensing my apprehension, his hand still held mine as he kicked forward, then back. He stepped side to side, and I followed as best I could. I laughed while I stumbled and tripped. And each time I did, to my surprise, Merek wrapped an arm around my waist, straightening me, and redirecting me. Reassuring me. We fell into this rhythm of messing up and laughing at my failed attempts. Once in a while I went right instead of left and stepped on his foot. His arms encircled my waist again as I staggered between his legs, and we tried to catch up to the moves.

After three songs, the rapid rhythm rested, and the tempo lowered. A slow song filled the sound system, and Merek pulled me toward him.

"Dance with me." His arm wrapped around my back, resting above my behind. His other hand reached for mine and pulled it up between us. We pressed against one another, and he kissed my forehead as Sam Hunt's crooning sound slowed the bar. Merek twirled me slowly. His hips swaying steadily, reminding me too much of compromising positions with him. My body relaxed into the steady pace he set. My head rested on his shoulder. He embraced me tighter. The music spoke for us.

Taking time.

Getting to know someone.

Smiling like that.

The song finished, but we remained swaying. Merek's hand released mine and slid down my body to surround my back with his other arm. My hand slipped up his chest to circle around his neck. I pressed into him, pulling him tight against my body. We stood like this while the red-light haze returned, and the music roared back to life. Merek and I were caught in an intense gaze, asking questions of one another. His head lowered. My toes tipped upward.

"Merek?" A screeching sound came from my left. "Merek Elliott, is that you?" I turned in time for a woman to leap at Merek. Releasing me, he caught her in his arms. Her feet off the ground, they wrapped around his waist as her arms circled his neck. She pulled back abruptly, looking at his face.

"I knew it was you. Where've you been? I've missed you."

I'd stepped out of the way of this reunion, noting Merek's hands held her by her ass, holding her against him. He jostled her like he could drop her, and then he stopped. His hands released her quickly and she slid down his body. His hands rose, like he surrendered. The woman clung to him. His head rotated. His eyes wide. He reached for me, but I shook my head infinitesimally, taking a second step back. His hands came to the woman's arms and removed them from his neck, pressing her back.

I spun and bounced off a hard body behind me.

"Professor Peters?"

"Lance?" I gasped. Lance Webber was a former student of my Writing 201. He was incredibly good looking, with short, dark hair, trim scruff, and a tender expression in his eyes. His warm hands engulfed my tiny arms with thick fingers. He swayed on his feet.

"Professor Peters!" A drunk slur hissed in my ear behind me.

"Grant," I whispered, another equally good-looking young man from Writing 201. His blue eyes smiled at me. His mouth opened enough his tongue sliced over lush lips. Gia wanted me to proposition one of my students once. Not only would it have been unethical, I didn't have the courage to be a cougar; but if I did, Grant Mullens would have been the man to seduce. His body language screamed *I like to have sex*. His smile seduced. His voice rolled over a woman's body in a tone that made her want to undress herself.

"Professor Peters, come dance with us," Grant said, placing his hands on my hips from behind, and tugging me back against him.

I was old enough to be the mother of these men, or close enough, but a lusty look from either of them, and I might forget myself for a while.

Lance still held my arms to steady me, or possibly him.

My brain finally caught up to what happened before me. Merek had run into an old lover. Someone who may have been a regular. Someone who might have been a one-night stand. It didn't matter. His comfort in this bar proved he'd been here frequently. And it pissed me off.

I nodded my acceptance and the three of us danced through the remainder of the song. My hips swayed in rhythm with the man behind me, while one of Lance's wrists rested lazily over my shoulder. My body was led into a seductive roll between the men, and I reveled in the attention, momentarily forgetting Merek and his reunion with a floozy.

"Emme." Merek's sharp voice reached me over the twangy music. Ignoring him at first, his hand enveloped my waist and pulled me from the college student sandwich. I collided with his body, but he held me tight against him. Softened dark eyes and a questioning expression speared me to the dance floor.

"Hey," Grant said, "get your own girl, old man."

Merek's hand gripped Grant's t-shirt without releasing me. "I have a girl." He shoved Grant back and Lance stepped between the men.

"Back off, Grant," my young protector warned.

Chapter 40
Side Streets Sidetrack

[M.E. 2]

"Yes, back off, Grant." My deep voice was full of venom. Steam practically spilled out of my ears. Was she trying to make me jealous? After Melissa jumped at me? Emme reached out a hand, raising it to separate me from this awkward situation. I reached for that hand and tugged her back to me. We'd only taken two steps when Grant's voice flitted toward us.

"Damn, I'd tap that."

I nearly tore her arm out of the socket, twisting back with a raised fist for this Grant guy. She tugged hard, as a counterbalance to my efforts, almost falling backward in her attempt to stop me.

"He's drunk, just let him be," she argued, holding fast.

"Do you know him?" My first thought was she'd been with another man while she'd been with me. Someone younger. Then I remembered, this was Emme. She swallowed hard, frightened to tell the truth.

"Emme," I demanded, and she flinched.

"They're former students."

"And he fucking wants to *tap you*," I snarled, spinning to face her. "Is he who you want?" I sounded like a deranged man. We were making a scene in the middle of the dance floor, and I didn't care.

"I want to go home," she snapped. "Just take me home." I stopped straining. Her words crushed me. The night was ruined. I thought we were finally getting somewhere. Longing to reconnect with her, I thought we were finally making progress when the moment was ruined by that stupid girl. Melissa. I barely remembered her name, and I didn't want to remember any part of her. Just like I didn't want these college punks thinking anything about Emme, especially *tapping* her.

Slipping my fingers through hers, I led her out of Rowdy's. I'd practically raced to Rowdy's, praying the atmosphere would break the tension between us. Our current pace was turtle-slow compared to that earlier rush. With each step, I felt like a dead man walking. One step closer to losing her, each step we took. We remained silent until we were almost to the fire department parking lot. I dragged her down a side street and tugged her hand to halt.

"I can't do this." My voice gently pleaded. My lips twisted in frustration when she spun to face me. "I don't like where this is going."

"I thought we were going home," she said, innocently.

"Not literally, Emme. Just us. Where are *we* going? I'm going crazy without you. I don't know what's happening to me. I'm forty-two years old and I feel like a teenager in the throes of first love."

She stared at me, blinking in surprise. No words responded to mine. Frustrated, I ran a hand over my hair.

"You were holding that girl," she said, softly, looking me directly in the eye.

"Those boys wanted to fuck you," I retaliated.

"They were drunk college kids."

"She's from the past," I sighed. We were at an impasse for a moment.

"There are so many of them, aren't there?" she whispered.

"The past is always going to be there, Emme. Always. I can't take it back. I can't erase it. I can't make it go away. All I can do is move forward, which I've been doing for seventeen years, since Janice left me with Jacob and Cassie. Day by day, then month by month. Do you know what that's like?"

She nodded, but I didn't let her speak. "I don't want to keep looking back," I sighed, shaking her hand in mine. "I only want to go forward."

My heart raced, my pulse beat in my throat choking out the words I wanted to say, so instead I said, "Everything is getting so fucked up. It's why I didn't date. I didn't share myself or my kids with someone. It's messy, but you said you wanted messy. Why do I feel like messy is more complicated than you expected? Too overwhelming for you? It's freaking suffocating me!" My voice rose with each question, filling the otherwise silent dark street with my defeat.

"I don't want to suffocate you," she said, still keeping her voice low. Her hand released from mine, and I walked a step away, spun around and returned to face her.

"You're not suffocating me, Emme. You're breaking my heart."

The words hung heavy in the fall air

"How?" she asked, completely confused.

"You keep running away from me. You shut down when something happens, like with Cassie and Mitzi. We needed to work through that together, not apart." I sighed. I regretted what happened with Cassie, and while I briefly wanted my mother who always had the right answers, I needed Emme. She seemed like a woman who could support me with my struggles and fears for Cassie. She was a great female role model, and Cassie was missing the only motherly figure she had, my mother.

"I'm...I'm sorry. I'm just used to being alone. Working through things by myself. Handling things on my own. Feeling alone," she answered. I understood.

"Me, too," I exhaled. "But I don't want to be alone anymore."

She stared at me once again, my words holding us in place. The silence fell between us. When I couldn't take the pressure weighing on my chest, I said, "I'll take you home. This whole night has been one big..."

"Mistake?" she whispered. My heart crushed and crumbled down to the sidewalk.

"I was going to say disaster. One disaster after another."

"You seemed like you wanted it over," she stated. "You rushed to Rowdy's."

"I just wanted to speed this night up..."

"To finish it," she interrupted.

"To start it," I said, at the same time.

Surprising her one more time, I cupped her face, staring into her eyes for a moment. The intense, questioning emotion flitted between us again, like when we stood on the bar dance floor before Melissa interrupted. Emme looked away first, but I tugged her to me.

"Don't run," I begged, holding her tight against my chest. "Don't do it."

I was losing her. I could feel it with every fiber of my being. She was slipping away from me. The kids setting up this date, threw us off. We were forced into this awkward situation, and we should have gone some place quiet to talk. Instead, I rushed to Rowdy's. I thought the easygoing surroundings would break the tension, and for a while, it did.

The Sex Education of M.E.

Touching her was driving me insane and I just wanted to drag her off to the back hall and bury myself inside of her. I wanted to reignite the spark in her that seemed immune to me.

Then that stupid girl leapt for me. For a second, I lost my head, blindsided by her, I held her up against me. We'd had a night or two together, but that was months ago. She wasn't as eager to see me again then, as she was tonight. It ruined the moment for Emme and I. That intense moment we had when she finally wrapped her arms around me and she let me pull her close. I wanted to feel that connection with her again, and I didn't know how to regain it.

We drove in silence back toward the neighborhood. My hand didn't leave hers. I was afraid to release her. Afraid that if I let her fingers go, she would walk away—abandon me when I finally found someone like her.

"I already told you Nate had an affair," she broke the silence. My thumb rubbed up and down the back of her hand. "What I didn't tell you was that I caught him." I risked a quick glance at her while I drove.

"He was making all these crazy excuses. Working late. Going in on Saturday. All practical excuses, if it had been tax season. But it wasn't. Then one night I heard him on the phone late at night. It was three in the morning. I couldn't make out what he was saying, but I heard his voice. Tender. Sweet. He didn't use that tone with me." She took a breath.

"A few weeks later, I picked up his phone. The screen was locked but a text message appeared. She missed him. Whoever she was, she missed him. A quick search of his recent calls showed hundreds to one number." She continued to stare out the front window.

"I don't want to ever feel again, the way I felt then. The helplessness. I had put my career on hold to raise our children who were still younger than toddlers. I had nothing. Even with Nate, I had nothing. I vowed that my children would be my focus. I would devote myself to them. It was the reason I took Nate back even after the woman called our home and played a tape of them together."

"My children came first for nearly eighteen years, Merek. And I'm being selfish, but I want me back. I wanted something for me, that wasn't related to Nate or the girls. I wanted to be wanted. Can you understand that need?" She swiped at her cheek to clear a tear. I could understand her, maybe more than she knew.

"Seeing that woman in your arms was like a cold splash of water. A wake-up call. While I knew there were others, this was so visibly in my face."

"The past, Emme," I interrupted her. "The past."

"In my head, I know that. Just like with Cassie and Mitzi. I know you had nothing to do with what happened. I actually blame me. If I had been home, she would not have gone out. If I had been home, she could have called me. She knew I was out with you. She didn't want to ruin it. She didn't want me to worry. I put my child at risk because I wanted to be wanted."

"Emme, no. No, that's not what happened." My thumb pressed harder, and I pulled over to the side of the road.

"Look at me." My hand came to her chin, forcing her to face me. My thumb swiped a tear by her lips. "This wasn't either of our faults. We're adults, and we also deserve to be adults. We deserve…things. There are a million scenarios to prevent what happened, but none of them involve us, because this could have happened another way, another day."

She nodded, agreeing with me. "I'm frustrated, and I'm caught between what I think I deserve and what I think I should do."

"What you should do is reach for what you deserve. They should be the same thing." I didn't know Nate Peters, but he didn't sound like a great man. While I'd never be perfect, I couldn't see how his lack of attention made him an honorable husband. Having an affair clearly dishonored Emme, but his unfaithfulness had nothing to do with me. What I did know of relationships was that trust was built, and that took time. And I wanted that time with Emme.

"Just take me home," she muttered as another tear fell. Her body language let me know she shut down. She turned away from me. The Emme I had experienced, the one who strived to take what she wanted, was closed off in the woman sitting next to me. I pulled back into traffic and headed for the neighborhood.

Chapter 41
Home

[M.E.]

"What are we doing here?" I snapped, as we pulled up in front of Merek's house.

"We're going inside my house. You're going to take me up on my offer for a ride. On me. Then we're going to make love and make up with one another." The words were definitive, and he exited the truck before I could speak. He came around the vehicle quickly and opened my door.

"Why are we at your house?" I couldn't even comment on his directive for what we were about to do.

"Because I'm tired of pretending. I want you in my bed. In my house." He reached for my hand and tugged me forward. I should protest. My brain screamed to stop. Be rational. Question his motives. My body, however, cried out to lose control. I followed his lead to the sidewalk where we were suddenly stopped by a white haired, older woman walking her dog.

"Ms. Carmichael," Merek addressed her. "Good evening."

"Hello, Mr. Whittington." She flirtatiously spoke his name. "What a lovely night." She looked up at the stars before returning to face us.

"Am I finally meeting the Mrs. Whittington?" she asked in my direction. Merek squeezed my hand as he answered.

"Ms. Carmichael, you know I'm not married," he teased.

"Well, then who's this tart?" Feigned shock rang out her elderly voice with a faint smile and a wink at me.

"My girl...," Merek said, cutting himself off while squeezing my hand a second time, and shaking his head in dismay.

"You said you weren't available," she shrieked, in mock horror, her hand covering her heart.

"I'm not," he said, and looked at me, bringing my hand to his mouth, and kissing it.

"Ah, so you'll be Mrs. Whittington soon?" She winked at me.

"Oh, I don't…" Merek leaned forward toward this quirky old woman, stopping me. He cupped his hand like he was about to tell her a secret. Whispering loudly, he said: "She doesn't know that yet."

Ms. Carmichael covered her mouth in surprise, then laughed before looking up at me. Her eyes softened and she smiled like she knew a secret, as if I hadn't just heard their conversation. She shook the dog's leash and walked around us.

"You know you just started a rumor," I said, stumbling behind him as he nearly dragged me down the side path of his house. He didn't answer me.

"You've been tugging me all over tonight. First down the street toward the bar, then in the bar. Why are you pulling me all over like you're in a rush to get—"

His mouth crashed mine as soon as we were in the door. Our lips argued, biting and nipping. He was right. We were both angry and frustrated.

"I was in a rush," he said, pulling away slowly, but keeping his mouth mere millimeters from mine. "I've been racing toward this moment tonight. The one where I have you alone." His mouth covered mine again, this time slowing in pace to savor my lips from top to bottom.

"Emme, if I don't get my mouth on other parts of you soon, I'm going to spontaneously combust." I chuckled at the severity of his comment, but his mouth covered mine again as if he absorbed the laughter, devoured it for its flavorful essence.

He maneuvered us toward the stairs, hardly releasing my lips as we moved. At the base of the staircase, he released me, then took my hand and climbed the stairs. He was no longer tugging but leading me.

We entered his room and he sat on the edge of the bed. His hands roamed upward over my body, removing the jean jacket. His head came forward to rest against my abdomen and my arms wrapped around him. We remained like this for a moment before his mouth covered my breast over the material of my dress. Reaching for the thin straps, he slipped the dress down my body to pool on the floor. I stood before him in a strapless bra, boy short underwear, and borrowed cowboy boots. Standing abruptly, his presence forced me to step over the dress while he dragged his shirt out of his jeans, then he pulled it over his head. He kicked off his boots and removed his jeans.

"Take off the rest," he demanded, seductively. "Leave the boots on...for now."

My body trembled with excitement at his commanding voice. My core screamed for me to follow orders. He sat back on the bed in only his boxers. Then he lay back, watching as I removed my underwear and bra. The sense of exposure was overwhelming. I'd never stripped before anyone like this and the need to cover myself was powerful. But the lust in his eyes gave me the confidence to continue.

"Climb me," he commanded, his hands crossing behind his head. I straddled his hips, but one hand on my hip encouraged me to move upward.

"Higher," he demanded. I walked on my knees over him to cover his chest.

"Remember what I said in the truck?" His voice was like water over river rocks. "You're taking this ride, Emme. Because you can trust me." With that he slipped his body lower, and my core covered his face. We did what he directed, and I've never felt more wanton, more sexually carefree, in my life. His heavier stubble against my thighs added to the sensory overload of his tongue between sensitive folds while I rode his face. I fell forward, unable to hold my own weight. On hands and knees, he devoured me, and I screamed his name in relief. He was correct. We were angry and frustrated, and this physical release drained the negative energy out of me.

Within seconds, he flipped me and covered my body. Lifting my hips, he slammed into me while my backside rested against his thighs. He balanced above me on his knees, moving my body in the way he wanted to give him the satisfaction he desired. His thumb came between us as he slid aggressively in and out of me. The friction on that sensitive nub, sparked a new fire. The tender tingles rose from my toes.

"Merek," I choked, knowing I was about to implode.

"Come on, darlin'. I'm so deep inside. I want to feel you explode around me." His demanding tone took me over the edge again and then he stilled. The pulse of him inside of me set off a wave of aftershocks. My orgasm didn't seem to be ending. My knees clamped at his sides, holding him in me. His grip on my hips was so tight I was sure I'd see fingerprints later. Filled to the hilt had new meaning to me. There was no way to tell where he ended, and I began.

Slowly, he released my hips, lowering them to the bed. He slipped out of me and fell to his back. An arm came over his face, covering his eyes. We both exhaled rapidly, filling the room with our heavy breathing.

"I think I just saw another universe," he said, breathlessly.

"What?" I softly laughed.

"You make me see stars, Emme, but that was so intense, I think I just discovered a new universe." His arm dragged to his side and his head rolled to face me. "You're my universe, Emme," he said softly.

"The moon, the stars, asteroids, meteors, and all the black space in between." His tone was serious while the image of infinity filled my head. "You're everything to me."

I rolled my body to take his mouth tenderly with mine. We kissed slowly, softly, while our breaths regulated and returned to normal. Kissing was breathing. His oxygen became mine, and vice versa. Time ticked, our mouths clicked, and minutes rolled on as our lips joined over and over and over again, keeping us connected.

"Are you still angry?" he muttered, forcing me onto my back with the motion of his body.

"No. I strangely feel much better," I said, kissing those dimples, tracing one with my tongue. His mouth captured it and sucked it into his.

"Ready to make-up now?" he asked softly, the tip of his tongue outlining my lips.

"Yes," I sighed, feeling the weight of his length pressed into my thigh. He slipped into me gently, filling me with affectionate anticipation. We sighed in unison as we reunited again after only a short time apart.

"Merek," I said into his shoulder. He pulled back to look at me under him.

"You're everything to me, too." My voice was hardly more than a whisper. He stilled inside me and rolled us, so he was on his back. He pulled me down to take my mouth hard. His tongue lingered. His lips savored. Suddenly, he released me. Pushing me gently to sit upright over him, he took my hands with his to support me.

The Sex Education of M.E.

"Take a ride with me, Emme," he said, and while the line was straight from the history of our relationship, his meaning was not an innuendo. The future was going to be one hell of a drive.

Chapter 42
Back From Outer Space

[M.E.]

"Dad?" The faint cry wafted up from the lower level of Merek's home. He covered me with most of his body, pinning me to the bed.

"Dad?" The voice grew louder, closer.

"Merek?" I whispered.

"Hmmm," he muttered sleepily.

"Merek, I think your kids are home."

His head shot upright. His neck twisted so he could look at the clock on the stand near his bed.

"Shit," he said, leaping off of me. I sat upright, taking the sheet with me for coverage.

"Stay," he demanded, holding out his hands, his naked body standing at the end of his bed. He reached for something on the floor and picked up the white t-shirt that had been under his plaid shirt. Slipping it over his head after stepping into a pair of basketball shorts, Merek turned and exited his room, closing the door behind him.

My heart raced. I didn't know what to do. Do I dress and climb out the window? My eyes traveled to the one on the left of the room. There didn't appear to be a tree close enough. I twisted to look at the window over the bed. No tree there either. My arm wrapped over the sheet covering me, I could feel the rapid thud of my heart through my chest.

Shaky fingers combed through my wild hair.

We were caught.

I covered my mouth with a shaky hand, stifling the growing laughter.

Oh my God, we were caught by his kids.

My body began to tremble as I suppressed the need to burst out laughing.

Oh my God, we were caught by his kids, and I was still in his bed.

The Sex Education of M.E.

A squeak leaked from my lips. *Oh my God, we were caught by his kids, I was still in his bed, and I'd have to do a walk of shame to get out of here.*

The need to laugh stopped. Hysteria was taking over. I fell back and cackled.

This could not be happening, I told myself. If I worried about rumors from an old lady, the gossip from his children would be immeasurable.

Neighborhood headline reads: *Mrs. Peters Got Caught Having Sex with Mr. Whittington.* Two neighbors. In the bedroom. With uncontrollable lust. But this wasn't a game any longer. Merek almost called me his girlfriend. He told the old lady I was going to be his wife.

I sat up again, my heart racing anew. *Could I marry again?* The thought had never crossed my mind. I enjoyed my independence. I was a modern woman. I didn't need a man to complete me. I could live alone.

The thought stopped me.

While I was all those things, the bottom line was—I didn't want to be alone. While I was independent, I wanted to be able to lean on someone. While I was a modern woman, I still believed in tradition and romance. While I didn't need a man to complete me, Merek did fulfill my needs. Allowing these thoughts to consume me, Merek returned. He quickly closed the door again and stepped toward the bed. He climbed over me, knocking me gently backwards and covering my body. He wasn't only pinning me; it was as if he was holding me down, so I couldn't leave.

"What's going on?" I asked, shakily.

"It's late. They wanted to come home. I'd texted them earlier to say we were stopping by the house to have a drink."

"My girls..." My voice faded with humiliation.

"They know you're here."

"How late is it?"

"Two in the morning." I struggled to sit up, but the size and strength of Merek kept me still.

"I can't spend the night," I shrieked quietly. His head lowered so his forehead rested on mine.

"I know," he exhaled, softly. His forehead rolled over mine before he pulled back. "But Emme, I don't want you to leave." His words lingered between us.

"I hate that you have to go. I hate that we each go to bed at night alone. I don't like that you have to leave after what we've done when all I want to do is hold you the rest of the night."

"Merek, I..." My hand tenderly wiped down his cheek.

"This is messy," he interrupted me with a tender peck. "But we can work it out, right?" He pulled back, his eyes roaming over my face. His expression hopeful and frightened.

"We...we can," I offered softly. His mouth twisted, and then curved on one side. That lopsided grin grew until both sides matched and those deep dimples were exposed.

"Yeah?" he questioned.

"Yeah." I nodded. His mouth came to mine, keeping me hostage for a few more minutes with delicate attention to my lips. Sucking and tracing, it was as if he wanted to memorize my mouth before I had to go.

"Merek," I nervously laughed. "How am I going to get out of here?" He rested his forehead against mine again. "I sent the kids to their rooms." He chuckled. His hand wrapped around the nape of my neck.

"I hate this," he whispered.

"I know." That intense gaze we had earlier in the night returned. Eyes questioned, trying to read thoughts, and draw out answers, but there wasn't a need. We'd just have to take things day-by-day, month-by-month. Only this time we were moving forward together, working toward something, not trying to step away from the past.

Chapter 43
Liking and Licking

[M.E.]

"Professor Peters?" The knock on the door and the soft address made me spin away from my desk. In the doorway of my office stood Grant Mullens, that seductive smile on his lips, but a sheepish expression on his face. In his hand he held a vase of flowers.

"Professor Peters, I wanted to apologize for the other night." He held out the flowers. It had been years since a man had given me flowers. It was the small things that mattered, and I always wished that Nate would spontaneously bring flowers to me. Instead, he felt they would just die anyway, so what was the point.

"Thank you, Grant. This is so sweet of you," I said, reaching out for the vase.

"Oh, yeah, well, these aren't from me. I stopped in the English Office to find out your office hours and the secretary asked me to bring these down to you."

"Oh. Oh," I said, feeling awkward as I set the arrangement on the corner of my desk. A beautiful array of yellow sunflowers, purple sprigs, and white daisies brightened my little corner of the university. I smiled in spite of myself, even if they weren't an apology from Grant.

"So, yeah, I just wanted to say I'm sorry about the other night. Lance told me I was out of line, and I don't want to get kicked out or a bad grade or anything. So I wanted to say I was sorry." He slipped his hands into the back pockets of his jeans. Rolling on the balls of his feet, I realized that the man-looking person before me was still barely out of childhood at twenty-something-years old. I could never have slept with someone so young, but it didn't hurt to take a second look at him. He was a gorgeous man. Hopefully, he was a good man, too.

"I wouldn't dock your grade, Grant. All in good fun, right? Did you enjoy the bar?" I asked.

"Yeah, but we left early. Might have had too much fun, if you know what I mean." He winked and the playful, flirtatious side of my student returned.

"I know what you mean."

"You okay, Professor Peters? You seemed like you were running from something the other night."

I stared at this young man. I was running the other night. Running from the past. Running from the history of being cheated on and the fear that it could happen again. Running from the past of a man who played the field, but was ready to settle at home plate. No more running away, though. We needed to face things as they happened, together.

"I'm fine, Grant. Thanks for asking." I was fine. I was better than fine, actually. "Thanks for bringing down the flowers." I nodded in the direction of the arrangement.

"Sure. Okay, see ya in class," he said with a feeble wave. After he left my doorway, I pulled the card from the bouquet.

Thanks for the ride.

I smiled to myself. Merek. Reaching for a flower, I stroked the delicate petal. I had a few minutes before class, so I texted him.

Thank you for the flowers.

Yeah? You're welcome, darlin'

They're beautiful.

So are you. I blushed at Merek's response.

I lck you, too.

I smiled to myself then did a double take. *Wait, what?*

You lick me?

Shit, where was autocorrect when you needed it? I'm typing my correction when he responds. **I like you.**

Smiling, I laughed. Out loud. Then another message appeared.

But if you want me to lick you, I can do that, too.

Suddenly, another body part smiled.

Maybe soon. I need to get to class.

There was no response after that, and I gathered my things for my short story course with a cheesy grin on my face and the potential for a wet problem between my legs. I walked briskly to the classroom hoping to ward off the sudden ache with some stimulating conversation about short stories.

"Ew," Jonathan Martinez shivers in his seat as we finished a passage with an older couple. "Old love," he muttered, loud enough he grabbed the room's attention. Looking up from the story, I questioned him.

"What's 'old love'?" Air-quotes emphasized the phrase.

"You know, when old people are all cutesy with each other and stuff."

I blinked in utter surprise.

"What's 'and stuff'?"

"You know, when they're all kissy and say cute things to each other. They're silly over each other." He shivered exaggeratedly from his seat.

"OTP," Andrea said next to him. "I think it's adorable."

"What's 'OTP'?" I asked, feeling older and older by the minute. I worried I was about to get an inappropriate education.

"OTP. One true pair, Professor," Andrea explained, like I was a child. "The grandfather and the nurse." She waved her hand over the short story. I laughed. I was certainly learning a lot today in my own class.

"Okay, back to Jonathan for a moment. What's your definition of old? Remember this is the 1700s. The grandfather isn't as old as yours might be, considering we live almost double the amount of time." Holding my breath, I awaited his answer, expecting what he was about to say.

"Over forty," he squeaked, shifting his eyes from me to the girl sitting next to him. I laughed, shaking my head.

"I'm over forty," I stated, still smiling.

"Yeah, well, you're different. You don't seem that old," Andrea assured me.

Out of the mouths of twenty-year-olds.

Class eventually ended on that note, and I couldn't contain my excitement to see the flowers sitting on my desk. They were thoughtful and a true novelty for me. Considering it had only been two days since Merek and I decided we were going to work at building something more, it was a sweet gesture. Romantic even.

I entered my small space, which had one window, one desk, an extra chair and a large messy bookcase, to stare at the flower arrangement. Standing before my computer, I jumped when I heard a voice.

"So, this is where you work?"

Merek's voice filled the cozy space, and I spun to face him. I couldn't contain the beaming smile on my face.

"Hey! What brings you here?"

Stepping into my office, he closed my door, and leaned against it.

"Cassie had some medical forms that needed to be handed in because she started a week late. Thought it was easiest just to bring them here myself." The comment brought the excitement of seeing him down a notch. Things would be raw for a little while as we wove our way through how a relationship might work.

"But I had another matter to discuss with you." His hand slid up the door and flicked the lock. "You don't have another class yet, right?" His listening skills were unbelievable. It appeared he had my class schedule memorized from a conversation.

"Nope. Nothing until one. Why?" I smiled slowly, the tension between us rising, but it didn't have to do with the issue of Cassie and her late start. This was something else, and that mischievous grin of his began to spread. Those dimples appeared under his salt-and-pepper stubble.

"Licking," he stated definitively, his mouth still tweaked upward. My underwear nearly melted. For some reason, I backed up against my desk, as if he was going to attack me. In many ways, I wanted him to pounce. His hand flipped the light switch. My office grew darker, but not too dark, as the one window had open blinds. Lights off signaled my office was closed, and that was good enough. Merek stalked toward me.

"Don't you have to work?" I questioned, just filling the silence as those dark eyes sparked.

"I do, but there was a small emergency. A flame was started, and I've come to put it out."

"A fire," I smirked, swallowing hard as his body came up against mine. "Good thing you're a fireman."

"That's commander to you," he teased.

"Yes, sir," I whispered. His eyes closed, and his hands tugged on my hips.

"You have no idea what that just did to me," he grinned, opening his eyes to reveal darkness ablaze with desire. The material of my pencil skirt rose. My bare legs were exposed. Impulsively, my feet spread apart.

"Are we really going to do this here?" My voice came out strangled but thrilled and paranoid.

"Yes," he confirmed as he knelt on one knee and then the other. My underwear came down to my ankles. My skirt pushed up to my hips. Merek's mouth came to my center. I gripped the edge of my desk, holding myself upright with the lip assault on my lower region.

"I could get fired," I whispered, one hand coming to his hair, holding his head against me while his tongue parted my folds and lapped at me.

"Good thing I'm a *fire man*," he mocked, blowing against the tender skin that needed his mouth back where it had been.

"That was a terrible line." I inhaled sharply as his mouth sucked my lower lips. All thoughts of losing my job evaporated as I lost control to Merek and his mouth. The blaze lit rapidly within me, and I ignited quickly. My legs shook afterward, and my body trembled. I needed to sit down.

He kissed my inner thigh as he pulled up my underwear. He stood methodically, dragging his body close to mine. His mouth captured mine, paying the same attention to my lips as he had below. He nipped and sucked in the same manner, then released his tongue to dance with mine. Kissing for too brief a time, he pulled back. I was dazed and sated, but I still needed more of him.

"That was...unexpected. Incredible, but unexpected." I reached for his belt and tugged the strap. "What about you?" I nervously questioned, uncertain I could follow through with going down on Merek in my office.

"This was all for you. An office visit. I make them, as well as house calls," he teased.

Old love came to mind. Merek was excessively playful, and silly.

"Want to share my lunch?" I asked. I still had more than an hour before my next class. His mouth kissed me.

"I just did."

I laughed. "Oh my God, Merek, I…" I what? I like him. It was more than that. I adored him. He made me feel young again. Forget old love, or rather embrace old love. I loved how silly he could be. I loved that he sent me flowers. I loved that he just gave me an orgasm in my office, and he asked for nothing in return. I loved him. Plain and simple, old school, and all. I loved Merek. Instantly, I knew the words would be too much for him. Our start to a relationship was all backwards and bumpy roads, and I didn't want to do anything to jeopardize it. I'd keep those words tucked away for a while. I was fine with that. Just fine.

"You what?" he asked, jostling my hips.

"I need to make that up to you." My eyes shifted down to my toes then back up to his face.

"Tonight," he said. "My shift isn't done until midnight. I'll come to you. Another house call."

Merek and I had talked after getting caught at his house. We discussed how we'd work it out. How we could still use the apartment as our escape, but the place was further in town and twenty minutes from where we lived. We were three blocks and two minutes away from each other. We had to come up with another plan.

"I have a proposition for you," he'd said. My eyes rolled. "I propose, we date. Real dates. Dinner, dancing, movies, whatever you'd like." I remembered nodding my head to agree.

"I only have one hard limit," I said, and watched as his face grew thoughtful.

"Okay," he'd replied, hesitantly.

"We still have to have sex. And kissing. Lots of kissing."

Epilogue
Go Large or Go Home

[M.E. 2]

Marshall was already seated in the front row bleacher seats, the seat next to him empty. I took mine with a heavy thump.

"Well, imagine my surprise seeing you here," he smirked, before standing and leaning over me. "Great seats."

"Emme," he breathed, reaching out to hug her. They connected over me, and I slapped his stomach hard.

"Get off my girl," I said. Marshall pulled back and smacked my shoulder. Emme sat next to me and laughed. It was a glorious fall day; not quite releasing summer with its blue skies and mild temperature, not quite embracing the cold that can come in a Midwest September. I slipped my arm around Emme's seat, and she turned to face me. Without a thought, I kissed her.

I faced forward, feeling the weight of my brother's eyes on me.

"Watch the game," I muttered through closed lips, but my brother stared.

"Oh my God, I really won," he scoffed.

"Won what?" Emme asked over me.

"Nothing," Marshall and I yelped at the same time. Marshall slapped my shoulder again and sat back in his seat. Within minutes, the beer man called out and Marshall raised his hand for an order. I knew Emme would only sip hers, but I didn't comment. I'd drink what she didn't finish. With the cups passed down the row, Marshall waited until we each had ours.

"What should we drink to?" he teased. Emme sat forward and waited for me to respond.

"I know," Marshall continued. He coughed as he said: "Commitment." He tapped my plastic cup and drank heartily.

"You can be an ass," I laughed as I took a drink.

"What's that all about?" Emme asked quietly, smiling as she took a sip of beer.

"Nothing," I shrugged. Emme's hand rubbed down my arm and her fingers laced with mine. The touch wasn't meant to start anything, but the feel of her hands on me were flicks of light from an ember fire.

"Nothing important," I said, turning to kiss her shoulder. Pulling my head up, her eyes met mine and I kissed her again. I couldn't help myself. Every single time we were together, I couldn't keep my lips from her. She couldn't keep her hands away from me. She told me how Nate and she weren't very affectionate outside of the bedroom, and while I wasn't one for public displays of affection, I never minded holding her hand or wrapping an arm around her. In fact, I liked the feel of it and did it often.

I kissed her again. She pulled back, thinking my intent was for something quick, but my hand reached up to cup her cheek, drawing her back to me. I lengthened the kiss, holding her lips to mine. Commitment, Marshall toasted. Devotion, that's what this was. I was devoted to showing Emme over and over how much she meant to me. Kissing her was an important act to confirm my feelings. I'd waited nearly twenty years to share this intimate expression with someone, and I didn't want the sensation to end.

"Get a room, will ya?" Bridge drawled in her Irish brogue, breaking me away from Emme while she sidestepped over my legs to get to the seat on the other side of Marshall. "Oh wait, you already have one, at Marshall's." She smirked, raising her eyebrows mischievously. "I don't know whether to hose you down, or hose me down," she said with a huff. "You're looking at that girl like she's a peanut and you want to crack her open." She sighed. "Pregnancy hormones," she muttered. Emme laughed.

"I appreciate those hormones," Marshall commented.

"Well, it'd be nice if you appreciated a few other things," she remarked in her heavy accent.

"Aww, baby, you know I love you," Marshall said, and I did a double take at his use of those words.

"That's what you keep saying," Bridge laughed, shaking her head. "Then this babe will be born, and you'll be running for the hills."

"Hey Bridge, when you due again?" I chuckled, a thought coming to me.

"December," she said. "Why?"

"Blackhawks season?" Mmmm. "Boxseats are in order, Marshall," I smirked, raising my eyebrow.

"Not gonna happen," Marshall laughed, shaking his head.

"Oh, it's gonna happen," I teased. The second Marshall saw that newborn baby, he'd be on his knees, begging Bridge to marry him. Commitment was next for my baby brother. "I'd like full service wait staff, too, please."

"You two are so strange," Bridge commented, tossing out her wild red hair.

"Nah," I said. "We're just committed." That made Marshall spit out his beer.

Later that night, Emme and I were in my kitchen. She leaned against my counter while I dropped pasta in the boiling pot of water.

"You know, you've called me 'your girl,' a few times," she swallowed slowly, taking a sip of her wine. "Are you saying I'm your girlfriend?"

"I..."

"I'm a little old to be called that," she wrinkled her nose, looking too cute as I could see the wheels start spinning behind her eyes. We'd been together for more than a month, juggling our schedules and that of our kids, trying to work in real dates and sexy time when we could, where we could. I wasn't lying when I told her I wanted her in my bed. I didn't like her always having to leave and sneak back home to her house where we would each end up sleeping alone. We had a weekend away planned for October, where we'd finally get a whole night alone and a real breakfast date.

"Maybe woman friend," I teased. I could be demonstrative, and call her my woman, like I possessed her, but I didn't think Emme would appreciate that. Besides, she owned me, not the other way around. I liked calling her my girl, like we were young. I wasn't pretending we were, but it felt right calling her that.

"Ew, that sounds worse," she chuckled.

"Emme, are you fishing for a label?" We weren't fuck buddies. We were more than friends with benefits. I wasn't lying when I said I could see Emme as my wife, but we were taking our time getting to that point.

"You can call me Uber. I can call you rider," I teased.

"That was still the worst pick up line," she said, her voice falling short. I approached where she stood against the counter. Bracing my feet on either side of hers, I took her face in my hands, tilting it up to me.

"Emme, I don't want to pick you up, I want to keep you. I want to see you every day. Be in you every night. I want to hold you and touch you. I want to tell you about my day. I want to know the thoughts I see dancing behind those eyes. I don't want one-time sex and one-night stands. I don't want benefits. You are the benefit. I want you to be my friend and my lover. I want to fuck you and make love to you and kiss you and own you, because you own me, when you kiss me like you do, and make love to me, and fuck me. So deep, Emme, I feel you so deep around me and in me, it scares the crap out of me. I didn't know I'd been biding my time, waiting for you, Emme. Now, I don't want to waste time. And I don't need a label for this."

She stared at me, but within minutes, I had her perched on the counter, thrusting forward in the motion of sex, while my hands roved her breasts and her mouth captured mine. I don't know who lurched for who first. It didn't matter. All that mattered was Emme pressed against me. She was in my hands and on my mouth and in my heart.

"God, I love you," she muttered against my lips. I stilled. My hands stopped roving. My mouth released hers. Our eyes met.

"I'm sorry. I shouldn't have let that out. Verbal vomit. Can't control." Her mouth did that spewing thing, like when we first met. My lips covered hers to stop her. Our mouths melded. One hand came to the back of her neck. The other laced fingers with hers. I pulled back after sucking her lower lip.

"Don't take it back," I whispered. "I love you, too." The words weren't difficult. Our mouths crashed again.

"Whipped. Chained. Spanked. Tied up. Unrestrained." I muttered between kisses.

"You didn't mention plugged or flogged." She snickered against my mouth.

The Sex Education of M.E.

"Still waiting to experience those before I add them to the list," I teased.

"Well, how hard can it be?" she laughed, wrapping her arms and legs around me while she balanced on the edge of the counter.

"Hard," I smiled. "Very hard." I thrust forward to prove my point. But the truth was Emme taught me to love again, and with her, that wasn't difficult at all.

L.B. Dunbar

Thank you for taking the time to read this book. Please consider writing a review on major sales channels where ebooks and paperbooks are sold.

More by L.B. Dunbar

Lakeside Cottage
Four friends. Four summers. Shenanigans and love happen at the lake.
Living at 40
Loving at 40
Learning at 40
Letting Go at 40

The Silver Foxes of Blue Ridge
More sexy silver foxes in the mountain community of Blue Ridge.
Silver Brewer
Silver Player
Silver Mayor
Silver Biker

Sexy Silver Foxes
When sexy silver foxes meet the feisty vixens of their dreams.
After Care
Midlife Crisis
Restored Dreams
Second Chance
Wine&Dine

Collision novellas
A spin-off from After Care – the younger set/rock stars
Collide
Caught

Smartypants Romance (an imprint of Penny Reid)
Tales of the Winters sisters set in Green Valley.
Love in Due Time
Love in Deed
Love in a Pickle (2021)

The World of True North (an imprint of Sarina Bowen)
Welcome to Vermont! And the Busy Bean Café.
Cowboy

Studfinder

The Sex Education of M.E.

Rom-com standalone for the over 40
The Sex Education of M.E.

The Heart Collection
Small town, big hearts - stories of family and love.
Speak from the Heart
Read with your Heart
Look with your Heart
Fight from the Heart
View with your Heart

A Heart Collection Spin-off
The Heart Remembers

THE EARLY YEARS
The Legendary Rock Star Series
Rock star mayhem in the tradition of King Arthur.
A classic tale with a modern twist of romance and suspense
The Legend of Arturo King
The Story of Lansing Lotte
The Quest of Perkins Vale
The Truth of Tristan Lyons
The Trials of Guinevere DeGrance

Paradise Stories
MMA romance. Two brothers. One fight.
Abel
Cain

The Island Duet
Intrigue and suspense. The island knows what you've done.
Redemption Island
Return to the Island

Modern Descendants – writing as elda lore
Magical realism. Modern myths of Greek gods.
Hades
Solis
Heph

L.B. Dunbar

A Nibble of *After Care*.
Meet Tommy Carrigan and Edie Williams...

1
The Introduction

"Is that your daughter?" A pretty blonde sat next to me on the edge of the pool. I fidgeted with the scarf wrapped around my head and smiled.

"Yes." The beautiful brunette was mine, and even though she was eighteen, she was child-like in spirit, laughing as two little girls splashed her. Watching the younger two frolicking in the water reminded me of my own children at that age. Life was much different then.

"Both yours?" I asked, shifting only my eyes to the twenty-something woman, adjusting the scarf once again on my head, waiting for her to notice it. There wasn't a way to miss it. The thin material made no sense in the heat of the Hawaiian sun, but the traditional paisley patterned bandana in bright yellow made sense to someone like me. I was a breast cancer survivor. If you didn't know, the head wrap gave it away.

She nodded in response to me, and we remained silent a moment.

My eyes closed as I faced the brilliant blue sky, soaking up the sunshine, a welcome reprieve from the frigid temps we left behind in Chicago. I desperately needed this vacation. *Party of three, please.* I looked forward to family time with my grown children. The doctors told me we had much to celebrate. I smiled despite myself as I looked back at the two babes dousing my daughter.

"She's good with kids," the young woman remarked, and I stared at my own child on the verge of womanhood. She'd make a great mother one day. Tears prickled my eyes. I didn't want to think dark thoughts, but they often crept in. Silently, I hoped I'd get to see the day she mothered a child of her own.

"Cannonball." A loud male screech erupted from my other baby—more a child than a man at the age of twenty-two. He catapulted into the huge, oddly shaped pool, covering his sister in a tidal wave of water, and drowning the two little girls.

"Caleb," I shouted but the mother next to me laughed. A man with dark, chin length hair caught one of her daughters under the arm, hoisting her upward from the vigorous aftershock of my son's jump. Masie held the other. Tiny arms wrapped around my daughter's neck, holding tight like a second skin. Laughter surrounded all of them.

"That's Ava," the woman pointed to the dark-haired one matching her apparent father. "She's six. And the blonde, choking your daughter is Emaline. She's four."

My eyes drifted back to the collection of young people but froze on the man with rock star good looks. Deep set eyes, a thin scrap of scruff around his jaw, and the midnight color of his wet hair, added to what I imagined was a brooding look on an average day. Smiling at his child made all the difference in his appearance.

"You can ask," the woman said. "Yes, it's him."

I turned to her. Her features were equally striking while softer than his. A playful look filled her blue eyes. Puffy, pink lips conjured images of them kissing each other enthusiastically. Passionate enough to create two small daughters. I sighed. It had been a long time since someone kissed me like that. Even the man who created two children with me had fallen out of practice years before everything happened.

"He's Gage Everly."

I blinked at her, shaking my head in confusion. "I'm sorry. Should I know him? Do I know you?" My eyes opened wider, a tingle of fear that somehow, I didn't recognize him when it should be obvious who he is. Not only had the cancer taken my hair, maybe it had also taken my memory. I chuckled, knowing that couldn't possibly be true.

"Gage Everly, lead singer of Collision?" Her brow rose in question, as if I should recognize him or the name of the band.

"I'm so sorry," I said again, cursing the terrible habit I had of apologizing for everything. *I'm sorry I wasn't younger. I'm sorry you no longer love me. I'm sorry I got cancer.*

I shook my head to acknowledge I didn't recognize him.

She chuckled softly and clapped her hands once before covering her cheeks. "Oh my, how refreshing." Her blue eyes beamed brighter than the sky overhead.

"I think it's just because I'm old," I weakly smiled, reaching for the bandana once again. My hair had moved from the stages of peach-fuzz to crazy C-shapes and kinky curly Qs, going in all directions. I didn't need the material covering my head, but sometimes, I felt safer wearing it. My hair color hadn't returned to my natural fading brown, but a mixture of white and dirty blonde.

You can dye it whatever color you want when approved, Nurse Marjorie had told me. *Purple's very popular for people your age.* Her sweet, innocent voice intended to encourage me. Instead, I wanted to erase the smirk on her lips.

Your age. I was forty-three. I should have been in the prime of my life. Where was the return of my sexual libido that everyone promised me would happen? Oh, right, it walked out the door with a younger model—blonde, thin, and cancer-free under her skin.

The new hair combination caused conflicting emotions. On one hand, the brilliant color reminded me of my growing age. On the other hand, the change from lackluster to vibrant aided to the new persona I wanted to adapt. It was time for a change.

"Oh." My companion's eyes opened wide, "Oh, I wasn't implying . . . I mean . . . It's just that . . ." Her hands waved in front of her as she swung her thin body toward me. "It's just everywhere we go people know it's him. It's nice to meet someone who doesn't recognize Gage."

I smiled. I didn't know how to respond. A child squealed and I turned my attention to the pool, noting my son in a deep conversation with her husband. Masie still held one girl while the other tried to climb her father. When Caleb was younger, he'd wanted to be a guitarist. It had been his life's ambition, until he discovered baseball. The sport became my ex's dream for our son. Watching Caleb, his body straightened, his awe trained on the man before him—someone I didn't recognize, but surely Caleb did.

A gruff voice behind us bellowed, "Please step away from him."

My body twisted to face the sound, rich in baritone, tough as a boulder, and rugged like gravel under bare feet. I shivered despite the heat. Two thick arms crossed a midnight-colored T-shirt stretched over the barrel chest of an older man, likely in his forties with silvery hair curling at his neck and salt-and-pepper facial scruff. He wore black pants, balancing himself with a wide stance on thick legs. Regardless of tinted aviators, the weight of his eyes bored into me. Rock star sprang to my mind.

"It's okay, Uncle Tommy," the woman said. "They're only talking."

"Well, we all know where talking can lead." His knuckles met his neck and he scratched at the hint of hair under his jaw. The sound traveled to me, and a thrill tickled my sun-heated shoulders. His pouty lips crooked in one corner as I sensed him teasing the girl. It was obvious he knew her secrets. "But seriously, he's on vacation. He doesn't need a groupie and some wannabe—"

"Excuse me?" I interjected, attempting to make my voice as knife sharp as his but failing miserably as he removed the aviators. Two deep set circles of coal returned his focus on me and the will to breathe escaped me. He stole my breath, literally, and I self-consciously tug at the scarf once again. There was no way he couldn't notice the bright material, but he kept his eyes pinned to mine.

Out of respect, I told myself.

To hold me prisoner, my mind whispered back.

Take me, I foolishly screamed, and then the warmest blush I've ever experienced crawled over my skin, prickly, tickly, tingly like the tiny tap of a million feet. I shivered again. The motion snapped his attention and he turned away.

"Tommy, this is..." the young mother paused. "I'm sorry, I didn't catch your name."

"Edie," I said, holding out my hand while the other fingers found security in touching the fabric just above my ear. "Edie Williams."

"This is Tommy Carrigan. He's the band's manager." She turned to look up at him over her shoulder, her smile affectionate. "He's a giant teddy bear when he isn't acting like a grumpy eagle." She pouted as she spun back to me.

"Don't ruin my reputation before I make an impression, sweetheart," he teased with a hint of a Southern drawl, his eyes redirected to the pool, but his shoulders loosened a little. Oh, he'd made an impression all right. A deep one, right between my thighs just from the sound of his voice.

Then I noticed my hand still lingering in the air, waiting for him to reach out and shake mine. When he didn't, I awkwardly lowered it, fussing with my scarf one more time.

"Don't mind him," the woman said. "By the way, I'm Ivy. Ivy Everly, and I'm happy to meet you."

Her smile put me at ease. For some reason, I was just as pleased to meet her.

Funny how a random introduction changed everything.

(L)ittle (B)its of Gratitude

It takes a village to publish a book, and this holds especially true with this one. I want to first thank Ana Ivies and the women of Ana's Attic: After Dark, who were honest in educating me, and the women (and a few men) in my reader group, Loving L.B. who helped select name, occupation and minor details of this older couple.

Thank you to the steadfast friendship of Shannon at Shanoff Designs for the beautiful cover and Kiezha Ferrell at Librum Artis for edits.

A million thanks to ALL THE BLOGGERS #bloggersarelove and the hard work they put in for free to help share the love of books and authors. Additional thanks to Give Me Books for another fabulous release day blitz and Heather Roberts at Social Butterfly PR for a blog tour and marketing. I can't fulfill my dream without this village of support.

HUGE thank you to Emerson Shaw and Brandy L. Rivers for hardcore beta edits. I am indebted to you forever for helping me be better. More hugs to Tammi Hart, Kali McQuillen and Sylvia Schneider for feedback and assurance that #OldLove works. AND love, love, love to Karen Fischer, who is an incredible proofreader/beta reader. I've come to rely on you so heavily for support and I appreciate that you keep giving it to me, Karen.

To my family, especially my #OldLove – for keeping it hot after all this time, and the four flames that came from that heat – MD1, MD2, JR and A.

About the Author

www.lbdunbar.com

L.B. Dunbar has an over-active imagination. To her benefit, such creativity has led to over thirty romance novels, including those offering a second chance at love over 40. Her signature works include the #sexysilverfoxes collection of mature males and feisty vixens ready for romance in their prime years. She's also written stories of small-town romance (Heart Collection), rock star mayhem (The Legendary Rock Stars Series), and a twist on intrigue and redemption (Redemption Island Duet). She's had several alter egos including elda lore, a writer of romantic magical realism through mythological retellings (Modern Descendants). In another life, she wanted to be an anthropologist and journalist. Instead, she was a middle school language arts teacher. The greatest story in her life is with the one and only, and their four grown children. Learn more about L.B. Dunbar by joining her reader group on Facebook (Loving L.B.) or subscribing to her newsletter (Love Notes).

+ + +

Connect with L.B. Dunbar

Made in the USA
Monee, IL
13 April 2023